The Spell

William Dana Orcutt

Alpha Editions

This edition published in 2024

ISBN : 9789361478864

Design and Setting By
Alpha Editions
www.alphaedis.com
Email - info@alphaedis.com

BOOK I

MASTER OF FATE

I

"Now, Jack, here is a chance to put your knowledge of the classics to some practical use."

Helen Armstrong paused for a moment before a Latin inscription cut in the upper stones of the boundary wall, and leaned gratefully upon her companion's arm after the steep ascent. "What does it mean?"

Her husband smiled. "That is an easy test. The ancient legend conveys the cheering intelligence that 'from this spot Florence and Fiesole, mother and daughter, are equi-distant.'"

The girl released her hold upon the man's arm and, pushing back a few stray locks which the wind had loosened, turned to regard the panorama behind her. It was a charmingly picturesque and characteristic Italian roadway which they had chosen for their day's excursion. On either side stood plastered stone walls, which bore curious marks and circles, made—who shall say when or by whom?—remaining there as an atavistic suggestion of Etruscan symbolism. The whiteness of the walls was relieved by tall cypresses and ilexes which rose high above them, while below the branches, and reclining upon the stone top, a profusion of wild roses shed their petals and their fragrance for the benefit of the passers-by. In the distance, through the trees, showed the shimmering green of olive-groves and vineyards—covering the hillsides, yet yielding occasionally to a gay-blossoming garden; and, as if to complete by contrast, the streaked peaks of Carrara gave a faint suggestion of their marble richness. In front, Fiesole rose sheer and picturesque, while villas, scattered here and there, some large and stately, some small, some antiquated and others modernized, gave evidence that the ancient Via della Piazzola still expressed its own individuality as in the days when the bishops of old trod its paths in visiting their see at the top of the hill, and Boccaccio and Sacchetti, with their kindred spirits, made its echoes ring with merry revelling. But, inevitably turning again, the modern pilgrims saw far below them, and most impressive of all, the languorous City of Flowers, peacefully dreaming on either side of the silver Arno.

All this was a familiar sight to John Armstrong, whose five years' residence in Florence, just before entering Harvard, made him feel entirely at home in its outskirts. He preferred, therefore, to fix his eyes upon the face of the girl beside him. She was tall and fair, with figure well proportioned, yet the characteristic which left the deepest impress was her peculiar sweetness of expression. Among her Vincent Club friends she was universally considered beautiful, and a girl's verdict of another girl's beauty is rarely exaggerated. Her deep, merry, gray eyes showed whence came the vivacity which ever made her the centre of an animated group, while the sympathy and understanding which shone from them explained her popularity.

The announcement of her engagement to Jack Armstrong was the greatest surprise of a sensational Boston season, not because of any unfitness in the match,—for the Armstrong lineage was quite as distinguished as the Cartwrights',—but because Helen had so persistently discouraged all admiration beyond the point of friendship and comradeship, that those who should have known pronounced her immune.

But that was because her friends had read her character even less correctly than they had Armstrong's. They would have told you that she was distinctly a girl of the twentieth century; he discovered that while tempered by its progressiveness, she had not been marred by its extremes. They would have said that her character had not yet found opportunity for expression, since her every wish had always been gratified; he would have explained that the fact that she had learned to wish wisely was in itself sufficient expression of the character which lay beneath.

He watched her in the midst of the social life to which they both belonged, entering naturally, as he did, into its conventionalities as a matter of course, and he rejoiced to find in her, beyond the enjoyment of those every-day pleasures which end where they begin, a response to the deeper thoughts which controlled his own best expression. He could see that these new subjects frightened her a little by their immensity, as he tried to explain them; he sympathized with her momentary despair when she found herself beyond her depth; but he was convinced that the understanding and the interest were both there, as in an undeveloped negative.

This same power of analysis which enabled him to discover what all could not surmise had separated Armstrong, in Helen's mind, from other men, nearer her own age, whom she had known. She could hardly have put in words what the difference was, but she felt that it existed, and this paved the way for his ultimate success. His personal attributes, inevitably tempered by the early Italian influence, marked him as one considerably above the commonplace. At college he had won the respect of his professors by his strength of mind and tenacity of application, and the affection of his fellow-students by his skill in athletics and his general good-fellowship. Now, eight years out of college, he had already made his place at the Boston bar, and was regarded as a successful man in his profession. But beyond all this, unknown even to himself, Armstrong was an extremist. The seed had been sown during that residence in Florence years before, when unconsciously he had assimilated the enthusiasm of an erudite librarian for the learning and achievements of the master spirits of the past. Latin and Greek at college had thus meant much more to him than dead languages; in them he found living personalities which inspired in him the liveliest ambition for emulation.

These were some of the subjects to which he introduced Helen. Little by little he told her of the fascination they possessed for him, of the treasures hidden beneath their austere exterior. But the girl was perhaps more interested by the charm of his presentation than by the possibilities she saw in the subjects themselves. She felt that she could understand him, and admitted her respect for the objects of his enthusiasm, but she was convinced that these were beyond her comprehension, and frankly rebelled at the necessity of going back into dead centuries for them.

"I love the present, and all that it contains," she replied to him one day when something suggested the subject during one of the many walks they took together; "I love the sky, the air, the sunshine, and the flowers. Why should I go back to the past, made up of memories only, when I may enjoy all this beautiful world around me? And you, Jack—I should not have you if I had lived in the past!"

As her friends had said, she possessed strong ideas about marriage, and expressed them without reserve. Until Armstrong's irresistible wooing, she had decided, as a result both of observation and of conclusion, that admiration and attention from many were far to be preferred to the devotion of any single one, and that matrimony was neither essential nor desirable except under ideal conditions.

"There are so many things which seem more interesting to me than a husband," Helen asserted. "I'm afraid that I agree too much with that wise old cynic who said that 'love is the wine of life, and marriage the dram-drinking.' I insist on remaining a teetotaler."

Thus Armstrong felt himself entitled to enjoy a certain degree of pride and satisfaction in that he had succeeded in convincing her at last that the ideal conditions she demanded had been met.

Even on board the steamer, at the start of their wedding journey, as the familiar sky-line of New York became less and less distinct, Armstrong read in his wife's eyes, still gazing back at the vanishing city, the thoughts which inevitably forced themselves upon her—a last remnant of her former doubt. When she turned and saw him looking at her, she smiled guiltily.

"We are leaving the old life behind us," she said. "With all the philosophy you have tried to teach me, I have not fully realized until now what a change it means."

"Do you regret it?" he asked her, half rebellious that even a passing shadow should mar the completeness of their happiness.

Helen quickly became herself again, and threw back her head with a merry laugh at the seriousness of his interrogation. "Regret it! How foolish even to ask such a question! But you cannot wonder that the importance of the event should force itself upon me, now that we are actually married, even if it never did before. It makes so much more of a change in a woman's life than in a man's."

Helen sighed, and then looked mischievously into his face. "With you superior beings," she continued, "it simply signifies a new latch-key, a new head to your household, and the added companionship of a woman whom you have selected as absolutely essential to your happiness. You keep your old friends, give up for a time a few of your bad habits, and transfer a part of your affections from your clubs to your home. To the woman, it means a complete readjustment. New duties and responsibilities come to her all at once. From her earliest memory she has been taught to depend upon the counsel and guidance of her parents, but suddenly she finds herself freed from this long-accustomed habit, with a man standing beside her, only a few years her senior, who is convinced that he can serve in this capacity far better than any one else ever did. Even with a husband as superior as yourself, Mr. John Armstrong, is it not natural that one should recognize the passing of the old life, while welcoming the coming of the new?"

After landing, they had lingered for a fortnight in Paris, but, beneath the keen enjoyment of the attractions there, Armstrong had felt an impatience, unacknowledged even to himself, to reach Florence, which contained for him so much of interest, and whither his memory—let him give it sway— ever recalled him. He felt that his *dei familiares* were patiently waiting for him there, indulgent in spite of his long absence, yet insistent that their rights again be recognized. Having dropped his engrossing law-practice, he yearned to take advantage of this opportunity, now near at hand, to devote himself to the girl he had won, and at the same time to gratify this long-cherished wish to study more deeply into the work of those early humanists who had foreshadowed and brought about that mighty thought revolution, the wonderful breaking-away from the deadly pall of ignorance into the light and joyousness and richness of intellectual life known as the Renaissance. Helen would no longer fail to understand them when she saw them face to face. He would lead her gently, even as Cerini the librarian had led him; and together they would draw from the old life those principles which made it what it was, incorporating them into their new existence, which would thus be the richer and better worth the living. So now that he had actually reached his goal, it was natural that his contentment at finding himself in Florence with his wife was intensified by the joy of being again amid the scenes and personages which his imagination had taken out from the indefiniteness of antiquity, and invested with a living actuality.

The sharp contrast of his two great devotions came to John Armstrong as he stood at the cross-roads on the edge of San Domenico. The one had exerted so powerful an influence on what he was to-day—the other must influence his future to an extent even greater. The one, in spite of the personality with which he had clothed it, was as musty and antiquated as the ancient tomes he loved to study; the other, as she stood there, her cheeks aglow after the brisk walk, her face animated with enthusiastic delight, seemed the personification of present reality. What a force the two must make when once joined together, contributing, each to the other, those qualities which would else be lacking!

"I must take you yet a little higher," Armstrong urged at length; "these walls still cut off much of the glorious view."

In a few moments more they had partly ascended the Via della Fiesolana, which at this hour was wholly deserted. With a sigh, half from satisfaction and half from momentary fatigue, Helen turned to her companion. She caught the admiration which his face so clearly reflected, but, womanlike, preferred to feign ignorance of its origin. Glancing about her, she discovered a rock, half hidden by the tall grass and wild poppies, which offered an attractive resting-place. Seating herself, she plucked several of the brilliant blossoms, and began to weave the stems together. At last she broke the silence.

"Why are you so quiet, Jack?"

"For three reasons," he replied, promptly. "This walk has made me romantic, poetic, and hungry."

Helen laughed heartily. "I am glad you added the third reason, for by that I know that you are mortal. This wonderful air and the marvellous view affect me exactly as a fairy-story used to, years ago. When I turned I fully expected to find a fairy prince beside me. You confess that you are romantic, which is becoming in a five-weeks'-old husband, but why poetic?"

"'Poetry is but spoken painting,'" quoted Armstrong, smiling; "and I should be pleased indeed were I able to put on canvas the picture I now see before me."

"Since you cannot do that, suppose you write a sonnet."

Armstrong met her arch smile firmly. The girlish abandon under the influence of new surroundings awoke in him a side of his nature which he had not previously realized he possessed. Stooping, he gently held her face between his hands and looked deep into her responsive eyes before replying:

"'Say from what vein did Love procure the gold
To make those sunny tresses? From what thorn
Stole he the rose, and whence the dew of morn,
Bidding them breathe and live in Beauty's mould?
What depth of ocean gave the pearls that told
Those gentle accents sweet, tho' rarely born?
Whence came so many graces to adorn
That brow more fair than summer skies unfold?
Oh! say what angels lead, what spheres control
The song divine which wastes my life away?
(Who can with trifles now my senses move?)
What sun gave birth unto the lofty soul
Of those enchanting eyes, whose glances stray
To burn and freeze my heart—the sport of Love?'"

Helen made no reply for several moments after Armstrong ceased speaking. Then she held out her hand to him and looked up into his face.

"I never knew before that you were a real poet," she said, quietly.

"I wish I were—and such a poet! My precious Petrarch, for whom you profess so little fondness, is responsible for that most splendid tribute ever paid to woman."

Helen was incredulous.

"That sanctimonious old gentleman with the laurel leaves on his head and the very self-confident expression on his face?"

Armstrong nodded.

"Who spent all his life making love to another man's wife from a safe distance?"

"Yes; this is one of his love-letters."

"Then if I accept those lines you just repeated with so much feeling, I must be Laura?"

"But not another man's wife."

"I should have been if you had acted like that, Jack. Let me see how you look with a laurel wreath made of poppies."

She drew his head down and tied the flowers about his forehead. Then, pushing him away from her, she clapped her hands with delight.

"There! if the noble Petrarch had looked like that, Madonna Laura could surely never have resisted him."

"Had Madonna Laura resembled Madonna Helen, the worthy Petrarch would have had her in his arms before she had the chance," laughed Armstrong, improving his opportunity as he spoke.

"Very gallant, Jack, but very improper." Helen pursed her lips and looked up at him mischievously. "But let us forget your musty old antiquities and talk of the present. Do you realize that this is the end of our honeymoon?"

"No," he replied, holding her more closely and laughing down at her; "it has only just begun."

"Of course," assented Helen, disengaging herself, "but to-morrow we are to exchange the very romantic titles of 'bride' and 'bridegroom' for the much more commonplace 'host' and 'hostess.'"

"Oh! I am relieved that you are not going to divorce me at once." Armstrong was amused at her seriousness. "But it was your idea to invite them to join us, was it not?"

"I know it was—and now I must make a confession to you. I thought that in five weeks we both would be glad enough to have some little break in our love-making. But I did not realize how rapidly five weeks could pass. Still"—Helen sighed—"what is the use of having a villa in Florence unless you can invite your friends to see it?"

"Then you have not become tired of your husband as soon as you thought you would?"

"Nor you of your wife?" Helen retorted, quickly. "Mamma suggested it first. She said that so long a wedding trip as we had planned was sure to end with one or both of us becoming hopelessly bored unless we introduced other characters into our Garden of Eden."

"Did she say 'Garden of Eden'? That family party included a serpent, if rumor be correct."

The girl laughed.

"But there could not be one in ours, because I would never give you the chance to say, 'The woman did it.'"

"Your mother forgets that we are exceptions."

"She says there may be some difference in men, but that all husbands are alike."

"Trite and to the point, as always with mamma." Armstrong paused and smiled. "Well, I think even she will be satisfied with the success of her suggestion. How many do our guests number at present?"

Helen dropped the flower she was idly swinging and began to count upon her fingers.

"Let me see. There is Inez Thayer—I am glad that she could visit us, so that at last you can know her. It is strange enough that you should not have met her until the wedding. You cannot help liking each other, for she is interested in all those serious things you love so well. The girls used to make sport of our devotion at school because our dispositions are so unlike: she is thoughtful, while I am impulsive; she is carried away with anything which is deep and learned, while I, as you well know, have nothing more important in life than you and my music."

Helen paused for a moment thoughtfully. "Sometimes I wish I could really interest myself in those ancient deities you worship."

"You could if you only knew them as I do," he urged, quietly. "The present is the evolution of the past, but it has been evolved so fast that many of the old-time treasures have been forgotten in the mad pace of every-day life."

"But we can't remember everything," Helen replied; "there are not hours enough in the day. I can't even find time to read our modern writers as much as I wish I could, and I think one ought to do that before going back to the ancients."

"All modern literature is based upon what has gone before," insisted Armstrong.

"Wait a moment." Helen's face again became thoughtful. "I have it!" she cried, triumphantly. "'The gardens of Sicily are empty now, but the bees still fetch honey from the golden jars of Theocritus.' That is what you mean, is it not? I remember that from something of Lowell's I read at school."

"Splendid!" he laughed, with delight. "Who dares to say that you are not in sympathy with the past?" He bent his head down close to hers. "Would you not prefer to hold those 'golden jars' in your very hands, sweetheart, rather than merely read about them?"

"But, Jack, 'the gardens of Sicily are empty now.' Think how lonesome we should be." Helen threw back her head and drew in a long breath of the exhilarating air.

Armstrong was still insistent. "I wish I could make you see it as I do," he said. "The present of to-day is bound to be the past of to-morrow. What I want to do is to assimilate all that the past can give me, so that I may do my part, however small, toward giving it out again, made stronger and more effective because of its modern application, thus helping this present to become worthy of being considered by those who come after us."

Helen looked up at him with undisguised admiration. "Oh, Jack, that sounds so wonderful, and I wish I could enter into it with you, but I simply cannot do it. Inez will be just the one. At school, as I told you, she went in for the classics and all that, while I—well, I was sent there to be 'finished.' Don't look so disappointed, Jack. Truly I would if I could."

"I shall not give you up yet," he answered, smiling at Helen's intensity, notwithstanding his genuine regret. "Tell me something more about Miss Thayer, since you insist upon her becoming your substitute."

"Inez is a darling, in spite of her superiority," Helen replied, gayly, "and I simply could not have been married without her for a bridesmaid. She would have sailed two weeks earlier except for our wedding. As it was, she came over with her cousins, and has been travelling with them until time to join us here at the villa."

"De Peyster is still devoted, I judge?"

"Poor Ferdinand! His persistency has quite won my sympathy. He simply will not take 'no' for an answer, but travels back and forth between Boston and Philadelphia like any commercial traveller. Going over, he has a bunch of American Beauties under one arm and a box of bonbons under the other; returning, nothing but another refusal to add to those Inez has already given him."

"He is not a bad sort of chap at all, when you get past his peculiarities," Armstrong added.

"Ferdy is a splendid fellow, in his own way," assented Helen, warmly, "and any girl might do a great deal worse than marry him; but he is not Inez' style at all. I believe her trip to Europe is really to get away from him. I know he thinks that is the reason, and is simply inconsolable."

"De Peyster would be a good match," remarked Armstrong, thoughtfully. "He has plenty of money and plenty of leisure, and he ought to be able to make his wife fairly comfortable."

"But that is not what Inez wants. She has great ideas about affinities, and Ferdy does not answer to the description."

"Then there is your uncle Peabody," Armstrong prompted, helpfully.

"Yes, there is dear Uncle Peabody. You will enjoy him immensely."

"Does he live up to his reputation of a man with an 'ism'?"

"Oh, Jack! Some one has been maligning him to you. That is because he is the only original member of our family, and really the most useful."

"Indeed! If that is your estimate of him, it shall also be mine. I was prepared for a well-developed specimen of the *genus* crank."

"Wait till you see him." Helen laughed at her husband's mental picture. "He is a crank, in a way, but he is a mighty cheerful one to have around."

"He believes in making an air-plant of one's self, in order to help him forget his other troubles, does he not?"

"Who has been making fun of dear Uncle Peabody? I must have him tell you about his work himself. It is true that he believes most people overeat, and it is true that he is devoting his life and his fortune to finding out what the basis of proper nutrition really is; but as for starving—wait till you see him!"

"You have relieved me considerably," Armstrong replied, gravely. "From what I had heard of your uncle I had expected nothing less than to be made an example of for the sake of science—and you have already discovered that I am really partial to my meals."

"You can be just as partial to them as ever, Jack. But, seriously, I know you will find him most interesting, and I shall be surprised if his theories do not give you something new to think about."

"His theories will not do for me," said Armstrong, assuming a position of mock importance, "for I have always been taught that a touch of indigestion is absolutely essential to genius."

"Splendid!" cried Helen. "That will be just the argument to start the conversation at our first dinner and keep it from being commonplace. I have been trying to think how we could get Uncle Peabody interested. It is only that first dinner which I dread, and you have helped me out nobly."

"That makes two," suggested Jack.

"Yes, two. Then there are the Sinclair girls, who have been studying here in Florence for nearly a year. They will come up from their *pension*. That makes four—and the others, you know, are Phil Emory and Dick Eustis, who arrive in Florence from Rome to-night. I don't need to tell you anything about them."

"There is a whole lot you might tell me about Emory if you chose."

Armstrong looked slyly into his wife's face.

"Shame on you, Jack!" Helen cried, flushing; "the idea of being jealous on your wedding trip!"

"I am not jealous *now.*" He emphasized the last word.

"Well, I am glad you are over it."

"It looks like a very jolly party," he hastened to add, seeing that Helen's annoyance was genuine, "and I can see where we become old married folk to-morrow. You and Uncle Peabody will act as chaperons, I presume, Phil and Dick will look after the Sinclair girls, while I am to devote myself to Inez Thayer. Is that the programme?"

"Exactly. I am so anxious that Inez should appreciate what a talented husband I have. She has heard great stories about your learning and erudition, so now you must live up to the picture."

"Then suppose we start for home if you are quite rested. It is plainly incumbent on me to make sure that my knowledge of the classics proves equal to the test."

II

The Armstrongs had installed themselves in the Villa Godilombra, near Settignano. The date for the wedding was no sooner settled than Jack cabled to secure what had always seemed to him to be the most glorious location around Florence. Years before, his favorite tramp had been out of the ancient city through the Porta alla Croce to La Mensola, whence he delighted to ascend the hill of Settignano. Every villa possessed a peculiar fascination for him. The "Poggio Gherardo"—the "Primo Palagio del Refugio" of the *Decameron*—made Boccaccio real to him. The Villa Buonarroti, whither Michelangelo was sent as a baby, after the Italian custom, to be nursed in a family of *scarpellini*, always attracted him, and times without number he had stood admiringly before the wall in one of the rooms, gazing at the figure of the satyr which the infant prodigy drew with a burning stick taken from the fire. In those days he had been seized with a secret yearning to become an artist, and often he had tried to reproduce the satyr from memory, but always the ugly visage assumed a mocking, sneering aspect which caused him to relinquish his cherished ambition in despair.

But the Villa Godilombra appealed to Armstrong for a different reason. It stood high up on the hill, affording a wonderful view of the village of Settignano and the wide-spreading valley of the Arno. The villa itself, with its overhanging eaves, coigned angles, and narrow windows, set on heavy consoles, was essentially Tuscan, and impressive far out of proportion to its size. It would have seemed too massive but for an arcade at either end, the one connecting the house itself with its chapel, the other leading from the first floor through a spiral stairway in one pier of the arcade to what originally, in the days of the Gamberelli, had been an old fish-pond and herb-garden. In front of the villa a row of antiquated stone vases shared the honors with equally dilapidated stone dogs along a grassy terrace held up by a low wall, while beyond this and the house was the vineyard.

Armstrong had studied the plans of the house and grounds from a distance, because, after his disappointing experience with Michelangelo's satyr, he had firmly determined to become an architect and to build Italian houses in America. He had walked up and down the long bowling-green behind the villa, carefully noting the number of statues set upon the high retaining wall and figuring the height of the hedges. One day old Giuseppe, the sun-baked gardener who had watched the boy first with suspicion and then with interest, invited him to enter, and his joy had been complete. Giuseppe showed him the fish-pond and the grotto, lying in the shadow of the ancient cypresses, made up of varicolored shells and stones, with shepherds and nymphs occupying niches around a trickling fountain. He led him to the balustrade at the end of the bowling-green, and pointed out the panorama which terminated in the hills beyond the southern bank of the river.

Parallel with the back of the villa was another wall which supported a terrace of cypress and ilex trees. Behind this was the *salvatico*, without which no self-respecting Italian villa could maintain its dignity, with stone seats beneath the heavy foliage offering a grateful relief from the glare of the sun. And here and there were white statues of classic goddesses, to relieve the loneliness had it existed. An iron gate, let into the wall opposite the main doorway of the villa, led into a small garden, this leading in turn into another grotto, which, with its fountain and statues, formed an extension of the *vista*. On either side a balustraded flight of steps led up to an artificial height—the Italians' beloved *terrazza*—flanked by rows of orange and lemon trees, growing luxuriantly in their red earthen pots; while against the wide balustrades rested the heavily scented clusters of the camellia and the rose-tinted oleander.

Twelve years is a short space of time in Italy, where age is reckoned by the millennial, so it seemed perfectly natural, when Armstrong arrived in Florence, to find Giuseppe still at his old post and included in the lease as a part of the Villa Godilombra. The old man expressed no surprise, no delight—yet at heart he was well pleased. The previous tenants of the villa had been the unimaginative family of a German-American brewer, and their preference for beer over the wonderful *vino rosso* which he himself had pressed out from the luscious grapes in the vineyard filled his heart with sorrow. He confided to Annetta, the red-lipped maid Armstrong had engaged for Helen, that he "was glad to serve an 'Americano molto importante' rather than a *porco*." And Giuseppe took great satisfaction in placing upon that last word all the emphasis needed to express six months' accumulated disgust.

From the moment the Armstrongs arrived, Giuseppe's admiration for Helen knew no bounds. To him she was the personification of all that was perfection. Not that he expressed it, even to Annetta—he would have forgotten mass on Good Friday sooner than so forget his place. It was rather that devotion which is born and not made—occasionally, but not often, found in those who enter so intimately into the life of those they serve, yet who must always feel themselves apart from it. Hardly a day had passed since the Armstrongs had assumed possession of the villa that Helen had not found the choicest *fragole* at her plate, each juicy berry carefully selected and resting upon a bed of its own leaves at the bottom of the little basket. Her room was ever redolent with the odor of the flowers he smuggled in, always unobserved; and his instructions to the more frivolous Annetta as to her duties toward the *nobile donna* were such as to cause that young woman to throw her head haughtily on one side, with the observation that she was probably as well acquainted with the requirements of a lady's maid as any gardener was apt to be, even though he *were* old enough to be her grandfather.

This particular tiff had taken place while Armstrong and his wife were making their excursion to Fiesole. On their return they had found Giuseppe in a morose mood, which quickly vanished when Helen told him, in her broken Italian, that she expected guests upon the morrow, and depended upon him to see that every room was properly decorated, as he alone could do it. The old man could hardly wait to arrange the chairs upon the veranda, so eager was he to seek revenge upon his youthful tormentor.

"Did she ask you to arrange the flowers, young peacock-feather?" asked Giuseppe of Annetta when he found her in the kitchen. "Did she trust you even to bring the message to old Giuseppe? No. With her own lips the *Eccellenza* praised the one servant on whom she can rely."

"She knows you are good for nothing else," Annetta retorted, with a scornful laugh and a toss of her pretty head; "and she wishes to get you out of the way while we attend to the really important matters. See," she cried, as the tinkling of the maids' bell punctuated her remarks, "the *nobile donna* will now give *me* commands."

Giuseppe could not so far forget his dignity as to reply to such an outrageous slander, so he contented himself with casting upon Annetta his most withering glances as she hastily brushed past him, holding back her skirts lest they be defiled by touching the old man. He watched her angrily until she vanished through the door, then, with the choicest maledictions at his command, he shuffled into the garden—into his own domain, where the present generation of ill-bred servants, as he explained to himself, could vex him not.

Mrs. John Armstrong's first dinner at the Villa Godilombra was an unqualified success. Uncle Peabody had arrived early that morning; his optimism had set its seal of approval upon the evident happiness of the bridal couple, and he had already established himself as chief reflector of the concentrated joy which he saw about him. Inez Thayer was received into Helen's welcoming arms soon after luncheon, and was at once installed in the best guest-chamber for an extended visit. Two dusty *vetture* brought the Sinclair girls, Emory and Eustis, in time for dinner, each driver striving to deliver his passengers first in anticipation of an extra *pourboire*. The company was therefore complete, and each member quite in the spirit of the occasion.

The great candelabra cast their light upon the animated party seated about the table in such a manner that the old paintings hanging upon the walls of the high room were but dimly visible. The long windows were open, and the light breeze just cooled the air enough to mellow the temperature, without so much as causing the candle-flames to flicker. Giuseppe's choicest flowers, deftly arranged upon the table by Helen's skilful hands, contrasted pleasantly with the antique silver and china which had once been the pride of the original owner of the villa; and the menu itself, wisely intrusted by Helen to the old Italian cook, was rife with constant surprises for the American palate. Even the wines were new—if not in name, at least in flavor, for Italian vintages leave behind them their native richness and aroma when transplanted. Never was any *vino rosso* so delicious as that which Giuseppe made, even though unappreciated by his former master; never such *lacrima Christi* as that which Armstrong secured in a little wine-shop near the Bargello; never such *Asti spumante* as that which sparkled in the glasses, eager to share its own bubbling happiness in return for the privilege of touching the fair lips of the beautiful *donne Americane*.

"We had a friend of yours on board ship, Miss Thayer," said Emory, speaking to his left-hand neighbor as they seated themselves.

"A friend of mine?" queried Inez. "I can't think who it could be."

"Ferdy De Peyster," replied Emory.

Inez cast a quick glance at Helen. "Really?" she asked. "I thought he was going to spend the summer at Bar Harbor."

"Changed his mind at the last moment," he said. "Could not resist the charms of Italy. Do you know, Helen"—Emory addressed himself to his hostess—"De Peyster has developed a mania for art."

Helen laughed. "No," she replied, "that is news indeed. It is a side of Ferdy's nature which even his best friends had not suspected. Is he coming to Florence?"

"Can't say; but he is evidently planning to leave Rome. We left him at the Vatican, in the Pinacoteca, standing before Raphael's 'Transfiguration.'"

"With a Baedeker in his hand?" queried Jack.

"No, studying Cook's Continental Time-table."

"What a detective you would make, Mr. Emory," suggested Mary Sinclair as the laughter subsided.

"I have a better story about De Peyster than that."

Eustis waited to be urged.

"Give it to us, Dick," said Jack, helpfully.

"It was at Gibraltar," began Eustis. "We were in the same party going over the fortifications. De Peyster, you know, enlisted at the time of the Spanish war. Some family friend in the Senate obtained for him a berth as second lieutenant, and his company got as far as Key West. He rather prides himself on his military knowledge, and he confided to me that he had his uniform with him in case he was invited to attend any Court functions. Well, all the way around De Peyster explained everything to us. The Tommy Atkins who was our guide was as serious as a mummy, but confirmed everything Ferdy said. When you reach the gallery at the top, you remember, the guide points out the parade-ground below, and it happened that there was a battalion going through its evolutions."

"'Ah!' said De Peyster, 'this is very interesting.'" Then he described each movement, giving it the technical military name. At last he turned to our guide and said, patronizingly: 'I'm a bit disappointed, sergeant, after all I have heard of the precision of the English army. I have often seen American soldiers go through those same movements—just as well as that.'

"The sergeant saluted respectfully and gravely. 'Quite likely, sir,' he said, 'quite likely. These are raw recruits—arrived yesterday, sir!'"

"De Peyster was a sport, though," added Emory. "When he saw that the joke was on him he handed Tommy a shining sovereign and said: 'Here, sergeant, have this on me, and drink a health to our two armies—may comparisons never be needed.'"

Helen clapped her hands. "Good for Ferdy! He is all right if people would only leave him alone."

"Too bad he has so much money!" Eustis was reflective. "If De Peyster had to get out and hustle a bit you would find he had a whole lot of stuff in him."

"Of course he has," Uncle Peabody agreed.

"Do you know Mr. De Peyster?" Inez asked, surprised.

"No," replied Uncle Peabody, "I don't need to after hearing Mr. Eustis's summary. On general principles, every one has 'a whole lot of stuff in him.' The trouble is that people don't give it a chance to come out."

"Your confidence is evidently based upon your general optimism?" Armstrong remembered that Helen had mentioned this as a cardinal characteristic.

"Yes, but proved by a thousand and one experiments. Our present subject, who now becomes No. 1002, is apparently handicapped by the misfortune of inherited leisure. It is rarely that a man of possession reaches his fullest development without the spur of necessity. More frequently we see one extreme or the other—too much possession or too much necessity."

"That is all very well as a theory, but does it really prove anything as regards De Peyster?" questioned Armstrong. "Personally I think optimism is a dangerous thing. This confidence that everything is coming out right is what makes criminals out of bank cashiers."

"There is a vast difference between real and false optimism," replied Uncle Peabody. "I knew a man once who called himself a cheerful pessimist, because every time he planted a seed it grew down instead of up. He came to expect this, so it did not worry him any. He was a real optimist, even though he did not know it."

"What would be your prescription for a case like Mr. De Peyster's?" queried Bertha Sinclair.

"A good wife, possessed of ambition, sympathy, and tact," Uncle Peabody replied, promptly. "This, my dear Miss Sinclair, is your opportunity to assist me in proving my argument. Will you be my accomplice?"

"I? Why, I don't even know Mr. De Peyster," Bertha protested. "You must find some one else."

"Very well," sighed Mr. Cartwright. "You see how difficult it is for science to assert its laws."

Helen caught sight of Inez' cheeks and hastened to her friend's relief.

"Uncle Peabody, do you know that you are responsible for the first difference of opinion which has arisen between my husband and me?"

"My gracious, no! Can it be possible?"

"It is a fact. I stated to him only yesterday that perfect digestion was the only basis on which health and happiness can possibly rest. You taught me that, but Jack asserts that a touch of indigestion is absolutely essential to genius."

"How does he know? Has he a touch of indigestion?"

"Not a touch," laughed Armstrong, "and that proves my statement. I really believe I might have been a genius if my digestion had not always been so disgustingly strong."

"Don't despair, my dear boy."

Uncle Peabody looked at Jack over his spectacles. "Genius is a germ, and sometimes develops late in life. If your theory is correct, a few more gastronomic orgies such as this will make you eligible."

"But is there not something in what I say?" Armstrong persisted, seriously. "Is it not true that good health is against intellectual progression? Is not good health the supremacy of the physical over the mental? The healthy man is an animal—he eats and sleeps too much. Pain and suffering have not developed the nervous side, which is so closely connected with the intellectual. When the physical side becomes weakened, then the brain begins to act."

Uncle Peabody listened attentively and then removed his spectacles. "My dear Jack Armstrong," he said, at last, "I can see some fun ahead for both of us, and Helen has placed me still further in her debt by her choice of a husband. Your argument is not a new one. It was invented a great many years ago in France by some clever person who wished to have an excuse for late nights, absinthe, and cigarettes. Do you mean seriously to advance a theory which, if logically carried through to the end, would credit hospitals and homes for the hopelessly depraved with being the highest intellectual establishments in the world?"

"But look at the examples which can be cited," Armstrong continued, undisturbed. "Zola produced nothing of importance after he adopted the simple life, and Swinburne's poetry lost all its fire as soon as he 'reformed.'"

"Can you prove in either case that the question of nutrition or digestion entered into the matter at all?"

"Oh, it may have been a coincidence, of course; but many other cases might be added."

Uncle Peabody was silent for a moment. "Let me give you a simple problem," he said, at length. "Helen tells me that you have an automobile now on its way to Florence?"

Armstrong assented.

"When it arrives I presume you will engage a chauffeur?"

"What has an automobile to do with nutrition, Mr. Cartwright?" demanded Mary Sinclair. "Surely an automobile has no digestion."

"My application is near at hand. When you engage that chauffeur I presume you will insist that he knows the mechanism of the machine, understands the application of the motive power and other details which enter into safe and successful handling of the car?"

"Naturally," replied Jack. "I am not introducing my machine here for the purpose either of murder or suicide."

"Exactly. That is just what I wanted you to say. Now, every human stomach is an engine which requires at least as intelligent handling as that of an automobile. Upon its successful working depends the mechanical action of the body. We may disregard the additional dependence of the brain. Petroleum in the automobile is replaced by what we call food in the human engine. Too much of either, unintelligently applied, produces the same unfortunate result. Now I ask you, John Armstrong, would you engage as chauffeur for your automobile a man who knew no more about the mechanism of its engine, or how to feed and handle it properly, than you yourself know about your own body engine?"

"No," Armstrong admitted, frankly, "I would not."

"But which is more serious—a damage resulting from his ignorance or from your own?"

"Look here, Mr. Cartwright," said Jack, laughingly, "you promised that there was fun ahead for us both. At present it seems to be mostly for you and our friends."

"Who started the discussion?"

"Helen; but I admit my error in being drawn into it. I had not expected to be convicted upon my own evidence."

Helen rose. "I must rescue my husband from the calamity I have brought upon him. Come, let us have our coffee in the garden."

III

If one could have looked within Uncle Peabody's room after the other guests had snuffed out their candles, he would have discovered its inmate seated beside the flickering light with an open letter in his hand. He had read it over many times since its receipt nearly three months earlier, announcing in Helen's characteristic way her engagement and approaching marriage. No one else had ever come so closely into his life, and he felt a certain responsibility to satisfy himself that the girl had made no mistake in the important step which she had taken. Now that he had actually met her husband, he again perused the lines which had introduced his new nephew to him.

"It has actually happened at last," the letter began, *"and your favorite wager of 'a thousand to one on the unexpected' has really won. In other words, I, Helen Cartwright, condemned (by myself) to live and die an old maid as penalty for being so critical of the genus homo, now confess myself completely, hopelessly in love, and so happy in my new estate that I wonder why I ever hesitated.*

"It is all so curious. The things which interested me before now seem so commonplace compared to the events to come in connection with this broader existence which is opening up before me. How infinitely more gratifying it is to feel myself living for and a part of another's life, how comforting to know that some other personality, whom I can love and respect, feels himself to be living for and a part of my life. It adds to the seriousness of it all, but how it increases the satisfaction!

"I wish I could describe John Armstrong to you, but now that I am about to make the attempt I realize how difficult a task I have undertaken. He is eight years older than I, but sometimes he seems to be years younger, while again I feel almost like a child beside him. No, Uncle Peabody, it is not a similar case to that little Mrs. Johnson whom you quoted when you were last home as saying that a woman feels as old as the way her husband treats her. I know this will pop into your mind, so I will promptly head you off. The fact is that Jack is a very remarkable man. He is handsome, with great strength of character showing in every feature, he is tall and athletic,—but it is his wonderful mental ability which will most impress you. Think of a man playing on the Harvard 'Varsity eleven, rowing on the crew, and yet graduating with a summa cum laude!

"Jack is a superb dancer, thus disproving the common belief that a man can't be clever at both ends; and at the Assemblies, even before we were engaged, I used to anticipate those numbers which he had taken more than all the others. Besides this, his conversation was always so original,—touching frequently upon topics which were new to me. His particular fad is what he calls 'humanism' and his particular loves the great writers of the

past,—his 'divinities,' as he calls them. You probably understand just what all this means, but, alas! most of it is beyond my comprehension! What he tells me interests me, of course,—it even fascinates me. I can follow him up to a certain point; then we reach my limitations, and I am forced to admit my lack of understanding. That is when I feel so like an infant beside him. He is as patient as can be, and insists that when once I am in Florence, where the air itself is heavy with the learning of the past, I shall be able to comprehend it all, and it will mean the same to me that it does to him. I wish I felt as confident!

"*We are to be married in April, and Jack has taken the Villa Godilombra in Settignano for the season. We expect to arrive there early in May, and we want you to come to us for just as long a visit as you can arrange. You won't disappoint me, will you, dear Uncle Peabody? We all have been broken-hearted that you have so long delayed your return, and one of the events in our plans for Florence to which I am looking forward with the greatest eagerness is this visit with you. Write and tell me how your work progresses, but don't say 'I told you so.' This would show that you really expected it all the time, and your favorite argument would lose its force. Just say that you will come to us at Settignano.*"

The letter itself showed that Helen had changed much during the months which had elapsed since he had last seen her. There was a more serious undertone and a broader outlook,—due undoubtedly to Armstrong's influence. Uncle Peabody wondered whether Helen could have been attracted to this man by her admiration for his mental strength rather than by any real sentiment, perhaps mistaking the one for the other. This was the point he wished to settle in his own mind, and this was why he had studied them both, from the moment of his arrival, much more carefully than either one of them realized.

Armstrong was a remarkable man, as Helen had said. Even in the few hours he had known him, Uncle Peabody found much to admire. It was true that his manner toward Helen showed indulgence, almost as to a child rather than to a wife; but his devotion was entirely obvious, and this relation was to be expected after reading Helen's letter. Still, Mr. Cartwright told himself, the existence of this relation necessitated a certain readjustment before a perfection of united interests could be attained. Armstrong was bound to be the dominating force, and Helen must inevitably respond to this new influence, strange as it now seemed to her. His knowledge of her sympathetic and intuitive grasp of his own pet theories gave him confidence to believe that this response would be equally prompt and comprehensive.

Henry Peabody Cartwright was distinctly a citizen of the world. Boston had been his birthplace, Boston had been the base of his eminently successful business operations, and his name still figured in the list of the city's "largest taxpayers." Beyond this, the city of his early activity had, during the past twenty years, seen him only as a visitor at periodic intervals. He had emerged from his commercial environment at the age of forty, with a firm determination to gratify his ideals.

Fortunately for him, and for mankind as well, his ideals were not fully crystallized when he set out to gratify them. Boston was entirely satisfactory to him as an abiding-place, but he felt a leaven at work within him which demanded a larger arena than even the outlying territory of Greater Boston covered. He started, therefore, in the late eighties for a trip around the world, with the definite purpose, as he himself announced, of "giving things a chance to happen to him."

"I have no schedule and no plans," he said to those who questioned him. "I shall 'hitch my wagon to a star,' but always with my grip near at hand, so that I may change stars upon a moment's notice."

There were no immediate family ties to interfere with the carrying-out of what seemed to his friends to be rather quixotic ideas. There may have been some youthful romance, but, if so, no one ever succeeded in learning anything of it from him.

"It is all perfectly simple," he once good-naturedly replied to a persistent relative. "The girls I was willing to marry would not have me, and those who would have me I was not willing to marry. I used to think that I would become more attractive as I grew older, but I have given up that idea now. Once I tried to rub a freckle off with sand-paper and pumice-stone and found blood under the skin; but the freckle—the same old freckle—is there to this day."

His devotion to women in the composite was consistent and sincere; the fondness which existed between himself and his brother's family was such that his departure had left a distinct void, and his visits home were events circled with red ink in the family calendar. He enjoyed these visits no less than they; but with never more than a day or two of warning he would announce his intention of leaving for Egypt or India or some spot more or less remote in his quest for the unexpected. To the reproaches which were levelled at him, he replied, with a smile which defied controversy:

"I am just as sorry not to be with you all as you can possibly be to have me away; but I have educated myself to the separation, and have thus overcome the necessity for personal propinquity."

On that first trip around the world Uncle Peabody found one of his ideals, although he did not realize its vast importance until several years later. Japan appealed to him, and the longer he remained there the more impressed he became with certain of the national characteristics. First of all, he marvelled at the evenness of temper which the people displayed, at their endurance, their patience. He watched the carefulness with which they weighed the importance of each problem before accepting its responsibility, and their utter abandon in carrying it through when once undertaken. This was twenty years before the Russo-Japanese war, and he had come among them with the existing Occidental estimate of their paganism and barbarity. It may have been a species of incredulity leading to curiosity which induced him to remain among them, but as a result of his sojourn he discovered that they were philosophers rather than fatalists, geniuses rather than barbarians.

He questioned his new hosts, when he came to know them better, and was told quite seriously and quite naturally that they never became angry, because anger produced poison in the system and retarded digestion; that upon digestion depended health; that upon health depended happiness, and upon happiness depended personal efficiency and life itself. They explained that forethought was one of the cardinal factors of their creed, but added that its antithesis, fear-thought, was equally important as an element to be eliminated. They called his attention to the fact that they did not live upon what they ate, but upon what they digested, and that by masticating their food more thoroughly than he did they secured from the smaller quantity the same amount of nourishment without needlessly overloading their systems with undigested food which could not possibly be assimilated.

This last theory did not altogether appeal to Peabody Cartwright at first. His friends at the Somerset Club still held memories of his epicurean proclivities, and they were not weary even yet of recalling the time when he had won a goodly wager by naming, blindfolded, five different vintages of Burgundy and Bordeaux. But the more he thought it over the more convinced he became that the something to which he had promised to give a chance had really happened to him. He pondered, he experimented—but he still continued to eat larger quantities of food than the Japanese.

A year later he was in Italy, and in Venice Mr. Cartwright suddenly discovered that he had found the geographical centre of the civilized world. With Venice as the starting-point, one could reach London or Constantinople, St. Petersburg or New York, with equal exertion. Venice, therefore, became his adopted home, although it could claim no more of his presence than any one of a dozen other cities in the four quarters of the globe. During the twenty years, he had succeeded in making himself a part of each one—had become a veritable citizen of the world, but by no means a man without a country.

Italy served to drive home the truths which Japan had first shown him. Three years after his experience there, a dingy, second-hand book-store in

Florence had placed him in possession of Luigi Cornaro's *Discorsi della Vita Sobria*. He read it with amazement. Here in his hand, written by a Venetian nobleman more than three hundred years before, at the age of eighty-three, was the text-book of the theories of life which he had accepted from the Japanese as new and untried except among this alien people! It gave him a start, and he journeyed to Turin, Berne, Berlin, Brussels, Paris, London, St. Petersburg, and even back to Boston, seeking to interest the famous physiologists in his discovery, which he believed was destined to exterminate disease and to transform those practising the medical profession into hygienic engineers.

Mr. Cartwright's name and personality preserved him from a sanitarium, but his theories as to self-control, forethought, and fear-thought received ample opportunity for personal experiment. He was as tenacious as if his future depended upon the outcome. A good-natured indulgence here, and an incredulous sympathy there, gave him his first opportunities for demonstration. He not only drew upon his fortune, but freely contributed himself as a subject for experiment. It had been slow, but he had learned patience from the Japanese. Disbelief gradually changed into doubt, doubt into question, question into half-belief, and half-belief into conviction. Quietly, surely, his own faith was assimilated by those high in the physiological ranks, and almost against their will, and before they realized the importance of their concessions, he had forced them to prove him right by their own analyses.

The last five years had been a steady triumph. He had found his ideals, but he had not attained them. He knew what his life-work was, and had the gratification of counting among his friends and collaborators the highest authorities the world recognized. The habits of generations could not be changed in a moment—some of them could never be changed; but the ball had been started and was gaining in size with each revolution. It no longer needed his gentle, persuasive push; it had its own momentum now, and he found it only necessary to guide its advance and to watch its growth.

Uncle Peabody's thoughts reverted to his work as he folded Helen's letter and placed it again in his pocket, where he had so long carried it. He regretted having his labors interrupted just now, but he found himself keenly interested to watch Helen's approaching evolution. His wagon was firmly hitched to this new star, and he had no notion of changing stars. So, with a murmured "Bless you, my children. May you live forever, and may I come to your funeral," he sought the repose which the others had already found.

IV

Mary and Bertha Sinclair were just completing a year's study in Florence, upon which they were depending to perfect their musical education; but both girls were sufficiently homesick after their two years' absence from Boston to be more than eager to exchange their *pension* for a week's visit with Helen, who brought to them a fresh budget of home news,—for which their eagerness increased as the date for their return to America drew nearer. Emory and Eustis, too, added familiar faces, so the days following the first dinner at the villa proved to be full of interest and enjoyment to all concerned.

The guests became familiar with each portion of the house and grounds, the mysteries of Italian house-keeping were contrasted with the limitations of boarding, and numerous topics of common import succeeded each other without surcease.

During the morning following the arrival of the guests, Armstrong touched tentatively upon the subject of visiting the library.

"We went there when we first came to Florence," Mary Sinclair replied; "and we saw everything there was."

Armstrong smiled indulgently, thinking of the little they had really seen.

"You know we are not very literary," explained Bertha, catching the expression upon his face.

"They are really more hopeless cases even than I," Helen added, sympathetically.

"Why don't you try Phil and me?" inquired Emory. "We went through the Vatican library, so we are experts. At least they said it was a library. The only books we saw there were a few in show-cases—the rest they kept out of sight."

"You would not recognize a real book if you saw it, Emory," Armstrong replied, with resignation. "There is no hurry. Perhaps Miss Thayer will go with me some day soon."

"Indeed I will," Inez responded, with enthusiasm. "There is nothing I wish so much to do."

"Good." His appreciation was sincere. "I shall take real delight in introducing to you my old-time friends, with whom I often differ but, never quarrel."

"Are they so real to you as that?" Inez asked, impressed by his tone.

"They are indeed," Armstrong replied, seriously. "I visit and talk with them just as I would with you all. But they have an aggravating advantage over me, for, no matter how laboriously I argue with them, their original statement stands unmoved there upon the written page, as if enjoying my feeble effort to disturb its serenity, and defying me to do my worst."

"I would much prefer to give them an absent treatment," asserted Eustis.

"Inez is clearly the psychological subject," Helen added. "At school she was forever putting us girls to shame by her mortifying familiarity with the classics. It is only fair that she should now be paid in her own coin."

"I accept both the invitation and the challenge," replied Inez, bowing to her hostess, and, walking over to the low wall on which Helen had seated herself, she threw her arm affectionately about her neck. "But you must not embarrass me with such praise, or your husband will suffer a keen disappointment. To study Latin and Greek out of school-books is one thing; to meet face to face the personalities one has regarded as divinities— even reading their very handwriting—is another. It makes one wonder if she ever did know anything about them before."

"That is exactly the spirit in which to approach the shrine, Miss Thayer!" cried Armstrong, enthusiastically. "Let us frame a new beatitude: 'Blessed is she who appreciates the glories of antiquity, for she shall inherit the riches of the past.'"

The contrast of the two girls in the rich Italian morning light was so striking that Uncle Peabody paused in his approach after a successful attack upon the rose-bushes, touched Armstrong upon the shoulder, and nodded admiringly in their direction. They were separated a little from the others, and were busily engaged in a conversation of their own, in which no man hath a part, quite oblivious to the attention they attracted. Inez was standing, and, even though seated, Helen's superb head reached quite to her companion's shoulder, and the fair hair and complexion were clearly defined against the darker hue of the face and head bent down to meet her own. Her eyes, looking out into the distance even as she spoke, reflected the calm, satisfied contentment of the moment, while in the brown depths of the other's one could read an ungratified ambition, an uncertainty not yet explained. Inez Thayer's face was attractive, Helen's was beautiful—that beauty which one feels belongs naturally to the person possessing it without the necessity of analysis.

Armstrong was evidently pleased with this comparison, as he had been with all previous ones. Italy, it seemed to him, formed just the background to set off to best advantage his wife's personal attractions. Uncle Peabody smiled contentedly at the undisguised satisfaction which was so clearly indicated in the younger man's face.

"If there had been any girls in Boston who looked like that when I was of sparking age," he whispered to Armstrong, "I should certainly have married and settled down, as I ought to have done."

"And allowed the world to perish of indigestion?" queried Armstrong, smiling.

"Scoffer! you do not deserve your good-fortune. Come, these roses are becoming all thorns. Young ladies, may I intrude upon your *tête-à-tête* long enough to present you with the trophies of my after-breakfast hunt?"

"A thousand apologies, Uncle," cried Helen, taking the roses in her arms and burying her face in their fragrant petals. "Oh! how beautiful! And how idiotic ever to leave this Garden of Paradise and immure yourselves within that musty old library. Do you not repent?"

"I place the decision wholly in Miss Thayer's hands," said Armstrong; but he glanced at Inez with evident expectancy.

"Then I decide to go," replied the girl. "I am quite impatient to meet the friends in whose good company Mr. Armstrong revelled before his present reincarnation."

"When?" asked Armstrong, quickly.

"Now!"

"Splendid! I will order the carriage at once."

"There is rapid transit for you!" exclaimed Eustis. "Jack believes in striking while the iron is hot."

"What a narrow escape we have had," murmured Mary Sinclair, with a sigh of relief.

"Very well," said Helen, resignedly. "It may be just as well to have it over. Jack has been looking forward to this ever since he turned his face toward Florence, and he will be quite miserable until he has actually gratified his anticipation.—But don't be away long, will you, Jack?"

"Miss Thayer will very likely find the staid company which we plan to keep quite as stupid as the rest of you anticipate," replied Armstrong, "so we may be home sooner than you expect."

Inez had already disappeared in-doors to put on her hat, and Armstrong started out to call a carriage. Helen intercepted him as he crossed the veranda.

"You won't mind if I don't go with you to-day, will you, Jack? If it were just to see the treasures at the library I would urge them all to go; but I know what is in your mind, dear. Truly, I will go with you some time, and you shall try your experiment upon me; but I am not in the mood for it just now. I ought not to leave the others, anyway."

"It is all right, of course," he answered. "I wish you did feel like going, but your substitute seems to be enthusiastic enough to make up for your antipathy."

"Don't call it that," Helen answered, half-reproachfully; "it is simply that I am ashamed to have my ignorance exposed,—and it will give you such a splendid chance really to know Inez. Now run along and have a good time, and tell me all about it when you come home."

The little one-horse victoria soon left the villa behind, and was well along on the narrow descending road before either of its occupants broke the silence. As if by mutual consent, each was thinking what neither would have spoken aloud. Helen had not seen the expression of disappointment which passed over her husband's face as she spoke. He would have given much if it might have been his wife beside him. He had studied the girl carefully, and had found in her an intuitive sympathy with the very subjects concerning which she disclaimed all knowledge. At first he had thought that she exaggerated her limitations because of his deeper study, but he soon discovered her absolute sincerity. It was a lack of confidence in herself, he inwardly explained, and when once in Florence he would give her that confidence which was the only element lacking to her complete understanding. But as yet he had been unable to get her inside the library, or even within range of the necessary atmosphere.

Inez Thayer's thoughts were upon the same subject, but from a different standpoint. Her last words to Helen, when Uncle Peabody had interrupted their conversation, framed a mild reproach. "If I had won a man like Jack Armstrong," Inez whispered to her, "I would not allow any one, not even you, to take my place on an excursion such as this, upon which he has so set his whole heart."

"You are a sweet little harmonizer, Inez," Helen had answered, smilingly, "but you are a silly child none the less. Jack and I understand each other perfectly. He knows my limitations, and, if I went, I should only spoil his full enjoyment. You will understand it and revel in it, and he will be supremely happy. If you were not so much better fitted naturally for this sort of thing, of course I should go rather than disappoint him, but, truly, the arrangement is much better as it is."

Inez had no opportunity to continue the conversation, but Helen had not convinced her. Hers was an intense nature, and she had much more of the romantic in her soul than her best friends gave her credit for. Her one serious love-affair had proved only an annoyance and mortification. Ferdinand De Peyster was in many ways a desirable *parti*, as mammas with marriageable daughters were quite aware. He was possessed of a handsome competency, was not inconvenienced by business responsibilities, and his devotion to Inez Thayer was only whetted to a greater degree of constancy by the opposition it received from its particular object. He was not lacking in education, having spent four years in the freshman class at Harvard; he was not unattractive, in his own individual way, and his one great desire, not even second to his striving for blue ribbons with his fine stable of blooded horses, was to have her accept the position of head of his household.

But Inez was repelled by the very subserviency of his devotion. Her love rested heavily upon respect, and this could be won only by a man who commanded it. John Armstrong fulfilled her ideal, and she wondered why Fate had not fashioned the man whom she had attracted in a similar mould.

Armstrong looked up from his reverie half guiltily, and for a moment his eyes met those of his companion squarely. Inez could not match the frank glance—it seemed to her as if he must have read her thoughts; but the heartiness of his words relieved her apprehension.

"What a bore you must think me, Miss Thayer! I have not spoken a word since we left the house."

"I must assume my share of responsibility for the silence," Inez replied, regaining her composure. "The seriousness of our quest must have had a sobering effect upon us both."

"But you won't find these old fellows so serious as you think," Armstrong hastened to say. "They were humanists and products of the movement which marked the breaking away from the ascetic severity preceding them. But, after all, they were the first to realize that life could be even better worth living if it contained beauty and happiness."

"You see how little I know about them, in spite of Helen's attempt to place me on a pedestal."

"Why, if it had not been for their work," he continued, enthusiastically, "the classics might still have remained as dead to us as they were to those who lived in the thirteenth century. Instead of studying Virgil and Homer, we should have been brought up on theological literature and the 'Holy Fathers.'"

"I feel just as I did at my coming-out party," Inez replied—"that same feeling of awe and uncertainty. I am eager to go with you, yet I dread it somehow. It is not a presentiment exactly,—it is—"

"I know just what you mean," Armstrong interrupted, sympathetically; "and, if you feel like that now, just wait until you see old Cerini, the librarian. It is he who is responsible for my passion for this sort of thing. Why, I remember, when I was here years ago and used to run in to see him at the Laurenziana, I never regarded him as a mortal at all; and I don't believe my reverence and veneration for the old man have abated a whit in the twelve years gone by."

The light vehicle had passed through the Porta alla Croce, and was swaying from side to side like a ship at sea, rattling over the stones of the narrow city streets at such a rate that conversation was no longer a pleasure.

"Just why Florentine cabmen are content to drive at a snail's pace on a good road and feel impelled to rush at breakneck speed over bad ones is a phase of Italian character explained neither by Baedeker nor by Hare," remarked Armstrong, leaning nearer to Inez to make himself heard.

With a loud snap of his whip and a guttural "Whee-oop," the *cocchiere* rounded the statue of John of the Black Bands, just missed the ancient book-stand immortalized by Browning in the *Ring and the Book*, and came to a sudden stop before the unpretentious entrance to the Biblioteca Laurenziana.

"You have been here before, of course?" he asked his companion as they passed through the wicket-gate into the ancient cloisters of San Lorenzo.

"Once, with Baedeker to tell me to go on, and with the tall Italian custodian to stop me when I reached the red velvet rope stretched across the room, which I suppose marks the Dante division between Purgatory and Paradise."

"This time you shall not only enter Paradise, but you shall behold the Beatific Vision," laughed Armstrong.

Passing by the main entrance of the library at the head of the stone stairs, Armstrong led the way along the upper cloister to a small door, where he pressed a little electric button—an accessory not included in Michelangelo's original plans for the building. A moment later they heard the sound of descending footsteps, and presently a bearded face looked out at them through the small grated window. The inspection was evidently satisfactory, for the heavy iron bar on the inside was released and the door opened.

"Good-morning, Maritelli," said Armstrong in Italian. "Is the *direttore* disengaged?"

"He is in his study, signore, awaiting your arrival."

Maritelli dropped the iron bar back into place with a loud clang and then led the way up the short flight of stone steps to the librarian's study. Armstrong detained Inez a moment at the top.

"I brought you in this way because I want you to see Cerini in his frame. It is a picture worthy the brush of an old master."

Maritelli knocked gently on the door and placed his ear against it to hear the response. Then he opened it quietly and bowed as Armstrong and his companion entered.

"Buon' giorno, padre." Armstrong gravely saluted the old man as he looked up. "I have brought to you another seeker after the gold in your treasure-house."

Cerini's face showed genuine delight as he rose and extended both hands to Inez. "Your wife!" he exclaimed; "I am glad indeed to greet her."

Armstrong flushed. "No, padre, not my wife, but her dearest friend, Miss Thayer."

The old man let one arm fall to his side with visible disappointment, which he vainly sought to conceal.

"I am sorry," he said, simply, taking Inez' hand in his own. "I have known this dear friend for many years, and have loved him for the love he gave to my work. I had hoped to greet his wife here, and to find that the *literæ humaniores* were to her the elixir of life that they are to me—and to him."

"When I tell her of my visit she will be eager to come to you as I have," said Inez, strangely touched by the keenness of his disappointment. "To-day she could not leave her guests."

"Will you first show Miss Thayer the illuminations and the rarest of the incunabula?" asked Armstrong, eager to change the subject; "and then will you let us come back here to talk with you?"

"With pleasure, my son, with pleasure. What shall I show her first?"

"That little 'Book of Hours' illuminated by Francesco d'Antonio, padre."

Cerini pulled up the great bunch of keys suspended from the end of his girdle and unlocked one of the drawers in the ancient wooden desk in front of him.

"I always wonder how you dare keep so priceless a treasure in that desk, and why it is not put on exhibition where visitors may see it," Armstrong queried.

Cerini laughed quietly. "There are many other treasures, my son, equally precious, as you know well, scattered about in these desks and drawers, where I alone can find them."

"How dare you take the risk?"

Cerini's face showed a gentle craftiness. "We are in Italy, my son. If any one could find these gems, any one could be librarian"—and the old man chuckled quietly to himself.

Inez' eyes were fastened upon a little purple velvet case inlaid with jewels. Cerini opened it carefully, exposing a small volume similarly bound and similarly adorned. Armstrong eagerly watched the interest in the girl's face as the full splendor of the masterpiece impressed itself upon her—the marvellous delicacy of design, the gorgeousness of color, the magnificence of the decoration and the miniatures. Inez drew in her breath excitedly and bent nearer to the magnifying-glass which it was necessary to use in tracing the intricacy of the work.

"Wonderful!" she cried, and then was silent.

"It belonged to Lorenzo the Magnificent, and represents the finest of the *quattrocento* work, my daughter," explained the old man, pleased as was Armstrong by her unfeigned admiration. "The patrons of the book in the fifteenth century considered gems of thought as the most precious of all jewels. The page containing them must be written upon the finest and the rarest parchment. They could not inlay costly stones, so they employed the most famous artists to place upon the page in beaten gold and gorgeous colors a representation of the jewels and miniatures as perfect as art at its highest could produce. Can you wonder, my daughter, that men brought up in the school of neo-Platonism should look upon the invention of printing as an evil and an innovation to be opposed?"

Inez would not permit Cerini to close the volume until she had feasted her eyes upon every page.

"Have you not prepared me for an anti-climax?" she asked, with a sigh, as Armstrong suggested a visit to the room of illuminations. "Surely there is nothing else here to surpass what I have just seen."

The librarian answered. "Nothing to surpass it, truly, but other volumes equally interesting."

The old man led them into a larger room filled with wooden cases whose glass tops were covered with faded green curtains. Costly tapestries lined the walls, but Inez' attention was quickly taken from them as Cerini pulled aside the curtains and disclosed the resplendent wealth beneath. Heavy choir-books, classic manuscripts, books of hours, breviaries embellished by Lorenzo Monaco, master of Fra Angelico, by Benozzo Gozzoli, whose frescos still make the Riccardi famous, and other artists whose names have long since been forgotten, but whose work remains as an everlasting monument to a departed art. Magnificent examples of every school, from the early Byzantine to the decadent style of the sixteenth century, combined to teach the present the omnipotence of the past.

From case to case they passed, their guide indicating the variations and the significance of the different schools, out into the great library itself, in which, with its noble yet simple proportions as laid down by Michelangelo, Inez found a relief after the gorgeousness and grandeur of the last hour. Armstrong pointed out to her the *plutei* upon which the great books rested, and to which they now remained chained as in the olden days, four centuries back, when they began their eternal vigil. Life outside the old walls had changed mightily since Cosimo de' Medici, the first grand-duke, laid their foundations. Cosimo, *"pater patriæ,"* the real founder of the collection, Pietro and Giovanni de' Medici had come and gone; Lorenzo il Magnifico had lived and died, bequeathing to them his illustrious name; Charles VIII. of France had destroyed the power of the house of the Medici, the Medici had again regained their own, the house of Lorraine had succeeded them, the separate states had been merged into a great kingdom—and still the volumes held their places at the end of their chains, as if to prove the immutability of learning as compared with the changeability of princes.

At Armstrong's suggestion, Cerini led them back into his study, where the old man again took his place at his desk, as his visitors seated themselves where they could best watch him and listen to his words. It was, indeed, as Armstrong had expressed it, a picture for an old master. Cerini was clad in the black silk soutane of his learned order, with the *biretta* upon his head. He was spare, and the skin upon his face and hands was as dried and colored as the ancient parchment of the books with which he lived. The dim light coming through the stained-glass window enhanced the weirdness of his aspect, and as one looked he seemed the personification of the ancient written manuscript vivified and speaking the words which one would have expected to read upon the page.

"My daughter," he was saying to Inez, "you, too, are a humanist, as my young friend and I are, or you could not manifest so true an understanding as you do. For humanism, my daughter, is not only the love of antiquity: it is the worship of it—a worship carried so far that it is not limited to adoration alone, but which forces one to reproduce. By the same token the humanist is the man who not only knows intimately the ancients and is inspired by them: it is he who is so fascinated by their magic spell that he copies them, imitates them, rehearses their lessons, adopts their models and their methods, their examples and their gods, their spirit and their tongue."

SLOWLY THE SPELL BEGAN TO WORK UPON INEZ' BRAIN. SHE WAS NO LONGER IN THE PRESENT—SHE WAS A WOMAN OF ITALY OF FOUR CENTURIES BACK

Then Cerini passed on in his conversation to the old-time writers themselves. The little study was poorly ventilated, and the air was heavy. The ancient tomes exuded their peculiar odor, and the low, sing-song voice of the speaker seemed far removed from the life they had just left outside. Slowly the spell began to work upon Inez' brain. She was no longer in the present—she was a woman of Italy of four centuries back. Petrarch, with his laurel-crowned head, rose up before her and recited verses written for Laura; Politian gave to her of his wisdom; Machiavelli discussed Florentine politics with her. It was not the voice of Cerini the librarian which she heard—it was the veritable voice from the dead and buried past. She furtively glanced at Armstrong and saw in his face a light which she knew Helen had never seen there, and in her heart she felt a guilty joyousness at the advantage she had gained. It was Leonardo sitting at the old desk now—Leonardo the master of art, of sculpture, the forerunner, the man-god against the god-man. She pressed her hand to her head; it was dripping moisture. Would he never stop? It was becoming fearsome, unbearable. Her eyes were fixed upon the aged priestly clad figure before her; she could not move them. What power held her, what magic controlled even her thoughts? She tried to speak to Armstrong, to tell him that she was ill, but her mouth seemed parched and she could not speak. She looked at Cerini's chair again. The old man was no longer there. Machiavelli had taken his place and was uttering diatribes against the state. She must cry out—she could not. She started to her feet—then she fell back, and all became a blank. When she revived, a few moments later, it was in the sunny enclosure of the cloister garden, whither Armstrong had anxiously carried her, and where the fresh air served to relieve the tension and to counteract the influence which had so overpowered her.

V

By mutual consent, Miss Thayer and Armstrong decided not to mention the rather dramatic finale to their first excursion to the library. Inez experienced the deepest mortification, while Jack blamed himself severely that he had not watched his companion more carefully. If he had done this, he repeated to himself, he might easily have anticipated and avoided the unpleasant climax to an otherwise thoroughly enjoyable morning. Miss Thayer, however, would not listen to his apologies: he had accepted her as a comrade, and she had proved herself unequal to the test. Armstrong tried to reassure her, but his efforts were not eminently successful.

The whole affair, in spite of their disclaimers, made a considerable impression upon them both. Armstrong knew that it had not been weakness alone; for even his brief acquaintance with her told him that strength was a salient point in her character. She was impressionable—he realized that—but surely not to the extent of losing all control over herself. Was it—and Armstrong feared lest Inez should read his mind as the thought came to him—was it that same irresistible influence of those ancient spirits, coming out from the past to her as they had so many times to him, recognizing her as a reincarnation of themselves, and claiming her, even for that, brief moment of unconsciousness, as a part of what had gone before?

Inez pleaded a headache upon reaching the villa, and asked that her lunch be sent to her room; but it was long after Annetta had left the tray upon the table that she was able to taste, even sparingly, the tempting delicacies which were placed before her. What can be more searching than a woman's self-examination? She had told Armstrong that she blamed herself for her weakness; so she did, but it was not wholly the weakness of losing consciousness. Who was this man, and what this influence which had so suddenly entered into her life and assumed such immediate control over her? She felt that she could resist either separately, but together they produced a power which she questioned her ability to oppose. And the strange part of it all was that no one was forcing it upon her. She knew perfectly well that she need never go to the library again unless she chose; but she knew equally well what her choice must inevitably be, if the opportunity were offered her.

Even as she recalled her experience, a thrill half of delight, half of apprehension, passed over her. What did it all mean? Armstrong compelled her respect, but it was ridiculous even to wonder whether or not the sentiments he inspired were of a more serious nature. The subjects in which he was interested appealed to her highest self and fascinated her, but beyond this what possible force could they possess to render her so immediately subservient to their demands? What was there about it all which made it seem so inexpressively delicious? And what of him, of this man above whose head the ancients had already placed the halo of their approval, who stood to her as the personification of ideal manhood?

These were some of the questions Inez Thayer asked herself that afternoon, wrestling within and striving honestly to decide her course; but even as she did so she found her thoughts again centering themselves upon Armstrong as she closed her eyes and allowed herself to be carried back to the experiences of the morning. She had no reasonable excuse to leave Florence, which instinctively she felt to be the safest thing to do; and, besides this, her spirit revolted at the thought that she could not meet the problem face to face and master it. She must do it, she would do it; and, having finally arrived at this determination, she came down, just before dinner, and joined her friends in the garden, where they were enjoying the soft close of the perfect Italian day.

"There you are!" Helen welcomed her with outstretched arms. "Is your headache better?"

"Yes, thank you," Inez replied, forcing a smile; "the air was very close in the library, and then, too, I found so much to make me thoughtful."

"Then you were not disappointed?" Emory asked.

"Disappointed? It was wonderful. You don't know how much you all missed."

"You look as if Jack had shown you some spooks," remarked Eustis; "you are as white as one yourself."

The color quickly returned to Inez' face. "I am always like that when I have one of these wretched headaches," she explained. "But, truly, I never had such a remarkable experience. I can quite understand Mr. Armstrong's devotion. I never knew before how fascinating such learning really is."

"Did he actually conjure up those old fellows and put them through their paces for you?" Emory asked.

Miss Thayer was in no mood for bantering. "It is not possible for you to understand without experiencing it yourself," she said, quietly.

"Or even afterward, I suspect," Bertha Sinclair added, slyly.

"I am so glad that you enjoyed it," said Helen. "I couldn't get much out of Jack, and I was afraid that you had passed a stupid morning and that the headache was the natural result."

"I shall never forget it—never!" Inez murmured.

Helen regarded her attentively for a moment. "I had no idea it would make so strong an impression on you," she said at length. "Now that it is over, you and Jack will both feel better satisfied."

"You must see Cerini, Helen, and let him show you those wonderful books and explain everything, just as he did to us."

"So I will, sometime," Helen smiled. "Perhaps he could bring out my dormant possibilities."

"It is time we dressed for dinner," remarked Mary Sinclair, rising. "You and Inez are already *en grande tenue*, but the rest of us are shockingly unconventional."

As the Sinclair girls hurried into the house, closely followed by the men, Helen leaned against the balustrade at the end of the bowling-green and watched the deepening color which touched alike the spires of Santa Croce and the turret of the Palazzo Vecchio, gleamed on the dome of the Cathedral and Giotto's tower, and spread like wine over the placid surface of the Arno. Beyond the river rose the basilica of San Miniato, its ancient pediment sharply outlined against the sky. Helen's thoughts wandered even farther away than her eyes. Inez watched her for several moments before slipping her arm about her waist.

"Oh, Inez!" Helen was startled for an instant. "Did you ever see such a wonderful spot as this?" she continued, recovering herself. "Some new beauty discloses itself uninvited hour by hour. Every time I come into the garden I find some lovely flower I never saw before, or meet some sweet odor which makes me shut my eyes and just draw it in with delight. Each time I look toward Florence the view is different, and each new view more beautiful than the last. Oh, Inez darling, is it an enchanted palace that Jack has brought me to, or is it just because I am so blissfully, supremely, foolishly happy?" Helen embraced her friend enthusiastically.

"Let us call it the enchanted palace, dear," Inez answered as Helen released her, "and you the modern Circe, with power to make all about you as beautiful and as happy as the ancient Circe to cast malign influences."

Helen laughed. "Why not take it further and say that the transformation of the ancient Circe is the final triumph of Uncle Peabody's labors? Had his theories been in force among the friends of Ulysses, the fair lady could never have turned them into swine. But tell me, did you not find Jack a very different person from what you had expected after seeing him here at home?"

"I did, indeed," assented Inez, soberly.

"Is he not simply splendid?" Helen's face beamed with pride. "It was just as much of a surprise to me. Of course, I have always known that he was interested in all these things, but it has only been since we were married that I have realized how much he actually knows.—I wish I thought there was even the slightest chance of his being able to lead me up to his heights, he is so eager for it. I shall give him an opportunity to try his experiment, of course, but the trouble is that in spite of the interest and fascination which I do feel, his hobby always seems to me to be hemmed in with needless limitations. For my part, I don't see why we can't take the best these master spirits of the past can give us, just as Jack says, but without ourselves becoming a part of the past.—You see how absolutely hopeless I am. I wonder how in the world he ever came to be attracted to me."

"You are the only one who wonders."

"Oh, I know that my hair is not red, and that I don't squint, and all that, but Jack is so fascinated by everything scholarly that I don't see why he didn't select an intellectual wife. Why, I don't even wear glasses!"

Inez smiled at the picture Helen drew. "The rest of us girls understand why he made just the selection he did, Helen."

"I never wanted to be intellectual before. Until now I have always considered the caricatures of the Boston Browning woman as typical of the highly educated species; but you are showing me that a girl can be human and intellectual at the same time."

"I wish I could show you that you make too much of a mountain out of this intellectual bugbear," Inez replied, candidly. "Your husband is a very unusual man. His interest in the humanities is beyond anything one can appreciate without seeing him as I saw him this morning. He longs to take you with him into this life, and if I were in your place I should let him be the one to discover my lack of understanding, if I really did lack it, instead of insisting upon it as a foregone conclusion. For myself, I don't take much stock in it. I remember too well how quick a certain Miss Cartwright was at school to grasp new ideas, and I have not noticed any serious retrogression since."

Helen pondered carefully over her friend's criticism before replying. "I suppose it does seem like obstinacy," she said, finally—"to him as well as to you; yet to myself it appears perfectly consistent. The one thing which gives me an idea of the extent of his devotion is my music. You know how I adore it, how much a part of my life it has always been—yet it means nothing to Jack, and he therefore takes no particular interest in it. He went to the Symphonies and the Opera with me while we were engaged, and to concerts and recitals, but I knew all the time that it was just to please me. I made up my mind that when we were married I would keep up my interest in this 'devotion' of mine only as much as I could without having it interfere with those things which he cared for or which we could enjoy together. But the fact that music means less to him than it means to me does not make me love him any the less."

"But you don't enter into this particular interest of his, even to please him, as he did to please you."

"Because I appreciate from the experience I have just mentioned how little real satisfaction it would give either one of us. Looking back, I feel that I was positively selfish to let him go to those concerts with me, and I shall never inflict them on him again. I am sure that he knows how I feel, and I think he ought to be grateful for my consideration."

Inez pressed Helen's hand. "You ought to know best, dear," she answered. "You both possess such wonderful possibilities that it would be a shame not to combine them. It seems to me that you might come to an appreciation of each other's interests by becoming familiar with them.—I wonder if you realize what a man your husband is?"

Helen leaned over and kissed her impulsively. "I realize more than I ever intend to let him know, dear child. He would become unbearably conceited were he even to guess how much he has already become to me. I really did not want to marry him—or to marry any one—but he swept away every objection, just as he always does, and now I find myself wondering how in the world I ever existed without him. Oh, Inez"—Helen's face became tense in her earnestness—"we girls think we know a whole lot about marriage. We anticipate it—we dread it; but, when one actually enters into her new estate, she knows how infinitely more it is to be anticipated, if happy, than her fondest dream. But if unhappy—then her dread must have been infinitesimal compared with the reality."

"'Marriage is either a complete union or a complete isolation,'" quoted Inez.

"As I tell you, Jack and I understand each other perfectly," Helen continued, confidently, "and that means so much to a girl. One of the first things I told him, after we became engaged, was that if our affection stood for anything it must stand for everything. If at any time while we were engaged, or even after we were married, he felt that he had made a mistake in thinking me the one woman in the world for him, he was to come to me frankly and say so, and together we would plan how best to meet the situation. Suppose, for instance, that Jack met some one whom he really loved better than me. It would be an awful experience, but how much less of a tragedy to recognize the fact than to live on, a hollow, miserable existence, such as we see in so many instances around us."

"And he has not confessed to you yet?"

"Not yet," Helen laughed, "and we shall have been married six weeks to-morrow. That is a pretty good start, is it not?"

"But how about yourself—have you the same privilege?"

"Of course; but that is not important, for I shall never see any one fit to ride in the same automobile with Jack."

"What did you say about my automobile? Has it arrived?"

Armstrong's face was filled with eager expectation as he came up behind Helen, followed by Uncle Peabody. He drew her affectionately toward him.

"You wretch!" cried Helen, "you have been eavesdropping."

"Not an eavesdrop," protested Jack, "and I can prove it by a witness. When I came down-stairs I looked for my beloved spouse upon the terrace and found her not. The gentle Annetta confided to me that you and the Signorina Thayer were in the garden; I set out upon my quest and found you here discussing my automobile or some one else's. Again I ask you, have you news of its arrival?"

"No, Jack—no news as yet; and you make out so good a case that I must absolve you. Since you insist on knowing, we were discussing the very prosaic subject of matrimony."

"Why discourage Miss Thayer from making the attempt simply because of your own sad case?" Armstrong queried, releasing his wife and seating himself beside her on the edge of the balustrade. "Marriage is a lottery—so saith the philosopher. We all know the preponderance of blanks and small prizes, yet each one feels certain that he will be the lucky one. Once in a while a chap pulls out the capital prize, and that encourages the others, though it ought to discourage them, because it lessens the chances just so much. But what I object to is the growling afterward, when each should realize that he is getting exactly what he ought to have expected."

"But it is not fair that both you and Helen should have drawn the lucky numbers," Inez declared. "It makes it so hopeless for the rest of us."

"There, Sir Fisher," cried Helen, "you have gained the compliment for which you strove. Art satisfied?"

"No one has drawn me yet," suggested Uncle Peabody, "and I am a capital prize—I admit it."

"It is a shame to throw cold water on Miss Thayer's beautiful sentiment," continued Armstrong. "Such thoughts are so rare that they should be encouraged; but the facts of the case are that the capital prizes in the men's lottery were discontinued long ago. No—among the girls they are still to be won at rare intervals, but the only way to distinguish the men is by looking up their rating in Bradstreet's, or their mother's family name in the Social Register. Other than this, one man is as bad as another, if not worse."

Inez looked at Armstrong for a moment with a puzzled expression, but failed to find any suggestion that he was speaking lightly. And yet—what a change in attitude from the morning! She hesitated to turn the subject upon what seemed to her to be forbidden ground, yet she could not resist opposing his expressions, even though they might be uttered flippantly. Her voice contained a reproach.

"You spoke differently of men this morning."

Armstrong turned to her quickly. "This morning?" he repeated. "Oh, but I was referring to the humanists, and to ancient ones at that. I am talking now of men in general, rather than of those rare exceptions, ancient or modern, who have succeeded in separating themselves from their commonplace contemporaries. Of course, my respect for the old-timers is supreme, because their great accomplishments were in the face of so much greater obstacles. Since then the world has had five hundred years in which to degenerate."

"Don't pay any attention to him, Inez," Helen interrupted, complacently. "He is simply trying to start an argument, and he does not believe a word he says. He really looks upon men as infinitely superior beings in the past, present, and future, and this self-abnegation on the part of himself and his sex is only a passing conceit."

"I refuse to be side-tracked," Armstrong insisted. "I grant that the conversation started more in jest than in earnest, but I maintain my position, none the less. Modern civilization has brought to us a wonderful material development, but intellectual advance, instead of keeping abreast of the material, has positively retrograded."

"You really make me feel ashamed to be living in such an abominable age," suggested Uncle Peabody.

Inez was serious. "I am quite incompetent to carry on this discussion with you, Mr. Armstrong," she said, disregarding the others, "and I admire, as you know, the marvellous accomplishments of these 'old-timers,' as you call them, wondering at their power to overcome the obstacles which we know existed. Yet I like to believe that the ages which have passed have marked an advance on all sides rather than a retrogression."

"So should I like to," assented Armstrong, "if I could; but look at the facts. William James has just succeeded in making philosophy popular, but Plato and Aristotle gave it to us before the birth of Christ. We enthuse over Shakespeare and Dante and Milton, but Homer and Virgil gave us the grandest of poetry two thousand years ago. The *quattrocento*, that period which so fires me with enthusiasm, gave us Raphael as an artist, together with Leonardo and Michelangelo as the foremost examples of humanists. Whom have we had since to equal them?"

"All this is beyond argument," Inez admitted. "But is this the fault of the men or of the times? Conditions are so changed that the same kind of work can never be done again. The telephone, the telegraph, railroad trains, fast steamships, the daily papers—everything distracts the modern worker from devoting himself wholly and absolutely to his single purpose; but with this distraction is it not also true that the modern worker gives to the world what the world really needs most under the present conditions? In other words, would not these same great men, if set down in the twentieth century, produce work very similar to what modern great men have given and are giving us?"

"I should be sorry enough to think so," affirmed Jack. "What a pity it would be!"

Uncle Peabody's mood had changed from amusement to interest. "If I really thought you were sincere in the attitude you take," he said, addressing Armstrong, "I could prescribe no better cure for your complaint than to force you to subject yourself, for one single week, to those same conditions which you seem to admire so much."

"If you refer to conveniences, Mr. Cartwright," interrupted Armstrong, "I will admit without argument that you are right. These are wholly the result of material development."

"Let us confine ourselves to intellectual achievements if you choose," continued Uncle Peabody. "Without an intellect, could one harness steam and electricity and make them obedient to the human will? Is not a wireless message an echo from the brain? What is the telephone if not a product of thought?"

"You and Miss Thayer are arguing my case far better than I can do it myself," replied Armstrong, undisturbed. "The triumphs of Watt and Edison and Marconi and Bell are all intellectual, even though utilitarian. Each of these men has proved himself humanistic, in that he has given to the world the best that is in him, and not simply modified or readapted some previous achievement. If they were not limited by living in an age of specialization they might even have been humanists. Right here in Italy you see the same thing to-day. The Italians are beyond any other race intellectually fit to rule the world now as they once did, and it is simply because they have been unable to withstand materialism that they have not reclaimed their own."

"Just what do you mean by 'humanism,' Jack?" Helen asked, abruptly.

"The final definition of modern humanism will not be written for several years," Armstrong answered. "The world is not yet ready for it, and I am afraid Cerini's creed of ancient humanism would strike you as being rather heavy."

"Let me see if I could comprehend it." Helen looked across to Inez, and the eyes of the two girls met with mutual understanding. "Can you repeat it?"

"I know it word for word," her husband replied, eagerly, delighted to have Helen manifest an interest. "It was the first lesson the old man taught me, years ago. 'The humanist,' Cerini says, 'is the man who not only knows intimately the ancients and is inspired by them: it is he who is so fascinated by their magic spell that he copies them, imitates them, rehearses their lessons, adopts their models and their methods, their examples and their gods, their spirit and their tongue.'"

Helen was visibly disappointed. "I thought I had an idea," she said, slowly, "but I was wrong. Inez used the word 'humanities' a few moments ago, and I once heard President Eliot say that this was simply another name for a liberal education—teaching men to drink in the inspiration of all the ages and to seek to make their age the best."

"You are not wrong, Helen," continued Armstrong, "unless you understand President Eliot to mean that the ages which have come since these great men lived have been able to add particularly to what has gone before. All that is included in what Cerini says."

"Then the present, which I love so well, means nothing?"

"It means a great deal." Armstrong laughed at the injured tone of Helen's voice. "The great material achievements of the present, which you just heard cited by Miss Thayer and Uncle Peabody, are of vast importance, but the age does not stand out as a period of intellectual progression. The achievements themselves, and the new conditions which they introduce, make that impossible."

"Can we not admire the past and enjoy what it has given us without becoming a part of it ourselves?" persisted Helen.

"Not if we remain true to our ideals. I spoke just now of Leonardo and Michelangelo as being the foremost examples of humanists. By that I mean that they represent the highest point of intellectual manhood. Da Vinci was a great writer, a great painter, a great scientist, a great engineer, a great mechanician, while Buonarroti was famous not only as a sculptor, but also as a painter, an architect, and a poet. And these men had to develop their own precedent, while all who have striven for more than mediocrity since then have propped themselves up on the work of these and other great masters. Can you wonder that my own great ambition, quite impossible of accomplishment, is to emulate these men—not in the same pursuits, but in some way, in any way, which enables me to give to the world the best that is in me. Should I gratify myself in this, that which I accomplished would be done simply in the fulfilment of my effort, and I should gain my recompense in the knowledge that it *was* my best. This is my understanding of Cerini's creed."

"All this is most interesting," admitted Helen. "It is indeed splendid to know the ancients intimately, and to receive their inspiration. It is fine to imitate them and to rehearse their lessons, but I don't see why we should bind ourselves down to the old-time limitations by using their methods when, to my mind, our own methods are so much better suited to modern conditions?"

"Your position is fully justified, Helen, if you really believe these methods to be limitations," replied Armstrong, seriously. "For my part, I do not feel this. I accept the Cerini creed without qualification. I grant you that many things of the past are limitations, but there are certain cardinal principles which must remain the same so long as the world lasts and which are not subject to what you call 'modern conditions.'"

"To be wholly consistent, Jack," pursued Uncle Peabody, "should you not adopt their tongue—as called for in the creed?"

"Not necessarily, as the 'creed' is, of course, idealistic; but the only reason I do not do so is because of the limitations which are placed upon us—this time by modern civilization. Cerini and I converse for hours together in the Latin tongue, but it is very seldom that I find the opportunity to do this. Why is it that Latin is used in medicine, in botany, in science, to give names to various specimens or species? Simply because French, German, Italian, English may be forgotten languages a few centuries hence, but Latin—the so-called dead language—will be as enduring then as now."

"I can never hope to become as much of an enthusiast as you, Mr. Armstrong," Inez said, finally, as the others gave up the argument in despair; "and I suppose you will never forgive me if I say that I fear it would be very uncomfortable for me if I did. You must simply let me browse around the edges as a neophyte while you and the master quaff the nectar and ambrosia of the gods."

"And I cannot even do that," added Helen, rising from the balustrade. "I cannot give up my dear present even to agree with my learned husband. You don't want me to say that I am sorry I am living among all these imperfect conditions when I really find them very satisfactory and enjoyable? It is wrong of you so to break down my modern idols. There are our guests," she continued, as a laughing group appeared on the veranda. "As penance I decree that you shall take each of us by the hand and lead us back to the villa—the Humanist flanked by the Pagan and the Christian. Arise, thou ancient one, and lead us on!"

VI

The visits which Armstrong and Miss Thayer made to the library became of daily occurrence. Encouraged by his companion's interest, and the eagerness with which she assimilated the enthusiasm which he and Cerini were only too willing to share with her, Armstrong promptly embraced a scheme for definite work suggested to him by the librarian. Inez at first proved only a sympathetic spectator, but by the third or fourth day she found herself a distinct part of the working force. She demurred half-heartedly, but when it became evident that she could really make herself of service she entered into it with characteristic intensity which increased from day to day.

Soon after the departure of the guests the automobile arrived, and transformed Armstrong from a Humanist into an Egoist and then into a Mechanist. For the moment the material concern took precedence over the intellectual.

"Of course I expect to have the chauffeur do the work once we are under way," he half apologized to Uncle Peabody, who with a good-natured interest watched him taking the precious machine to pieces; "but before I trust it to any one I must understand it thoroughly myself."

"Quite right, quite right," Uncle Peabody assented, cheerfully. "I believe in that theory entirely. I have noticed when my friends have found themselves stalled on the road that it never annoys them half so much if they can explain the reason why. Besides, from a secondary consideration, I suppose it adds something to the safety to know the machine yourself."

As the car had arrived in advance of the chauffeur, Armstrong had plenty of time to study the mechanism. It came to pieces with consummate ease. Its new owner had never claimed much knowledge along these lines, but the simplicity of this particular machine increased his respect for his judgment as a purchaser and his natural though hitherto undeveloped ability as a mechanic.

"These Frenchmen," he confided enthusiastically to Uncle Peabody, "have the rest of the world beaten to a stand-still in building automobiles. My hat is off to them."

"Would you not be even more comfortable if you removed your shirt as well?" suggested Uncle Peabody, mischievously, as he glanced sympathetically at Armstrong's face, from which the perspiration rolled down onto his collar in response to his unusual exertions and the heat of the full Italian sun.

"It is nearly to pieces now," Armstrong replied, complacently. "I will wait until it is cooler before I set it up again."

True to his word, Armstrong began work on the restoration early next morning, but the heat of the day found him still at his labors and in no cheerful frame of mind. Uncle Peabody's philosophical suggestions had proved unacceptable some hours before. Helen's remark that she did not believe the three extra pieces Jack held despairingly in his hand had come from that particular machine at all brought forth such a withering expression of pitying contempt that she flew back to the house in alarm. Even the servants found that the opposite side of the villa demanded their especial care. A truce was declared for the *colazione*, but Armstrong devoured his repast in silence, showing no interest in the animated conversation, and with scant apologies left the table long in advance of the others to resume his task.

At five o'clock a dusty *vettura* drove noisily into the driveway, and from his point of vantage, lying on his back underneath the automobile, Armstrong saw Mr. Ferdinand De Peyster alight. With a curse muttered, not from any antipathy to his visitor, but simply on general principles, he laboriously extricated himself from his position with a view to the extension of hospitality. De Peyster saw the movement and hastily approached.

Ferdinand De Peyster was a distinct individuality, which in a degree explained the criticism which some of his friends passed upon him. His foreign descent, though now tempered by two generations of American influence, was probably responsible for the fact that he was "different from other men." Always faultlessly dressed, his taste followed the continental styles rather than those which other men about him were in the habit of adopting, so while Americans in Florence were clad in flannels, *négligé* shirts, and white buckskins, De Peyster appeared at the Villa Godilombra immaculate in the conventional lounging-coat, tucked shirt and lavender gloves, with white spats over his patent-leather shoes. There was more of a contrast between visitor and guest at that moment than Armstrong realized as he emerged in his old clothes, thoroughly soaked through with perspiration, and with his hands and face grimy with oil and dirt.

De Peyster drew back instinctively as the full vision of Jack's figure presented itself. "Comprenez vous français?"

Armstrong stopped in his advance as he heard the question and noted the superior tone in which it was delivered. Then the humor of the situation appealed to him.

"Yes, sir," he replied, respectfully, "or English, if you prefer."

De Peyster's face brightened. "Ah! Mr. Armstrong brought you over with him?" he remarked, becoming almost sociable.

"Yes, sir," Jack replied, truthfully. "Is there anything I can do for you, sir?"

"I am Mr. De Peyster," said Ferdinand, with condescension—"a friend of your master's in America. Is he at home this afternoon?"

"Yes, sir—"

Before Armstrong could continue De Peyster approached nearer to him and lowered his voice. "I say—is there a Miss Thayer from America visiting here just now?"

A quick movement on De Peyster's part deposited a franc in Jack's grimy palm. Holding his hand in front of him, his astonished look alternated between the piece of silver and his friend's face until he found himself unable to keep up the farce.

"De Peyster, you are a fraud!" Armstrong laughed boisterously at the look of dismay in Ferdinand's face as a realization came to him. "Do you mean to tell me that the joys of a honeymoon and life in Italy have wrought so many changes that you don't recognize me?"

"But can you blame me?" De Peyster joined in the merriment. "Run and get some one to tell you how you look."

The sound of this unexpected hilarity reached the terrace, and Uncle Peabody, flanked by both of the girls, came rushing out fearful lest Jack's problem had resulted in temporary mental derangement. A glance at the picture before them, however, explained the situation better than words, and Helen hurried forward to greet her visitor while Inez followed behind.

"Ferdy De Peyster—in the flesh!" cried Helen. "What does this mean, and when did you reach Florence?"

Armstrong gave him no opportunity to reply. "He prefers to speak French, Helen, and he is just throwing his money around."

Then turning to De Peyster and exhibiting his *pourboire*, he repeated, "Comprenez vous français?" while both men went off again into a paroxysm of laughter.

"What is the joke?" Helen asked, looking from one to the other completely mystified.

"It is a good one—and on me," replied De Peyster. "I took him for the chauffeur, you know."

Helen looked at her husband. "Is it safe for me to laugh now, Jack?" she asked. "I am glad something has happened to put you in good-humor. Can you be induced to leave your work for the rest of the day and make yourself presentable to join us in the garden?"

Armstrong cast a despairing glance at the machine.

"Of course," he said. "I shall be fresher in the morning, anyway, and I am sure I can fix it up then."

"Nothing like knowing all about it yourself, Jack," Uncle Peabody remarked, innocently. "These French machines are so simple!"

"You take the girls back to the garden," Armstrong replied, emphatically, "and kindly devote your attention to your own theories, or I will put you at work on the blamed thing yourself to-morrow."

De Peyster greeted Inez effusively, paying but little attention to Helen and Uncle Peabody as they strolled back to the garden, while Jack disappeared in-doors.

"Oh, I say!" he exclaimed as they reached the balustrade. "How did Armstrong happen to find a place like this? Is it not simply splendid, Inez?"

Inez Thayer resented something—she did not quite know what. She had been expecting De Peyster's arrival daily, yet now that he had come she was still unprepared. She could find no fault with his attentions except that they had been too assiduous. Perhaps it was that, try as she could, she had been quite unable to convince him that his devotion was useless. He accepted each rebuff philosophically and bided his time.

Annetta skilfully arranged the chairs and laid the little table, placed, as Helen had taught her, in a spot commanding the exquisite view of the valley and San Miniato beyond. Luscious *fragole*, cooling *gelati*, seducing little Italian *paste*, as only Helen's cook could make them, and a refreshing Asti cup replaced the tea which the girls had decided would be less acceptable on this particular day; and by the time all was in readiness Armstrong joined them clothed in his proper mind and raiment.

The conversation turned upon the voyage across.

"We had an awfully jolly crowd on board," said De Peyster. "There were Emory and Eustis, who you say have just left you, and then there were three charming married women who insisted on my playing bridge with them every afternoon."

"They did not have to insist very hard, did they, Ferdy?" interrupted Helen—"with your reputation for gallantry."

Ferdinand smiled complacently. "Making up a fourth at bridge comes under the definition of 'first aid to the wounded,'" he replied, "but I did not object at all to being the doctor. Their conversation was so clever, you know."

"Clever conversation always helps good bridge," Armstrong interrupted, dryly; but De Peyster was already deep in his story.

"One afternoon they had a discussion as to how large an allowance for personal expenses would make each one perfectly happy,—funny subject, wasn't it? Well, one of them said ten thousand a year would take care of her troubles nicely; the second one was more modest and thought five thousand would do,—but what do you think my partner said? She was a demure little lady from Chicago and had only been married a year and a half."

"Don't keep us in suspense, Ferdy," said Helen, as De Peyster yielded to the humor of his recollections.

"Truly, it was awfully funny," he continued. "She looked rather frightened when the conversation began, and when they urged her to set a price she said, 'I would be perfectly satisfied if I could afford to spend just what I am spending.'"

"She had a conscience—that is the only difference between her and the other women," Armstrong commented.

"Perhaps," added Helen; "but I'll guarantee that in another year she will be getting a divorce from her husband on the ground of incompatibility of income."

"Then in the evenings," De Peyster went on, "the men got together in the smoke-room, but I think we drank too much. I always felt uncomfortable when I got up next morning."

"Another encouragement for my *magnum opus!*" exclaimed Uncle Peabody. "I am going to invent a wine possessing such qualities that the more one drinks of it the better he will feel next morning."

"If you succeed you will have clubdom at your feet," Armstrong replied, while De Peyster feelingly nodded assent.

"Would you mind if I invited Inez to drive with me to-morrow, Helen?" ventured Ferdinand, abruptly, looking anxiously at Miss Thayer. "I know you honeymooners won't mind being left alone if I can persuade her."

"By all means, Ferdy—unless Inez has some other plans. Jack has been making her ride his hobby ever since she arrived, and I have no doubt she will be glad enough to escape us for a little breathing-spell."

"If you put it that way I shall certainly decline"—Inez failed to show any great enthusiasm—"but otherwise I shall be very glad to go."

"Jack intends to put his automobile together to-morrow," Uncle Peabody remarked, "so it will be just as well not to have any one outside the family within hearing distance."

Armstrong tried to wither Uncle Peabody with a glance, but ran up against a smiling face so beaming with good-nature that even real anger would have been dispelled.

"For Helen's sake—" Jack began, but Uncle Peabody interrupted.

"For Helen's sake you will hasten the arrival of your chauffeur, if such a thing be possible."

The following day was an eventful one. First of all, as if in response to Uncle Peabody's exhortation, the chauffeur appeared. Mr. Cartwright departed for the city soon after breakfast, to be gone all day, and by the time the heat of the afternoon had subsided De Peyster drove up in state to enforce the promise Inez had given him the afternoon before. After watching them drive away, Helen slipped her hand through her husband's arm and gently drew him with her into the garden. They walked in silence, Helen's head resting against his shoulder, until they reached her favorite vantage-spot, when she paused and looked smilingly into his face.

"Jack dear," she said, quietly, "do you realize that this is almost the first time we have really been by ourselves since we took that walk to Fiesole?"

"But at least you have had an opportunity to show your villa to your friends!"

"Don't joke, Jack—I am not in the mood for it this afternoon. I don't know why, but I have been feeling very serious these last few days. Tell me, dear—are you perfectly happy?"

Armstrong looked surprised. "Why, yes—perfectly happy. What a curious notion!"

"I know it is, but humor me just this once. Are you as fond of me now as you were that day at Fiesole?"

"You silly child!" Jack drew her to him and kissed her. "Whatever has possessed you to-day?"

"I don't know, but you see I measure everything by that day at Fiesole. I believe it was the happiest day I ever spent. Since then, somehow, I have felt that we were not so near together. Of course, you have been away a good deal at the library and looking up things with Inez, which was just what I wanted you to do; and then we have had a good many here to entertain, which was also what I wanted; but I can't help feeling that you have not found here at home just what you should have found to make you perfectly happy. Tell me, dear, have I been to blame?"

Armstrong paused as if weighing something heavily in his mind. "Perhaps I have no right to go on with this work," he remarked, at length, "but the only way to stop it would be to leave Florence."

"You know I don't mean that, Jack."

"I know you don't. I am speaking simply for myself."

He was again silent, and Helen hesitated to break in upon his reverie. He seemed for the moment to be far away from her, and she felt an intangible barrier between them.

"I could not make any one understand." Armstrong was speaking more to himself than to her. "Ever since I left Florence years ago I have felt something pulling me back, and ever since I have been here I have been under influences which I can explain no more than I can resist. It must be this, if anything, that you feel."

"I think I understand," Helen hastened to reassure him. "Sometimes when I have been playing something on the piano I have the strangest sensation come over me. I seem to lose my own individuality and to be merged into another's. I feel impelled to play on, and an unspeakable dread comes over me lest some one should try to stop me. Is it not something like that which you feel?"

"Yes," replied Armstrong, "only a thousand times stronger than any one could put in words."

"I know exactly what you mean—and there is nothing for which you need blame yourself. You warned me before we left Boston that you had left here a second personality. I know that you confidently expected your own enthusiasm to excite my interest when once in the atmosphere. I wish that it had, dear, but I fear I am hopelessly modern."

Armstrong looked at his wife intently, yet he gave no evidence that he had heard her words.

"I have started on a great task at the library, Helen. The spirit of work is on me, and I feel that I have a chance to prove myself one of that glorious company. I may find myself unequal to the opportunity, but if we stay here in Florence I cannot keep away from it. If my absence from you makes you unhappy I must separate myself from these associations."

"No, indeed," cried Helen. "I would not have you stop your work for worlds. Even though I am unable to appreciate it, you know how interested I am in anything which adds to your happiness—and I am so proud of you, dear! That was one reason why I was glad that Inez could spend a little time with us. She, at least, can help you."

"She can indeed," replied Armstrong, frankly, "and she has already. I have never seen a girl with such natural intellectual gifts. Her arguments are so logical, her reasoning so clear, that I find even her disagreements most entertaining. What a pity she is not a man!"

"I knew you would like her," answered Helen. "Sometimes I think you ought to have married a girl like her instead of me, but"—Helen looked at him smilingly and drew closer to him—"but I am awfully glad that you didn't, Jack!"

"What nonsense, Helen!" cried Armstrong, coming to himself and drawing her to him. "Who is fishing now? I would ask no better chum than your charming, brown-eyed friend, but I am quite content that I possess as wife this sweet girl here in my arms who is trying to find a cloud in this cloudless sky."

"Oh no, Jack." Helen straightened up reproachfully. "But I like to hear you say these things—just as you did that day at Fiesole! And even if I should find a cloud it would be sure to have a silver lining, wouldn't it, dear?"

Armstrong smiled. "Yes, sweetheart, and, as Uncle Peabody says, 'all you would have to do would be to turn it around lining side out.'"

VII

Inez Thayer found herself overwhelmed by a varied mingling of conflicting emotions as she settled herself in the victoria, and listened without remark to the enthusiastic and joyous monologue to which her companion gave free rein. She felt herself absolutely helpless, borne along resistlessly like a rudderless ship by a force which she could neither control nor fully comprehend. She still longed for a valid excuse to leave Florence, yet in her heart she questioned whether she would now be strong enough to embrace the opportunity even if it came. She had dreaded the certain appearance of De Peyster, yet she had been eager to enter into the inevitable final discussion so that the episode might be closed forever. She said to herself that she hated Armstrong for the mastery which he unconsciously possessed over her, yet every thought of him thrilled her with a delight which nothing in her life had before given her. The color came to her cheeks even now, and De Peyster, watching her intently, thought it was in response to his own remark and felt encouraged.

The drive took them, as a matter of course, to the Cascine, where fashionable Florence parades up and down the delightful avenues formed by the pines and the ilexes. On this particular afternoon the heat encouraged them to take refuge on the shadier side toward the mountains, reserving the drive along the Arno until the brilliant coloring of the setting sun should show them both Bellosguardo and the city itself in their fullest glory. De Peyster was intoxicated by the enjoyment of his environment, and seemed quite content to accept his companion's passive submission to his mood. At length his exuberance of spirits became mildly contagious, and Inez threw off her apprehensions and forgot the dangers and perplexities which she felt surrounded her.

But her feeling of security was short-lived. De Peyster no sooner became conscious of her change of manner than he seized it as a long-awaited opportunity. Beginning where he had left off at the last attack, he rehearsed the history of his affection from the day he had first met her until the present moment. For the first time Inez experienced a sympathy toward him rather than a sorrow for herself. He was, even with his limitations, so deadly in earnest, his devotion was so unquestionable, his very persistency was so unlike his other characteristics, seeming a part of a stronger personality, that it forced her admiration. And yet how far below the standard she had set!

"You have not believed me, Ferdinand, when I have told you over and over again that what you ask is absolutely impossible." Inez spoke kindly but very firmly. "I truly wish it might be otherwise, but it is kinder that I make you understand it now instead of having this unhappiness for us both continue indefinitely. I know you mean every word, but I say to you now finally and irrevocably—it can never be."

De Peyster looked into her face searchingly. "You never said it like that before, Inez."

"Yes, I have—not once, but many times, and in almost the same words."

"But it is not the words that count, Inez. I don't care how many times you say it in the way you always have said it before. I expected to hear it again. But this tone, Inez, this manner is quite different; and for the first time I have a feeling that perhaps you do mean it after all."

"I do mean it, and I have meant it every time I have said it."

Inez was relentless, but she felt that this was the one time when matters could be finally settled, and the carriage had already begun the climb to Settignano.

De Peyster still gazed at her with uncertainty. Then a sudden light came to him and showed in his face, mingling with the evident pain which the thought brought him.

"I have it," he said, bending toward her to watch her expression more intently; "I have it. You are in love with some one else!"

Inez felt her face burn with the suddenness of the accusation. She hesitated, and in that moment's hesitation De Peyster had his answer. Still he was not satisfied. He must hear the words spoken.

"You told me last time that there was no one else," he said, reproachfully, "and I know you spoke the truth. Now there must be some one, and if there is I am entitled to know it. So long as my love for you cannot harm you, no power on earth can take it away from me; but if there is another who has a better right than I, that is a different matter. Tell me, Inez—I insist—do you love some one else?"

There was no retreat. Any denial of words would be useless, and it was the only way to end things after all. She lifted her eyes to his and spoke calmly, though the color had fled from her cheeks and her face was deathly pale. "Yes, Ferdinand, you are entitled to know it. I do love some one else, and I love him better than my life!"

"I knew it!" De Peyster exclaimed, dejectedly.

There was a long pause, during which he struggled bravely with himself.

"Tell me who it is," he said, at length. "Of course, this makes it different."

Inez could not help admiring the unexpected strength.

"No, Ferdinand, I cannot. This is my secret, and you must not question further."

"But it must be some one here, for you told me just before you sailed that there was no one."

"Perhaps here—perhaps elsewhere. You must leave it there, Ferdinand. If you care for me, as you say you do, I ask you to leave it there."

De Peyster bowed submissively and shared her evident desire for silence during the few moments which remained of their drive.

Helen and Jack met them at the villa, and were greatly disappointed that Ferdinand declined their pressing invitation to stay for supper in the garden. A promise that he would take tea with them on the following afternoon was all they could secure from him, and when Inez rushed up-stairs promptly upon his departure Jack looked at Helen meaningly.

"She must have turned him down good and hard this time, eh?"

"Poor Ferdy!" Helen replied, sympathetically. "I had no idea he could get so cut up over anything."

The automobile, even in the two days it had been a member of the Armstrong family, completely demoralized the entire establishment. Jack was beside himself with excitement and joy, his early experiments both with chauffeur and car being eminently satisfactory. He contented himself with short runs down to the city and back the first day after his man had succeeded in putting the car into its normal condition, but his impatience to start out again immediately after each return, even though luncheon was most unceremoniously shortened, produced almost as much dismay in the household as his bad temper while trying to reconstruct the machine.

"I want you all to have a ride in it at the earliest possible moment," he explained; "but before I risk any one's neck but my own I must satisfy myself that the car is all right and that the chauffeur knows his business."

The only event which diverted Armstrong was the return to the villa of Inez and De Peyster, for their evident discomfiture caused him real concern. On general principles he was interested in the outcome of the obvious errand which had brought De Peyster to Florence, and beyond this he had already come to look upon Miss Thayer as a most agreeable companion and assistant whose happiness and equilibrium he regretted to see disturbed.

After De Peyster's unceremonious departure and Inez' abrupt disappearance, he and Helen strolled out into the garden, where the table was already laid for supper.

"There is no use waiting for Inez," said Helen. "Poor child! It is a shame to have her unhappy when we are so contented. But where is Uncle Peabody?"

"I met him on the Lung' Arno and offered to take him home, but he said he was bound for Olschki's. Trying to find out if Luigi Cornaro wrote anything he had not discovered, he said."

"Perhaps he will come before we have finished. You sit there, Jack, where you can watch the sunset behind San Miniato, and I will sit next to you so that I can watch it, too."

Helen drew the light chair nearer, and smilingly looked up at him. "There," she said. "Is this not cozy—just you and I?"

Armstrong smiled back into her radiant eyes with equal contentment. "This is absolute perfection, but you don't imagine we can eat like this, do you?"

"I don't feel a bit hungry," she replied, cheerfully, making no attempt to move. "Uncle Peabody says we ought not to eat when we don't feel like it, and I don't feel like it now."

"But what does Uncle Peabody say about not eating when you have been knocking about in an automobile all day and have the appetite of a horse?"

"Oh, you men!" cried Helen, straightening up with a pout. "I don't believe there is a bit of sentiment in a man's make-up, anyhow. Eat—eat—eat—" and she piled his plate high with generous portions from every dish within reach.

Uncle Peabody's step upon the path gave warning of his approach.

"So I am in time after all," he said. "I was afraid I should be obliged to eat my evening repast in solitary loneliness. But is this the way you follow my precepts?" he continued, as his eye fell upon Armstrong's plate. "Can't you take it on the instalment plan—or are you anticipating forming a partnership with a stomach-pump?"

"It is my fault, uncle," replied Helen, contritely. "I can't make Jack romantic, so I tried to stuff him to keep him good-natured. That is always the next best thing with a man."

"Oh ho!" Uncle Peabody looked shocked as he drew a chair up to the little table. "So I have come right into a family quarrel, have I? Naughty, naughty, both of you!"

"I wish I could quarrel with him," said Helen, "but he is too agreeable, even in his aggravating moods."

"What have you to say to that pretty speech, John Armstrong?" asked Uncle Peabody.

"What can I say?" answered Jack, between mouth-fuls, "except that, speaking for myself, I am always much more romantic when I am not hungry. If Herself will indulge me for five minutes longer I will promise to be as sentimental as the most fastidious could desire."

"I do not care for manufactured sentiment," replied Helen; "and it is too late now anyway, for my own appetite has returned and my anger is appeased."

"Miss Thayer evidently has not returned yet?" ventured Uncle Peabody, interrogatively, as the supper progressed.

"Yes, she is up-stairs in tears, and Ferdy has gone away to throw himself into the Arno," Helen replied.

"Dear me, dear me!" murmured Uncle Peabody. "What a pity! I am not sure that I would have returned had I known that I should find so much trouble."

"Now that you have had this much, I think I will let you in for the rest," suggested Armstrong. "I will take you out to the garage after you have finished."

"More trouble there?"

"Yes—punctured a tire on the way up the hill."

"And you never said a word about it!" cried Helen. "No wonder you did not feel romantic!"

"Good! Peace is once more established, which is worth more than a new tire. Come, my appetite is satisfied—suppose we all go out to the garage."

Annetta interrupted their progress at the door.

"A gentleman to see the signora," she announced—"the same gentleman who took the Signorina Thayer to ride this afternoon—and would the signora see him alone?"

"Poor Ferdy," Helen sighed, aloud. "He wants me to intercede for him. You go on, Jack, and perhaps I may join you later. Show Mr. De Peyster out here, Annetta."

Ferdinand hardly waited to be ushered through the hallway. He was visibly suffering as he approached Helen with outstretched hand.

"I am so sorry, Ferdy," was all she could say before he interrupted her.

"Forgive me, Helen, for coming to you before I have regained control of myself; but I have made a sudden decision, and unless I carry it out at once I won't be able to do it."

"A sudden decision, Ferdy?"

"Yes, I am leaving Florence on the night train for Paris; but I could not go without seeing you again and leaving with you a message for—Inez."

"The night train to-night? Surely you are not going away without seeing Inez again?"

Helen's sympathy was strong in the face of his almost uncontrollable emotion.

"Yes, to-night, Helen; and I shall never see her again unless she sends for me."

"But what has happened to make things so hopeless now? She has refused you before, Ferdy, and I have always admired your pluck that you refused to give her up."

"But it is different now—there is a reason why I must give her up. There was none before, except that she did not think she cared for me. I was certain I could make her do that—in time. But now—"

"What is it now?" Her interest was sincere.

"You must know, Helen. Why do you pretend that you don't?"

"Why, what do you mean? I am not pretending. I know of nothing."

De Peyster was incredulous. "It's all right, Helen. We men would do the same thing, I suppose, to protect another chap's secret; but it is pretty rough on me, just the same."

Helen's mystification was complete. "Look here, Ferdy," she said; "this has gone too far. Inez has evidently confided to you something which she has never told me. I have not had a word with her since she returned, and I know nothing of what has happened except what I have surmised."

"Do you mean to tell me that Inez has been here all this time as your guest without your knowing that she has fallen in love with some one over here?"

"Inez in love! Ferdy, you are crazy! Who is it, and where did she meet him?"

"I don't know—she would not tell me, but it is some one she has met over here."

"I don't believe a word of it. She must have said it to make you understand that she could not marry you."

Ferdinand shook his head. "No. A girl could fool me on some things, I suppose; but when she speaks as Inez spoke she means every word she says. 'I do love some one else,' she said, 'and I love him better than my life.' Do you think Inez would say that if she did not mean it, Helen?"

Helen leaned against the arm of the settle. "I don't understand it, Ferdy—I don't understand it."

"But I do, and I am not strong enough to see her again or to stay here in Florence. I will not trouble her again unless she sends for me—anything sent in care of Coutts will always reach me. Or after she is married, and I am myself again, I would like to see her and congratulate—him. Forgive me, Helen, I am all unstrung to-night. Good-bye."

De Peyster was gone before Helen realized it. She sank upon the settle and rested her face on her hand. Inez in love, and with some one she had met in Italy! Who was it—when was it? She had come directly to the villa upon her arrival. She had said that she had met no one who interested her on the steamer. In Florence she had met no one otherwise than casually. All her time had been spent either with her or with Jack. Helen lifted her head suddenly. "With Jack," she repeated to herself. She rose quickly and looked off into the distance. The last bright rays were disappearing behind San Miniato. "I love him better than my life," Inez had said to Ferdinand. Helen grasped the railing of the balustrade for support. "With Jack!" she repeated again. "Oh no, no, no—not that!" she cried aloud—"not that!"

VIII

"How is the work at the library progressing?"

Helen asked her husband at breakfast a few mornings later.

"Famously," Armstrong replied, pleased that she had referred to the subject.

"Is it nearly finished?"

"Finished?" Jack laughed indulgently. "You evidently don't realize what a big thing I have undertaken. I find myself appalled by its possibilities."

"Indeed." Uncle Peabody looked up surprised. "Does this mean that you are likely to lengthen your stay in Florence beyond your original plans?"

"No, I think not," Armstrong replied. "We have been here less than a month now, and I ought to be able to put my material into shape during the two months which remain—especially with the splendid assistance Miss Thayer is giving me. I can add the finishing touches after we return home, if necessary."

"Will it take as long as that?" asked Helen, her color mounting.

"Surely you are not counting upon me for any such length of time!" exclaimed Inez, almost in the same breath. "My cousins are expecting me to join them in Berlin any day now."

"You would not desert your post of duty?"

"I must follow the direction toward which it points."

"Just what is this 'big thing' you have undertaken?" interrupted Uncle Peabody. "You forget that I have not yet been taken into your confidence."

Armstrong turned to his questioner seriously. "I have really stumbled upon something which has not been done before and which ought to have been undertaken long ago. You see, Cerini has there at the library hundreds of letters which belong to the Buonarroti archives. Many of them were written by Michelangelo, and many more were written to him. The correspondence is between him and men in all walks of life—popes, kings, princes, tradesmen, and even some from the workmen in the Carrara quarries."

"And you and Miss Thayer are translating these letters?" Uncle Peabody anticipated.

"Yes; but that is not the work which most interests me, except indirectly. Any number of volumes have been published upon the life and manners and customs of every age before and since that in which Michelangelo lived, yet practically nothing concerning this particular period. The artistic importance of the epoch has been written up with minute detail, but the intimate life of the people and its significance seems to have been wholly overlooked—probably because it was overshadowed. Very few of these letters have ever been printed, and they ought to form the basis of a great work upon this subject. Cerini has turned them over to me to see what I can do with them. At first I started with the idea of going through everything myself, but that would be a hopeless task unless we plan to live in Florence indefinitely. Now, Miss Thayer reads over the letters and takes out the important data, leaving me free to work on the book itself. We are really making splendid progress, and I shall be bitterly disappointed if Miss Thayer has to go away and leave me to finish it alone."

"I am sure Inez will stay as long as she can, Jack," Helen said, quietly. "She knows how welcome she has been, but we must not urge her beyond what she thinks is best."

She broke off suddenly; then, with an assumed nonchalance, said: "I wonder if I could not help in some way and thus get the work completed just that much sooner. Of course, I don't understand Italian, but perhaps I could do some copying or something. Don't you think three would accomplish more than two, Jack, even if one of them was a weak sister?"

Helen looked over to her husband with obvious expectancy, but she could not fail to notice the momentary hush.

"I know how ridiculous my proposition sounds," she continued, bravely, "but I would really like to try."

"Why, of course," Armstrong replied, hastily. "Miss Thayer's suggestion to leave and your willingness at last to come to my rescue have combined to give me two unexpected shocks—one unpleasant, the other delightful. Let me see. Miss Thayer and I have been developing a kind of team work, so this means a little readjustment."

"Never mind, if it is not perfectly convenient." Helen made an effort to appear indifferent.

"Of course it is convenient," Jack hastened to add, ashamed of his hesitation. "You know how much I have wanted you to do this, and I am perfectly delighted. I am sure it can be arranged and that you can help us a great deal."

"I wish you knew Italian, Helen, so that you could take my place," added Inez. "Then Mr. Armstrong would not accuse me of deserting my post of duty."

"Not at all," protested Armstrong, impulsively. "Even then I could not get along without your assistance. We can easily find something for Helen to do which will help the work along and encourage her in her budding enthusiasm. This is splendid! Helen interested at last in my dusty old divinities! Perhaps we can even infect Uncle Peabody."

"Perhaps," assented Uncle Peabody; "but for the present I shall devote myself to my own researches—even though your masterpiece is forced to suffer thereby. But I will ride down with you as far as the Duomo."

No one in the automobile, unless it was the chauffeur, could help feeling a certain tenseness in the situation as the car conveyed the party to its destination. Helen's action was the result of a sudden decision, quite at variance with all the conclusions at which she had arrived during the wakeful hours of the preceding nights. Armstrong had so long since given up all thought of having his wife co-operate with him in this particular expression of himself, and the work upon which he and Miss Thayer were engaged had settled down into so regular a routine, that he was really disturbed by Helen's change of base, although he had been entirely unwilling to admit it. Inez inwardly resented the intrusion, at the same time blaming herself severely for her attitude; and Uncle Peabody, who saw in the whole affair only a clever ruse on Helen's part instigated by a tardily aroused jealousy, was in danger, for the first time, of not knowing just what to do.

As a result of all these conflicting emotions, the efforts at conversation during the ride would have seemed ludicrous had the situation been less serious. Armstrong kept up a continuous and irrelevant conversation into which each of the others joined weakly with equal irrelevance. Each was trying to talk and think at the same time. The car reached the Piazza del Duomo almost abruptly, as it seemed, and Uncle Peabody alighted with considerable alacrity, waving a good-bye which was mechanically acknowledged as the machine slowly moved into the narrow Borgo San Lorenzo. At the library, Armstrong led the way through the cloister and up the stone stairs to the little door where Maritelli was this time waiting to give them entrance.

"I will take you to meet Cerini," said Armstrong.

"While I," interrupted Inez, "will seek out our table and get all in readiness for our triple labors."

A gentle voice called "Avanti," in answer to Jack's tap upon the door of Cerini's study, and the old man rose hastily as he saw a new figure by Armstrong's side.

"My wife, padre." Jack smiled at the admiration in Cerini's face as he took Helen's hand and raised it to his lips. "She could not longer resist the magnet which draws us to you and to your treasures."

"Your wife," repeated the old man, looking from Helen to Armstrong. "I have looked forward to this day when I might meet her here. But where is your sister-worker? Surely she has not given up the splendid task which she has so well begun?"

Helen flushed consciously at Cerini's praise of Inez. "No, father; Miss Thayer is already at her work, and Mr. Armstrong is equally eager to return to it. May I not stay a little while with you?"

"Have you time to show her some of the things here which we know and love so well?" asked Armstrong.

"Most certainly."

He turned to Helen. "If you will accept my guidance we can let these humanists resume their labors while we enjoy the accomplishments of those who have gone before."

Armstrong left them, and Cerini conducted Helen through the library, explaining to her the various objects of interest. It was quite apparent to Helen that the old man was studying her minutely, and she felt ill at ease in spite of his unfailing courtesy.

"You have known my husband for a long while, have you not?" Helen asked as they passed from one case to another.

"Yes, indeed—even before he came to know himself."

"Then you must know him very well."

Helen smiled, but the old man was serious.

"Better than you know him, even though you are his wife. But see this choir-book. It was illuminated by Lorenzo Monaco, teacher of Fra Angelico. Can anything be more wonderful than these miniatures, in the beauty of their line and color?"

Helen assented with a show of interest, but she was not thinking of the blazoned page before her. The old man's words were burning in her heart. Passing through a smaller room to reach Cerini's study, they came suddenly to a corner lighted only by a small window where Armstrong and Inez were at work. So intent were they that the approach of Helen and the librarian had not been noticed. Cerini held up his hand warningly.

"Quiet!" he commanded, softly. "Let us not disturb them. I have never seen two individualities cast in so identical a mould. One sometimes sees it in two men, but rarely in a man and a woman."

Helen felt her breath come faster as she watched them for a moment longer. Inez was pointing out something in the text of the original letter which lay before them. Armstrong's head was bent, studying it intently. Then Inez spoke, and her companion answered loud enough for Helen to hear.

"Splendid! And to think that we are the first ones to put these facts together!"

The expression of sheer joy upon her husband's face held Helen spellbound, and Cerini was obliged to repeat his suggestion that they return to his study by another route.

"It is just as you have seen it, day after day," said the librarian as he closed the door quietly, and Helen seated herself in the Savonarola chair beside his desk. "When I heard from him that he was to be married I hoped that his wife might be able to enter into this joy of his life; but, since that could not be, it is well that he has found a friend so sympathetic."

Helen told herself that the old man could not intend deliberately to wound her as he was doing.

"Why are you so sure that his wife cannot enter into it also?" she asked, quietly.

Cerini looked at her in evident surprise. "Because what I have seen during these weeks, and what you have seen to-day, can happen but once in a lifetime. You are more beautiful than his companion, but you are not so intellectual."

It was impossible to take offence at the old man's frankness because of his absolute sincerity. He spoke of her beauty exactly as he spoke of one of the magnificent bindings he had just shown her, and of Inez' intellectuality as if it were the content of one of his priceless tomes.

"I came to the library to-day for the definite purpose of joining in their work—" Helen began, hesitatingly.

"Surely not!" replied Cerini, emphatically. "You would not disturb these labors which mean so much in the development of them both? It would mean stopping them where they are."

"Could I not assist them at some point, even to a slight extent, and participate in this development myself?"

Cerini was mildly indulgent at her lack of understanding. "My daughter," he said, kindly, "some one has written that it is no kindness to a spider, no matter how gentle the touch, to aid it in the spinning of its web. Any one can work at translating, truly—almost any one can write a book—but few can accomplish what your husband and Miss Thayer are doing now. The book they are engaged upon in itself is the least of value. They do not themselves realize, as I do, that it is the influence of this work upon their own characters which is making it a success. They were humanists before they knew the meaning of the word. They come into the highest expression of themselves here in this atmosphere. You were born for other things, my daughter—perhaps far more important things—but not for this."

"You cannot understand, father," Helen replied, desperately. "I am his wife, and it is my place, rather than that of any other woman, to share with him any development which affects his life as deeply as you say this does. It must be so."

"Forgive me if I offend you, but this is not a matter which you or I can settle. It is perhaps natural that I cannot understand your viewpoint. The nature of my life and work gives me little knowledge of women; but this is not a question of sex—it is the kinship of intellects. You are his wife, and, as you say, it is your privilege to share with your husband any development, but it must be along a path which you are able to tread. I mean this in no unkind way, my daughter. I doubt not that you, perhaps, in all other ways, are quite capable of doing so, but this one single portion of his life it is quite impossible that you should share."

Helen had no response. Her heart told her that all Cerini said was literally true. She felt herself to be absolutely unfitted to understand or to supplement that particular expression of her husband's character. But the matter-of-fact suggestion of the librarian that Inez should fulfil to him that which she, his wife, lacked, almost paralyzed her power to think or speak. Cerini seemed instinctively to read what was passing through her mind.

"You think me unreal, my daughter—you think me impractical. I may be both. Here, within these old walls, I am not limited by the world's conventions, so perhaps I disregard them more than is right. Those whom I love signify nothing to me as to their personal appearance or their families or their personalities except in so far as these attributes may be expressions of themselves. Life to me would not be worth the living if in debating whether or not I ought to do a certain thing I was obliged to consider also what the world would think or what some other person might think. Let me ask you a question: Was your motive in coming here this morning the result of a desire to put yourself in touch with the spirit of your husband's work, or was it to separate these two persons in the labor they have undertaken?"

Cerini's question brought Helen to herself.

"If you are really free from the world's conventions," she responded, quickly, "you will understand my answer. My husband is everything to me that a wife could ask, and his happiness is the highest object my life contains. Miss Thayer is the dearest friend I have, and my affection for her is second only to the love I bear my husband. While this side of his nature was not unknown to me, until we came to Florence—even until to-day—I have never fully appreciated its intensity. Yet when I feel that to a certain extent, at least, his welfare depends upon a gratification of this expression, is it unnatural that I, his wife, should wish to be the one person to experience that development with him?"

"You did not feel this strong desire when you first came to Florence?"

"I did not understand it."

"Would your present comprehension have come at all if his companion had been a man rather than a woman?"

Helen flushed. "You are not so free from the world's conventions as you think."

"But you do not answer the question," the old man pursued, relentlessly.

"You think, then, that my desire is prompted by jealousy? Let us speak frankly," continued Helen as Cerini held up his hand deprecatingly. "The distinction in my own mind may be a fine one and difficult for another to comprehend, but I can say truly that no jealous thought has entered into any of my considerations. I could not love my husband and be jealous of him at the same time. On the other hand, it is probably quite true that were his companion a man I should not have recognized so strongly the importance of joining him in this particular work."

Cerini rose quietly, and took from the bookcase near his desk a copy of a modern classic.

"The author has expressed an idea here which I think explains your position exactly." He turned the pages quickly. "See here," he said, drawing closer to Helen and pointing to a paragraph marked with a double score in the margin. "'No man objects to the admiration his wife receives from his friends; it is the woman herself who makes the trouble.' Now I suppose the reverse of that proposition is equally true."

Helen smiled. "You mean that the reason I am not jealous of my husband in this instance is because he has given me no occasion?"

"Exactly."

"That is perfectly true."

"But you fear that it may not always be true?"

Helen was no match for the old man in argument, yet she struggled to meet him.

"Perhaps," she said; "there is always that danger. Why not avoid it by making this other companionship unnecessary?"

"But suppose you yourself are not temperamentally fitted to gratify this particular craving in your husband's life?" Cerini watched the effect of his words upon his companion. She was silent for several moments before she raised her eyes to his.

"I know that you are right," she answered, simply. "I have felt it always, but my husband has insisted that in my case it was lack of application rather than of temperament. I came here to-day to try the experiment, and you have shown me that my own judgment is correct."

"It is correct," agreed Cerini, delighted by Helen's unexpected acquiescence. "It was your husband's heart rather than his head which led him astray in his advice. You have just shown me your intelligence by coming so promptly to this conclusion; now you are going to manifest your devotion to him by leaving him undisturbed in this work which he has undertaken. It can only last during a limited period at best. It is the expression of but one side of his nature. Before many weeks have passed you and he will be returning to your great country into a complexity of conditions where this experience will become only a memory. These conditions will call to the surface the expression of his other characteristics into which you can fully enter. By not interfering with this character-building now going on, you, his wife, will later reap rich returns."

A tap sounded on the door of the study.

"There is your husband now," said Cerini, taking Helen's hand. "Tell me that you forgive me for my frankness."

Helen pressed his hand silently as he turned from her to admit Armstrong.

"Here you are!" cried Jack, as he entered with Inez. "We became so engrossed that I am ashamed to say I completely forgot our new convert."

"Your forgetfulness has given me the opportunity to become well acquainted with your charming wife," replied Cerini. "Is your work completed for the day?"

"Yes, but we shall be at it again to-morrow. You will come with us of course?" he asked, turning to his wife.

"I am not quite sure, Jack," Helen replied. "Monsignor Cerini has suggested to me another way in which I can help you, which may prove to be equally important."

She turned to Inez with an unflinching smile. "Our friend has been explaining to me the nature of what you and Jack are doing together. You must certainly plan to stay on for a while longer. I am sure Jack could never finish it without you."

IX

The human heart can play no more difficult rôle than to keep on with its every-day monotonous pulsations, so far as the world sees, when in reality every throb is a measured duration of infinite pain. Ten days had passed since De Peyster had so unconsciously been the cause of completely changing the even tenor of Helen's existence, and during this time she had drifted helplessly in the deep waters of uncertainty. What was the wise thing to do? Helen knew Inez too well to deceive herself into thinking that what was said to Ferdinand had been simply an expedient to accomplish his dismissal, and her observations since then had confirmed her early convictions. Inez was in love with Jack. Jack was obviously fond of her companionship. Their work in the library had brought them constantly together, and at home an increasing proportion of the time had been devoted to a consideration and discussion of the various topics which had developed and into which Helen did not enter. Yet there was nothing in all this which was not perfectly natural; in fact, it was, as Helen said to herself, wholly the outcome of what she had originally suggested.

Helen's convictions regarding Inez were confirmed, not by what her friend did, but rather by the efforts she made to avoid doing certain things. Never for an instant did Helen question Inez' loyalty to her, and she could scarcely refrain from entering into the tremendous struggle in which she saw her engaged. Each woman's heart was passing through fire, and Helen felt a new and strange bond of sympathy between her friend and herself because of their mutual suffering. But the struggle must continue. Helen must come to some decision wiser than any which had yet suggested itself to her before disclosing to any one, and to Inez least of all, that she possessed any knowledge of the situation.

Fortunately, at this crisis, the automobile became the controlling excitement. During the intervening days Jack had resisted the temptation, devoting himself assiduously to his self-appointed task, and satisfying himself with short excursions after his labors at the library were over. Now he could resist no longer. The book was assuming definite proportions, and, as he explained to himself and the others, the work would be all the better for a little holiday. So it was that the Armstrongs, with Miss Thayer and Uncle Peabody, made runs to Siena, Padua, and to all the smaller towns less frequented by visitors and consequently of greater interest. Miss Thayer forgot in the excitement the experience she was passing through; Uncle Peabody forgot Luigi Cornaro and the Japanese; Armstrong, for the time being, appeared indifferent to the hitherto compelling interests at the library; and Helen, at intervals, forgot her suffering and the heavy burden which lay upon her heart in her feeling of helplessness. New sensations, in this twentieth century, are rare, and the automobile is to be credited with supplying many. The exhilaration, the abandon, which comes with the utter annihilation of time and space, forces even those affairs of life which previously had been thought important to become miserably commonplace. The danger itself is not the least of the fascination.

"I would rather be killed once a week in an automobile," asserted Uncle Peabody while the fever was on him, "than die the one ordinary death allotted to man."

With the temporary cessation of the library work, there had been no occasion for separate interests. This, Helen felt, was most fortunate, as it gave her ample opportunity to arrive at her conclusions. It was all her own fault, she repeated to herself over and over again. Had she made an earlier effort to enter into Jack's interests, even though it had proved her inability, matters need never have arrived at so serious a pass. Now she was convinced that it was too late to become a part of them; she had done an irreparable injury to Inez, whom she loved as a sister, and had taken chances on disrupting her own and her husband's domestic happiness.

"As Jack said, I have found a cloud in the cloudless sky," she thought.— "And poor Inez!"

Thus the burden resolved itself into two parts—solicitude for Inez and how best to undo the harm Helen felt she had wrought. Her first attempt had proved a failure, and she could not see the next step. While the motoring fever lasted there was nothing to do but to plan; for the excitement was infectious, and one trip followed another in rapid succession. Household regularity became conspicuous by its absence. Meals were served at all hours and were rushed through with reckless haste, entirely upsetting Uncle Peabody's theories.

"You treat your stomach like a trunk," he protested to Armstrong one morning, "and you throw the food into it just about the way an average man does his packing."

"But you finish your breakfast just as soon as any of us," was the retort.

"Yes, but if you observe carefully you will note that I actually eat about one-quarter as much as you do in the same given time. And what I have eaten will satisfy me about four times as long, because I have thoroughly masticated it and assimilated all the nourishing portions of the food. When I think of the gymnastic performances your poor stomach must go through in order to tear into shreds the chunks of food you have bolted down I admit my sympathy is fully aroused."

"Sympathy is always grateful," Armstrong replied, unconvinced, "but every moment we lose discussing nutrition is a moment taken off the finest trip we have tried yet. The car is in splendid condition, the weather is ideal, and Pisa awaits us at the other end of our excursion."

"So it is to be Pisa, is it?" Uncle Peabody arose. "Do you know, Jack, I like you for the way you plan these charming rides, and that almost makes up for your lack of judgment in some other directions. An ordinary man would spend at least the day before in studying maps, asking advice, and in making plans generally. You, on the contrary, wait until breakfast is over, throw down your napkin, and then with a proper show of impatience say, 'Why do you keep me waiting? The car is ready to take us to the moon.' All this fits in exactly with my principles: it is the unexpected which always brings satisfaction."

"Uncle's praise is distinctly a man's approval," Helen protested. "From a woman's standpoint Jack's methods represent the acme of tyranny. No inquiries as to where we prefer to be spirited, no suggestions that our opinions are worth consulting, no suspicion that we are other than clay in the potter's hands; simply, 'The machine is ready. Please hurry.' Yes, we are coming," Helen hurriedly added, seeing Jack's impatience over the bantering, "we are coming!"

Giuseppe, Annetta, and the cook were avowed enemies of the motor-car, not only because of the effect it had produced upon the household arrangements, but also because of the intrusion of the French chauffeur which it had forced upon them. They would die rather than show the slightest interest in it, yet on one pretext or another they never allowed the machine to start out without regarding it with secret admiration and respect. Giuseppe, on this particular morning, was gathering roses on the terrace, Annetta was closing a shutter on the veranda, while the cook's red face peered around the corner of the villa. Giuseppe crossed himself as the engine started up, then jumped and fell squarely into his rose-basket as the chauffeur maliciously pressed the bulb, and the machine moved majestically past him, out of the court-yard, and into the narrow road.

"I don't blame these people for resenting the invasion of motor-cars and other evidences of modern progress," said Inez as they reached the level; "it is all so out of keeping with everything around them and with everything they have been brought up to regard as right and proper."

"But 'these people' represent only one portion of the Italians, Miss Thayer," replied Uncle Peabody. "Italian civic life contains two great contrasting factors—one practical, the other ideal. Each in its way is proud of the past; the first thinks more of the present and the future, while the second, opposed on principle to innovations, only accepts, and then under protest, those which come from Italian sources. This car we are riding in is of French manufacture. Were it Italian, you would find that it would have been greeted with smiles instead of scowls just now. And yet I like their patriotism."

"But it does seem a sacrilege for the wonderful old towers and walls here in Florence to be torn down to make room for prosaic twentieth-century trolley-cars," Helen added.

"And Mr. Armstrong says there is talk of a board road being built for automobiles between Mestre and Venice. What will dear old Italy be when 'modern civilization' has finished with her?" Inez asked.

"From present tendencies," remarked Uncle Peabody, gravely, "I expect to live to see the day when the Venetian gondola will be propelled by gasolene; when the Leaning Tower of Pisa will either be straightened by some enterprising American engineer or made to lean a bit more, so that automobiles may make the ascent, even as the Colosseum at Rome is already turned over to Buffalo Bill or some other descendant of Barnum's circus for regular performances, including the pink lemonade and the peanuts."

"Don't!" Inez cried. "It would be far better to go to the other extreme, which Mr. Armstrong would like to see."

The road was level and smooth, now that the rough streets of the city lay behind them, and there was nothing to think of until after reaching Empoli. Armstrong had been running the machine, and he turned his head just in time to hear Inez' last remark.

"I can imagine what the conversation is, even though I have not heard much of it," he said, "and I am sure that I agree with Miss Thayer. How about getting back to our work at the library to-morrow?" he added.

Inez flushed at the suddenness of the question, and Helen caught her breath. The time for her decision, then, was near at hand.

"I am as eager as you are to resume it," replied Inez, her face lighting with pleasure.

"Then it is all arranged," Armstrong said, decisively. "Helen and Uncle Peabody may have the machine to-morrow, and we will start in again where we left off."

The Arno winds around and about in a hundred curves between Florence and Pisa, leaving the road for some little distance at times, but ever coming back to it in flirtatious manner. The fields stretch away between the river and the road in undulating green. Small hamlets like San Romano, La Rotta, and Navacchio, and the more pretentious settlements of Signa, Empoli, and Pontedera give variety to the ride and add by their old-time strangeness to the beauties which Nature so bountifully supplies. But the climax comes at the end of the journey, after crossing the tracks at the very modern station and the bridge which spans the Arno. Over the roofs of the quaint twelfth-century houses rise the Cathedral and the Leaning Tower and the pillared dome of the Baptistry.

The motor-car was halted in front of the little doorway of the Hôtel Nettuno, where the host appeared with all his affability, offering opportunities for removing the dust accumulated by the ride, and a choice *colazione* to be ready as soon as might be desired. Helen was preoccupied during the preparations for luncheon, but Inez' excitement over her first visit to Pisa, and Armstrong's eagerness to watch the effect of the early impressions, saved her changed demeanor from attracting any attention.

"It is hard to realize that this is the city of Ugolino and the Tower of Hunger after this sumptuous repast," remarked Jack, lighting his cigarette with much satisfaction as coffee was being served.

"Probably the 'Nettuno' was not in existence at that time," suggested Uncle Peabody.

"Is this not where the wonderful echo is to be heard?" inquired Inez.

"Yes—at the Baptistry," Armstrong replied; "and you are sure to enjoy it— the sacristan makes up such a funny face when he intones."

"The echo at Montecatini, I understand, is taking a long vacation," observed Uncle Peabody.

"How so?" inquired Inez, innocently.

"The regular echo was ill, and the sacristan failed to coach the new boy properly. The visitor called, 'What is the hour?' and the echo came back, 'Four o'clock'!"

Jack and Inez led the way from the hotel, through the narrow walled streets and under the gateway to the Piazza del Duomo, where all the splendor of the marvellous group of buildings burst upon them. Helen pleaded fatigue and asked to be left in the Duomo while the others set out to climb the Leaning Tower and to inspect the Campo Santo; so Uncle Peabody insisted on staying with her. They sat down on one of the wooden benches beneath the lamp of Galileo, and Helen rested her head upon her hand. Uncle

Peabody watched her curiously for a moment. Finally he took her hand quietly in his. Helen started.

"I would do it if I were you, Helen," he said, deliberately.

"Do what?" she asked, surprised into confusion.

"Just what you were thinking of doing when I interrupted you."

"Do you know what I was thinking, then?"

"No." Uncle Peabody spoke in a very matter-of-fact way. "But I am sure it is the right thing to do."

Helen looked at him steadily, uncertain of just how far he had surmised her secret thought. There was nothing in the calm, unruffled expression which gave her even an inkling as to whether her peculiar sensation was caused by his intuition or her own self-consciousness. Then her gaze relaxed, and she laughed half-heartedly.

"You have mislaid your divining-cap this time," Helen said at length. "If you had really read my mind your advice would have been quite different."

Uncle Peabody was undisturbed. "In that case you will exercise your woman's prerogative and change it within the next twenty-four hours. When that has taken place you will find that my advice fits it exactly."

"I wish I had your confidence, Uncle Peabody." Helen rose suddenly and held out her hand to her companion. "Come, let us go into the sunlight, where things look more cheerful."

Uncle Peabody watched the figure militant as Helen preceded him down the broad aisle, past the small altars, and out into the air. He recalled this same attitude when Helen had been a child, and he remembered the determination and the strength of will which went with it at that time. He had forgotten this characteristic in meeting his niece grown to womanhood and in the midst of such apparently congenial surroundings. Now he felt that he knew the occasion for its reappearance.

Inez and Jack soon joined them, and together they returned to the hotel. A few moments later the car was gliding back toward Florence again, in the refreshing cool of the afternoon, with changed color effects to give new impressions to the panorama of the morning. They were almost home when Armstrong turned suddenly to Helen:

"How absolutely stupid of me!" he said, abruptly. "I met Phil Emory on the Lung' Arno yesterday and asked him to take dinner with us to-night." Armstrong looked at his watch. "We shall be just about in time, anyhow, but I am sorry not to have told you about it."

X

When Helen Cartwright had accepted Phil Emory as escort for the Harvard Class Day festivities, on the occasion of his graduation, every one had considered the matter of their engagement as settled; that is to say, every one except Helen and Emory. This view of the matter did not occur to Helen, even as a remote possibility, and Phil Emory had absolute knowledge to the contrary, since Helen herself had answered his question very clearly, even though not satisfactorily, some months before this event took place. But she liked him immensely none the less, and saw no reason why she should not throw confetti at him from the circus-like seats of the Stadium, or eat strawberries and ices with him and her other friends at the various Class Day spreads. In fact, she saw every reason for doing so, inasmuch as she thoroughly enjoyed it; and Emory was proud enough to act as host under any conditions whatever.

After graduation Emory probably had as good a chance as any one until Jack Armstrong entered the field. The younger man had become more and more intense in his devotion, but when he found himself out-classed by the force of Armstrong's attack he accepted his defeat generously and philosophically. No one contributed more to the jollity of the wedding breakfast or extended heartier congratulations to the bride and bridegroom.

Emory's visit at the Villa Godilombra, when he first arrived in Italy, was one of the pleasantest experiences of his whole trip thus far. Never had he seen a more glorious spot, and never had he seen Helen so radiantly beautiful. He had remarked to Eustis more than once during their stay that an Italian background was the one thing needful to show off Helen's charms to the greatest perfection. When he returned to Florence, therefore, he determined to see her again, making his belated duty call the excuse; so the fortunate meeting with Armstrong and the invitation which resulted fitted in most agreeably with his plans.

The automobile passed Emory in his *vettura* half-way up the hill. "Good-bye, old chap! Must hurry, as we have company coming for dinner!" cried Armstrong, gayly, as the machine glided past him, giving him only a vision of waving hands before he became enveloped in the cloud of dust. When he arrived at the villa he found Helen and Jack awaiting him as if they had been at home all the afternoon.

"This is a pleasant surprise, Phil," said Helen, cordially. "Until Jack told me you were in Florence I supposed you and Dick Eustis had at least reached London by this time."

"No," Emory replied, as they walked into the garden; "I only went as far north as Paris. Eustis continued on to London, and is there now, I expect, but I ran across Ferdy De Peyster in Paris. He had a frightfully sick turn, and I had to take care of him for a while."

"Ferdy was sick, you say?" Helen was eagerly interested. "You don't mean dangerously so?"

"No—not as things turned out; but I will admit I was a bit anxious about him for a time. He had been terribly cut up over something, and then caught a beastly cold on his lungs, and I thought he was in for a severe case of pneumonia. He was pretty sandy about it, and in a week he came around all right. I took him over to Aix, where I left him, and then I decided to sail home from Naples instead of Southampton."

"Did he tell you what the trouble was?" Helen was anxious to know how confidential De Peyster had been.

"Oh, an *affaire de cœur* he said; but he did not tell me who the girl was. He spoke of his call on you and Miss Thayer, here, shortly after we departed, but the poor chap was not very communicative."

"Forgive me for deserting you, Emory," interrupted Armstrong as he approached them from the house, closely followed by Annetta bearing a tray. "This is one part of the dinner which I never leave to any one else. These Italians know a lot of things better than we do, but mixing cocktails is not one of their long suits."

"By Jove! that is a grateful reward to a dusty throat!" said Emory, replacing the glass on the tray.

"And now to dinner," announced Helen. "Annetta bids us enter."

Uncle Peabody and Miss Thayer joined them at the table.

"I must tell you, Mr. Cartwright," said Emory, after the greetings were over, "that what you said about eating when I was here before made quite an impression on me, and I have been trying your methods a little."

"Good for you!" cried Uncle Peabody.

"I really think I ought to make a confession," Emory continued. "I had heard about your work and all that, but I had an idea that you were more or less of a crank, and that your theories were the usual ones which go with a new fad. But when you talked about understanding and running properly one's own motive power it appealed to me as being sensible. Then your idea that the appetite is given one to tell him what the system needs sounded reasonable to me; and when you insisted that this same appetite had a right to be consulted as to when enough fuel was on board I woke up to a realization that I had not always been that respectful to myself."

Uncle Peabody smiled genially. "Have you found the experiment very disagreeable?"

"By no means," replied Emory, decidedly. "Of course, I started in on it more as a joke than anything else, but I have been surprised to find how much more I really enjoy my food. Why, there are flavors in a piece of bread which I never discovered until I chewed it all to pieces."

"That is on the same principle exactly that a tea-taster or a wine-taster discovers the real flavor of the particular variety he is testing. That is one thing which gave me my idea. He sips a little and then thoroughly mixes it with the saliva, and in that way tastes the delicate aroma which the glutton never knows either in drink or food."

"How does the system work with the elaborate Continental *table d'hôte*, Mr. Emory?" queried Miss Thayer.

Uncle Peabody answered for him: "You became an object of suspicion to the head-waiter, and the *garçon* thought you were criticising the food."

"Exactly," laughed Emory. "But, all joking aside, Mr. Cartwright, I have become a confirmed disciple. I never felt so well, and I am eating about half as much as I used to."

"This seems to be developing into an experience meeting," Armstrong remarked. "Why don't you write out a testimonial for the gentleman?"

"I would gladly do so, but from what I hear he stands in no need of any such document."

Emory turned to Uncle Peabody. "It is a case of being 'advertised by our grateful friends,' is it not, Mr. Cartwright?"

"How long will you be in Florence, Phil?" asked Helen. "Are you just passing through again, or is this where you make your visit to the City of Flowers?"

"I have no definite plans. My steamer doesn't sail for a month, and I am moving along as the wind blows me. Are the Sinclair girls still here?"

"No; they sailed for home last week."

"Why don't you stay in Florence for a while and help Helen exercise the automobile?" suggested Armstrong. "Miss Thayer and I are working every day at the library, and it will prevent her becoming lonesome."

Helen looked inquiringly at her husband. This suggestion from him, and to Phil Emory of all men! The times had indeed altered! She saw that Emory was observing her, and felt the necessity of relieving the tension.

"You must not put it on that score, Jack," she said, quietly. "I am not at all lonely, but I should be very glad to have Phil join us to-morrow. What do you say, Phil?"

"I should like nothing better. But tell me about this work, Armstrong. Are you really boning down to arduous labor on your honeymoon?"

"It is a bit out of the ordinary, is it not?" admitted Jack, uncertain whether or not Emory's question contained a reproach. "I would not dare do it with any one except Helen, but she understands the necessity. I don't know when I shall get another chance."

"Jack is accomplishing wonders in his work," explained Helen, anxious to have Emory feel her entire sympathy; "you must have him tell you about it. In the mean time, while he is improving himself mentally, Uncle Peabody and I are entering somewhat into the social frivolities of Florence. To-morrow we are going to a reception to be given to the Count of Turin and the Florentine Dante Society at the Villa Londi. Jack scorns these functions, but you will be quite in your element. We will take you with us."

"It is not that I 'scorn' these things, as you say, Helen," protested Armstrong. "You give any one an entirely wrong idea. They are all right enough in their own way, but I can get these at home. This chance at the library, however, is one in a lifetime, and I feel that I must improve it."

"Of course," replied Helen, "that is what I meant to say."

Emory glanced from one to the other quietly. "I shall be most happy to go if you are quite sure I won't interfere with the plans you have already made. You know I am not on speaking terms with Italian."

"You won't have to be," Uncle Peabody assured him. "These Italians speak English so well that you will be ashamed of your ignorance. You will have no difficulty in making yourself understood."

Helen was rebellious at heart that Jack should have suggested Emory to relieve her loneliness. It was enough that he was willing to be away from her so much without taking it for granted and referring to it in such a matter-of-fact way. Inez as well came in for her share of the resentment, her very silence during the discussion serving to aggravate Helen's discomfiture. Helen deliberately turned the conversation.

"I can't help thinking of poor Ferdy, Phil. Have you heard from him since you left him at Aix?"

"No, but I should have heard if all had not been going well."

"What is the matter with De Peyster?" asked Armstrong.

"Oh, you did not hear what Phil told me about him before dinner, Jack. He has been very ill, and Phil took him over to Aix for a cure."

It was the first time De Peyster's name had been mentioned since his abrupt departure, and Inez flushed deeply as she listened.

"What was the trouble, Emory?" asked Armstrong, innocently.

"He came pretty near having pneumonia," replied Emory. "He was hard hit with a girl somewhere over here, and was thrown down, I suspect. Then he grew careless and was a pretty sick chap when I ran across him in Paris."

Armstrong had no idea of the result of his question. He glanced hastily at Inez and gulped down half a glass of wine, nearly choking himself in the process.

"There you go!" exclaimed Uncle Peabody, quite understanding the situation and wishing to relieve the embarrassment. "You will drown yourself one of these fine days if you don't listen to my teachings and profit by Mr. Emory's example."

But Emory was quite unconscious of the delicate ground upon which he trod. The days and nights he had spent with De Peyster were still strongly impressed upon his mind.

"I thought you might know something about this, Helen," he continued, "for Ferdy mentioned your name and Miss Thayer's several times while he was delirious. I could not make out anything he said, he was so incoherent. Later, when he began to improve, I asked him about it, but he evidently did not care to talk. But how stupid I have been!" He broke off suddenly and turned to Miss Thayer. "Here I have been sitting beside you all this time and never once offered my congratulations!"

Inez drew back from the proffered hand. The color left her face as suddenly as it had come. "What do you mean?" she stammered.

"Why, De Peyster told me you were engaged," Emory said, quite taken aback. "Have I said something I ought not to? He said you told him so."

"Mr. De Peyster had no right to say that!" Inez cried, fiercely, almost breaking into tears.

Emory was most contrite. "Ten thousand pardons," he apologized. "You must forgive me, Miss Thayer. Ferdy never suggested that it was a secret at all—and now I have given the whole thing away!"

Emory wished himself half-way across the Atlantic.

"I am very much annoyed," replied Inez, still struggling to contain herself—"not with you, but with Mr. De Peyster."

"But she is not engaged," Armstrong insisted, with decision.

"I think Inez had better be left to settle that point herself, Jack," Helen interrupted, pointedly.

"Then why does she not settle it?"

"I will settle it." Inez sat up very straight in her chair, her tense features making her face look drawn in its ashy paleness.

"Jack has no right to force you into any such position, Inez," Helen protested, indignantly; "he is forgetting himself."

"De Peyster is responsible for the whole thing." Emory struggled to step in between the clash of arms. "I recall the very words. 'Phil, old chap,' he said, 'you remember Miss Thayer? She is engaged. She told me she had found some one whom she loved better than her life.' Can you blame me for making such a consummate ass of myself?"

Armstrong's intense interest had taken him too deeply into the affair for him to heed Helen's protests.

"You never said anything of the kind, did you, Miss Thayer?"

"I am not engaged," replied Inez, very firmly, "and I cannot understand why Mr. De Peyster should have put me in this uncomfortable position."

"Of course not," assented Armstrong, with evident satisfaction. "De Peyster is a fool. I will tell him so the next time I see him."

"I think we had better change the subject," said Helen, rising, her face flushed with indignation. "The methods of the Inquisition have no place at a modern dinner-table."

XI

Inez Thayer had congratulated herself upon her success in keeping her secret. Since her searching self-examination and the harrowing experience during De Peyster's brief visit she had spent many hours inwardly debating the proper steps to take in order to solve her problem. She was certain that no one knew the real state of affairs, and with this certainty the only danger lay in its effect upon herself. But she knew all too well that this danger was indeed a real one. Day by day her admiration for Armstrong increased, and with that admiration her affection waxed stronger and stronger. Those hours together at the library—when they were quite alone, when his face, in their joint absorption in their work, almost touched hers, when his hand rested unconsciously for a moment upon her own—were to her moments in the Elysian Fields, and she quaffed deeply of the intoxicating draught. What harm, she argued to herself, since her companion was oblivious to her hidden sentiments—what disloyalty to her friend, since the pain must all be hers? And the pain was hers already—why not revel in its ecstasy while it lasted?

With her conscience partially eased by her labored conclusions, Inez threw herself into a complete enjoyment of her work. Helen's attitude toward her had not in any way altered, and she was still apparently entirely agreeable to the arrangement. Her suggestion to join them in their labors was the only evidence which Inez had seen that perhaps her friend was becoming restless, even though not ready to raise any objections; but when Helen herself gave up the idea, after her single visit to the library, Inez was convinced that she had misunderstood her motive. Nothing remained, therefore, but to accept her previous argument that she was simply following the inexorable guidance of Fate, with herself the only possible victim. It was uncomfortable, it was wearing, but she could not, she repeated over and over again, remove herself from the exquisite suffering of her surroundings until she was absolutely obliged to do so.

The episode at the dinner-table completely shattered the structure she had built, and its sudden demolition stunned her. This she vaguely realized as she and Helen left the men at the table and walked to the veranda for their coffee. Their departure was in itself an evidence of new and strained conditions, as both Helen and Jack regarded the coffee-and-cigar period as the best part of every dinner and a part to be enjoyed together. Helen had not yet acquired the Continental cigarette habit, but, as she had once expressed it, "Men are so good-natured right after dinner, when they are stuffed, and so happy when they are making silly little clouds of smoke!"

Inez hesitatingly passed her arm around her friend's waist, and when Helen drew her closely to her she rested her head against her shoulder, relaxing like a tired child.

"Who would have expected this outcome of such a happy day?" Inez queried, sadly, as the two girls seated themselves upon the wicker divan.

"Jack was a brute!" exclaimed Helen, almost savagely.

"It is all my own fault, Helen; but I could not tell them so in there."

Helen appeared astonished. "How do you mean? Are you really engaged, after all?"

"No, no, Helen; but you see when Ferdy urged me so hard for an answer I had to tell him something."

Inez glanced up at Helen to see how she took her explanation.

"So you told him you were engaged?"

"Not exactly that, but—"

"That you loved some one better than your life?"

Inez shrank a little as she answered. "Something like that," she admitted.

"And it was not true?"

Inez laughed nervously. "What an absurd question, Helen! You know I have seen almost no one since I came here."

"Except Jack," said Helen, impulsively.

Inez sprang to her feet. "What do you mean, Helen? You don't accuse me of being in love with your husband, do you?"

Helen pulled her down beside her again. "Don't be tragic, dear," she said, quietly. "I admit that the suggestion is unkind, after the display Jack made of himself at the table. I am provoked with him myself."

"Helen,"—Inez spoke abruptly, after a moment's silence—"I think I ought to leave Florence."

"Don't be absurd, Inez. You are worked up over this miserable affair, but you will forget all about it in the morning—when you get back to your work at the library."

"No; this time I really mean what I say. I ought to have gone when my visit was up a fortnight ago; but you were so sweet in urging me to stay, and the work had developed with such increasing interest, that I have just stayed on and on."

"I am sorry if you regret having stayed, dear. It certainly seemed to be for the best."

"But see what it has brought on you, Helen."

"I am not proud of my husband's behavior, I admit; but you have even greater cause to feel annoyed than I."

Inez seemed to be drifting hopelessly in her attempt to find the right thing to say.

"I have felt that I ought to go for a long time."

"A long time?" Helen echoed. "Has Jack behaved as badly as this before?"

"Not that; it is the library work which makes me feel so."

"I don't wonder you are getting tired of it."

"Tired of it! Oh, Helen, I wish you could get as much joy out of anything as I do out of this work. Tired of it!" Inez laughed aloud at the absurdity of the suggestion. Then she grew serious again. "I know I ought to leave it, yet I cannot force myself to make the break."

"I don't think I understand," said Helen, quietly, watching intently the struggle through which the girl was passing.

"I know you don't, and I don't believe I could make any one understand it," replied Inez, helplessly.

"You talk about it in this mysterious way just as Jack does," continued Helen. "There must be some sort of spell about it, for you both are changed beings since your first visit to the library."

"Then you have noticed it?" Inez looked up anxiously.

"Of course I have noticed it," admitted Helen, frankly. "How could I help it when you yourself feel it so strongly?"

"Do you blame me for it?"

"Why should I blame you, Inez? Is there any reason why I should blame any one?"

"No, except that the work takes your husband away from you so much."

"But I can't hold you responsible for that, can I? It is the work which draws you both, is it not—not each the other?"

Inez moved uneasily and withdrew her hand from Helen's lap. "Of course it is the work," she answered, quietly; "but, frankly, would you not rather have it discontinued?"

"No," replied Helen, without hesitation; "but I sincerely wish Jack might be less completely absorbed by it. I have no intention of opposing it, and I am willing to sacrifice much for its success, yet I see no reason why it should so wholly deprive me of my husband."

"It has opened up an entirely new world for me." Inez seemed suddenly obsessed by a reminiscent thought. Her troubled expression changed into one of rapt ecstasy. Helen watched the transformation, deeply impressed by the strange new light which she saw in the girl's eyes. "I must be more impressionable than I supposed," she continued, "for it all seems so real. I can see Michelangelo's face as I read his letters; I can see his lips move, his expression change—I can even hear his voice. I have watched him fashion the great David out of the discarded marble; I have heard his discussions with Pope Julius and Pope Leo; I have witnessed his struggle with Leonardo at the Palazzo Vecchio. The events come so fast, and the letters give such minute information upon so many topics, that I actually feel myself in the midst of it all. I know Vittoria Colonna as well as Michelangelo ever did, and I know far better than he why she refused to marry him. All these great characters, and others, live and move and converse with us these mornings at the library." Inez paused to get her breath. She was talking very fast. "I know it sounds uncanny," she went on, "but there is something in the very atmosphere which makes me forget who or what I am. Cerini comes and stands beside us, rubbing his hands together and smiling, and yet we hardly notice him. He is a part of it all. What he says seems no more real than the conversations and the communions we have with the others who died centuries ago. I realize how inexplicable all this must sound to you, because I find myself absolutely unable to explain it to myself. It must be a spell, as you say, but I have no strength to break it."

"It must be something," Helen admitted, gravely, "to affect both you and Jack the same way. I wonder what it is?"

Inez paid no heed to the interrogation. "You should see your husband, Helen, when he is at his work. You don't really know him as you see him here."

Helen felt herself impressed even more strongly than she had been during her visit to the library. Inez spoke with the same intensity and conviction which at that time had overwhelmed her previously conceived plans.

"Cerini said the same thing—" she began.

"Cerini is right," Inez interrupted. "Your husband is a god among them all. He is not a mere student, searching for facts, but one of those great spirits themselves, looking into their lives and their characters with a power and an intimacy which only a contemporary and an equal could do. Cerini says that his book will be a masterpiece—that it will place him among the great *savants* of his time. No such work has been produced in years; and you will be so proud of him, Helen—so proud that he belongs to you! Is it not worth the sacrifice?"

As her friend paused Helen bowed her head in silence. "So proud that he belongs to you," Inez had just said. Did he belong to her—had he ever belonged to her? The new light in Inez' eyes, the intensity of her words, both convinced and controlled her. What was she, even though his wife, to stand in the way of such a championship? What were the conventions of commonplace domestic life in the presence of this all-compelling genius? She felt her resentment against Jack become unimportant. With such absorption it was but natural that he should not act like other men.

The sound of voices in the hall brought both girls to themselves.

"Dare we come out?" asked Uncle Peabody, cautiously, pausing at the door. "These back-sliders are very repentant, and I will vouch for their good behavior."

"There is only one of us who requires forgiveness," added Armstrong, frankly, advancing to the divan. "I owe you both an apology; first of all to my wife, for not heeding her good advice, and then to my 'sister-worker,' as Cerini calls her, for adding to her discomfiture."

"If Inez will forgive you, I will cheerfully add my absolution," replied Helen, forcing a smile.

"I was really afraid that I was going to lose my right-hand man," continued Armstrong by way of explanation, "and my work must then have come to an abrupt conclusion."

"You give me altogether too much credit," replied Inez. "The work is already so much a part of yourself that you could not drop it if you lost a dozen 'sister-workers.'"

"It must never come to that, Jack," added Helen, seriously. "Inez will surely stay until the book is completed, and I shall do what little I can to help it to a glorious success."

"You are a sweet, sympathizing little wife." Armstrong placed his hand affectionately upon her shoulder. "Your interest in it will be all that I need to make it so."

Emory and Uncle Peabody instinctively glanced at each other, and for a moment their eyes met. It was but an instant, yet in that brief exchange each knew where the other stood.

BOOK II

VICTIM OF FATE

XII

All Florence—social, literary, and artistic—was at the Londi reception. The ancient villa, once the possession of the great Dante, fell into gentle hands when the present owner, thirty years before, entered into an appreciative enjoyment of his newly acquired property. The structure itself was preserved and restored without destroying the original beauty of its architecture; the walls were renovated and hung with rich tapestries and rare paintings; priceless statuary found a place in the courts and corridors, but with such perfect taste that one felt instinctively that each piece belonged exactly where it stood as a part of the complete harmony.

Florentine society possesses two strong characteristics—hospitality and sincerity. No people in the world so cordially welcome strangers who come properly introduced to settle temporarily in their midst; no people so plainly manifest their estimates of their adopted aliens. There is no half-way, there is no compromise. They are courteous always, they are considerate even when they disapprove; but when once they accept the stranger into their circle they make him feel that he is and always has been a part of themselves.

Uncle Peabody had won this place long since. His genial disposition and quiet philosophy appealed to them from the first by its very contrast to their own impulsive Latin temperament. It was an easy matter, therefore, for him to introduce his niece to those whom he counted among his friends, and this he made it a point to do when he discovered how much she would otherwise have been alone. Helen had ceased to urge Jack to accompany her, and he seemed quite content to be omitted. Their first weeks in Florence had been devoted to getting settled in their villa and in rambling over the surrounding hills, entirely satisfied with their own society. The house-party had taken up another week, and even before the guests had departed Armstrong began his researches at the library, which required a larger portion of each day as time went on. The moment when Helen and Jack would naturally have jointly assumed their social pleasures and responsibilities had passed, and the necessity for diversion of some kind prompted Helen gratefully to accept her uncle as a substitute.

"There is a countrywoman of ours—the Contessa Morelli," Uncle Peabody remarked, as he skilfully piloted Helen and Emory away from the crush in the reception-hall, indicating a strikingly attractive woman surrounded by a group of Italian gallants. "She came from Milwaukee, I believe, and married the title, with the husband thrown in as a gratuity for good measure."

"She looks far too refined and agreeable to answer to your description," Helen replied, after regarding the object of his comments.

"She is refined and agreeable," assented Uncle Peabody, "and—worldly. When you have once seen the count you will understand. She is a neighbor of yours, so you must meet her—the Villa Morelli is scarcely a quarter of a mile beyond the Villa Godilombra."

"Don't overlook me in the introduction, will you?" urged Emory, eagerly.

"Still as fond as ever of a pretty face, Phil?" queried Helen, laughing.

"Of course," he acquiesced, cheerfully; "but this is a case of national pride. You and she—the two American Beauties present—would make any American proud of his country."

Helen smiled and held up a finger warningly as she followed Uncle Peabody's lead. The contessa acknowledged the introductions with much cordiality, but to Emory's disappointment devoted herself at once to Helen.

"So you are from dear, old, chilly Boston," she said, breezily. "The last time I passed through was on a July day, and I was so glad I had my furs with me."

"Boston is celebrated for its east winds," volunteered Emory, calmly.

The contessa glanced at him for a moment to make sure that his misunderstanding was wilful.

"Yes," she replied, meaningly; "and I understand that in Boston the revised adage reads, 'God tempers the east wind to the blue-bloods.'"

"And I was just going to say some nice things about Milwaukee!" Emory continued.

"Then it is just as well that I discouraged you," the contessa interrupted. "No one who has not lived there can ever think of anything complimentary to say about Milwaukee except to expatiate upon its beer. That seems to mark the limitations of his acquaintance with our city."

The contessa turned to Helen. "Mr. Cartwright tells me that you and your husband are my mysterious neighbors, about whom we have had so much curiosity. You must let me call on you very soon."

Helen was studying her new acquaintance with much interest. Her features were as clearly cut as if the work of a master-sculptor, yet nature had improved upon human skill by adding a color to the cheeks and a vivacity to the eye which made their owner irresistible to all who met her; while the simple elegance of her lingerie gown, in striking contrast to the dress of the Italian women near her, set off to advantage the lines of her graceful figure. She was a few years older than Helen, yet evidently a younger woman in years than in experience. Uncle Peabody's comments had naturally prejudiced Helen to an extent, yet she could not resist a certain appeal which unconsciously attracted her.

"I hope we may see much of each other," the contessa continued, cordially, scarcely giving Helen an opportunity even for perfunctory replies. "Morelli is housed by the gout at least half of the time, and he bores me to death with his description of the various symptoms. I will run over to Villa Godilombra and let you rehearse your troubles for a change. But, of course, you have no troubles—Mr. Cartwright said you were a bride, did he not?"

The contessa noticed the color which came in Helen's face, and her experience, tempered by her intuition, told her that it was not a blush of pleasure.

"Where is your husband?" she asked, pointedly. "You must present him to me."

"He is engaged upon some literary work at the library," Helen replied.

"Oh, a learned man! That is almost as bad as the gout!" The contessa held up her hands in mock horror. "Then you will need my sympathy, after all," she said, with finality. "Oh, these husbands!—these husbands!"

It was a relief to Helen when other guests claimed the contessa's attention. Uncle Peabody had mingled with friends in the drawing-room, so she and Emory moved on in the same direction. Here she found many whom she had previously met, and for half an hour held a court as large and as admiring as the contessa's. Emory was quite unprepared to find his companion so much at home in this different atmosphere.

"By Jove, Helen," he whispered, as he finally discovered an opportunity to converse with her again, "one would think you had always lived in Florence. If it were not for the gold lace of the army officers and the white heads of the ancient gallants who flock about you, I should almost imagine we were at the Assemblies again."

"Every one is cordiality itself," replied Helen. "See Uncle Peabody over there! Is he not having a good time? He told me Professor Tesso, of the University of Turin, was to be here, and I presume that is he."

Following the example of the other guests, Helen and Emory strolled out into the main court, in one corner of which is the old well dating back to the time when the Divine Poet slaked his thirst at its stony brim. The sun streamed in through the narrow windows and lighted the terra-cotta flagstones where its rays struck, making the extreme corners of the court seem even dimmer. With rare restraint, the only decoration consisted of long festoons, made of lemons, pomegranates, eucalyptus, oranges, and laurel, fashioned to resemble the majolicas of Della Robbia and hung gracefully along the stone balcony, between which was an occasional rare old rug or costly tapestry. Passing slowly up the spacious stairway, stopped now and again by one or more of Helen's newly acquired friends, they reached the library, where some of the more valuable manuscripts and early printed volumes were exposed to view. A group of book-lovers were eagerly examining an edition of Dante resting upon a graceful thirteenth-century *leggio*, printed by Lorenzo Della Magna, and illustrated with Botticelli's remarkable engravings. From the balcony, leading out from the library, they gained a view of the carefully laid-out garden, brilliant in its color display and redolent with the mingled fragrance of myriads of blossoms.

Here Uncle Peabody rejoined them, bringing with him the scholarly looking professor from Turin.

"Helen, I want you to meet Professor Tesso. He was among the first who saw in my theories and experiments any signs of merit."

The professor held up his hand deprecatingly. "You give me too much credit, Mr. Cartwright. Judicially, we men of science are all hidebound and look upon every innovation as erroneous until proved otherwise. We could not believe that your theories of body requirements of food were sound because they differed so radically from what we had come to regard as standard. But when you proved yourself right by actual experiment we had no choice in the matter."

"Uncle Peabody has been very persistent," said Helen, smiling. "His own conviction in time becomes contagious, does it not?"

"That is just it," assented Professor Tesso. "What he had told us is something which we really should have known all the time, but we failed to recognize its importance. Now he has forced us to accept it, and the credit is properly his."

"I have invited Professor Tesso to take tea with us to-morrow afternoon, Helen, at the villa," said Uncle Peabody.

"By all means," Helen urged, cordially. "We shall be so glad to welcome you there."

The sudden exodus of the guests gave notice that something unusual was occurring below.

"It must be the arrival of the Count of Turin," explained Uncle Peabody. "Let us descend and take a look at Italian royalty."

With the others they entered the magnificent ball-room—a modern addition to the original villa made by Napoleon for his sister Pauline when she became Grand-Duchess of Tuscany. In the centre of the room, surrounded by his suite, stood the count, graciously receiving the guests presented to him by his host. Hither and thither among the crowd ran little flower-maidens bestowing favors upon the ladies and *boutonnières* upon their escorts. A few pieces of music played quietly behind a bank of palms, the low strains blending pleasantly with the hum of conversation.

As Helen and Emory stood with a few Italian friends, a little apart from the others, watching the brilliant throng, Cerini suddenly joined them. Helen had never thought of him outside the library, and it seemed to her as if one of the chained volumes had broken away from its anchorage. The old man saw the surprise in her face and smiled genially.

"I seldom come to gatherings such as this," he explained, even before the question was put to him; "but his Highness commanded me to meet him here." Cerini smiled again and looked into Helen's face with undisguised admiration. "This is where you belong," he assured her, quietly but enthusiastically—"this is your element. Do you not see that I was right that day at the library? You are even more beautiful than when I saw you before. There is a new strength in your face. You are a creation of the master-artist, like a marvellous painting which intoxicates the senses."

Helen had no answer, but the old man continued:

"I have just left your husband and his sister-worker. They are not beautiful—they represent the wisdom which one finds in books. The world needs both, my daughter. Be content."

And without waiting for a reply Cerini disappeared in the crowd of guests as suddenly as he had come.

XIII

Emory was the only one near enough to Helen to observe the interview with Cerini. The old man's words were uttered in too low a tone to reach his ears, but Emory saw Helen close her eyes for a fraction of a second and heard her draw a quick breath. Then she turned to him with a smile so natural that he nearly believed himself deceived, and found himself almost convinced that he must have been mistaken in what he thought he had discovered.

"Whose little old man is that?" Emory queried.

Helen laughed. Emory had a way of putting questions in a form least expected.

"Monsignor Cerini," she answered, "and he belongs to Jack."

"Oh, he is the librarian!" Phil recognized the descriptions he had heard at the villa. "Interesting-looking old chap; I don't wonder Jack likes him."

"He is a wonderful man," assented Helen; "but his knowledge almost frightens one. I feel like an ignorant child every time I meet him."

They strolled slowly through the brilliant throng out into the court, up the stairs, and into the library again. The room was wholly deserted, the other guests preferring to watch the spectacle below. No word was spoken until Helen threw herself into a great chair near the balcony.

"What an awful thing it is to have so little knowledge!" she exclaimed.

Emory looked at her in surprise. At first he could not believe her serious, but the expression on her face was convincing.

"Compared to Cerini?" he asked.

"Compared to any one who has brains—like Jack or Inez."

Emory studied his companion carefully. The impression made upon him a few moments before, then, was no hallucination.

"What did Cerini say which upset you, Helen?"

"Cerini?" Helen repeated. "Why, nothing. As a matter of fact, he was very complimentary—even gallant. Some of you younger men could take lessons from Cerini in the gentle art of flattery."

"I beg your pardon, Helen," Emory apologized; "I had no intention of intruding."

"Dear old Phil," cried Helen, holding out her hand impulsively, "of course you had not, and you could not intrude, anyhow."

Emory held the proffered hand a moment before it was withdrawn. "I can't help feeling concerned when I see something disturb you," he said, quietly—"now, any more than I could before."

Helen saw that she had not succeeded in deceiving him, but was determined that he should discover as little as possible. "I don't believe Florence is just the right atmosphere for me," she began. "I did not notice at first how much more every one here knows about everything than I do, and it makes me feel uncomfortable. That is what I meant. Of course one expects this supreme knowledge in a man like Cerini, but even those Florentines whom one meets casually at receptions such as this are as well informed on literature and art and music as those whom we consider experts at home."

"This lack of knowledge on your part does not seem to interfere any with their admiration for you," insisted Emory. "If Jack took the trouble to see how much attention you received he might have a little less interest in that precious work of his."

"You must not speak like that, Phil," Helen protested. "Jack is doing something which neither you nor I can appreciate, but that is our own fault and not his. I only wish I could understand it. Every one says that his book will make him famous, and then we all shall be proud of him—even prouder than we are now."

Emory rose impatiently. "You are quite right, Helen,—I certainly don't appreciate it, under the circumstances; but I shall put my foot in this even worse than I did yesterday with Miss Thayer, so I suggest that we change the subject. Come, let us see what is going on down-stairs."

Uncle Peabody met them in the court. "I was coming after you," he said by way of explanation. "Tesso has just left, and we also must make our adieux. Would you mind taking Mr. Emory and me to the Florence Club, Helen, on the way home? He might like to see it."

Their appearance in the hall was a signal for the unattached men again to surround Helen with protestations of regret that she had absented herself from the reception-room, and Emory watched the episode with grim satisfaction. Uncle Peabody appeared to take no notice of anything except his responsibility, and gradually guided the party to where their host and hostess were standing, and then out to the automobile. An invigorating run down the hill, past the walls which shut out all but the luxuriant verdure of the high cypresses, alternating with the olive and lemon trees, and through the town, brought them to the Piazza Vittorio Emanuele, where the car paused for a moment to allow the men to alight. Then, after brief farewells, Helen continued her ride alone to Settignano.

Uncle Peabody led the way up the stairs to a small room leading off from the main parlor of the club. Producing some cigars, he motioned to Emory to make himself comfortable at one end of a great leather-covered divan, while he drew up a chair for himself.

"I brought you here for a definite purpose," he announced as soon as the preliminaries were arranged.

"I think I can divine the purpose," replied Emory, striking a match and lighting his cigar.

Uncle Peabody looked at his companion inquiringly.

"It is about Helen, is it not?" continued Emory, without waiting for Mr. Cartwright to question him.

"It is," assented Uncle Peabody; "and your intuition makes my task the easier."

"It is not intuition," corrected Emory; "it is observation."

"Well, call it what you like—the necessity is the same. Perhaps I have no right to discuss this matter with you, but I understand you have known Helen for a good while and pretty well."

"So well that I would have married her if she had ever given me the chance," asserted Emory, calmly.

"What do you make out of the case?"

"The girl is desperately unhappy."

"She is. But how are we going to help her without making things a thousand times worse?"

Emory smoked his cigar meditatively. "I have been thinking of that, too," he replied at length, "but with no more success, apparently, than yourself. It is a rather delicate matter."

"There is no question about that." Uncle Peabody spoke decisively. "And this is all the more reason why we should talk things over together. We are the only ones who can possibly straighten matters out, and I am not at all certain that we can accomplish anything."

"Do you think Armstrong himself realizes the situation?"

"Not in the slightest. He is absolutely absorbed."

"How about Miss Thayer?"

Uncle Peabody looked at Emory interrogatively. "What have you observed about Miss Thayer?" he asked.

"That she is exceedingly sensitive upon the subject of her engagement," replied Emory, with feeling.

"Have you come to any conclusion as to the reason?"

Emory was surprised by the implied meaning in Mr. Cartwright's words. "Why, no," he said, slowly.

"I was here when De Peyster proposed to her," Uncle Peabody continued.

"Then she was the girl!"

"She was the girl," repeated his companion. "When she threw him over, she did not tell him that she was engaged, as he repeated to you, but that she loved some one else."

A wave of understanding passed over Emory.

"And the some one else was—Armstrong! What a stupid fool I've been!" Emory rose and walked to the window. Suddenly he turned. "Does Helen know this?"

"Without a doubt."

"Then why does she not put a stop to it?"

"Now you have at length arrived at my standpoint," replied Uncle Peabody, with satisfaction. "Helen knows it, I am convinced. Miss Thayer, of course, knows her own feelings. Armstrong is head over heels in this alleged masterpiece of his, and I give him credit for appreciating Miss Thayer's sentiments toward him as little as he does Helen's sufferings. Except for this I should not think of interfering, but under the circumstances I feel that between us we may have a chance to straighten things out before the principals know that there is anything which needs straightening."

"That is a fair statement of the basis of the conspiracy," said Emory, returning to his seat; "but have you worked out the details as carefully?"

"No," admitted Uncle Peabody, frankly. "That is a more difficult proposition, and I doubt if we can formulate any definite plan. It occurred to me that if we joined forces we would stand a better chance of hitting upon some expedient when the opportunity offered."

"Helen seems more or less reconciled, in spite of what we know she feels," said Emory, reflectively; "you heard what she said to Armstrong last evening about helping his work to a glorious success?"

"She is trying desperately to be reconciled, and she thinks she has concealed her real feelings," replied Uncle Peabody; "but she is eating her heart out all the time."

"Well, I wish I thought I could help her some way." Emory rose and extended his hand. "I have never looked upon myself as much of a success in matters like this, Mr. Cartwright, but there is nothing I would not do for Helen—even to helping her to get a divorce!"

Uncle Peabody smiled as he took Emory's hand and held it firmly. "I suspect you will have to eliminate yourself if you hope to accomplish anything. If I know Helen at all, she will never take another chance if this first venture turns out unfortunately. But let us hope that all will right itself, and that we may be the direct or indirect means of its so doing."

"Amen to that," assented Emory, warmly. "I have wanted Helen always, but I should be a brute if I did not want her happiness first of all."

"I thought I had made no mistake," replied Uncle Peabody. "I rather pride myself on my skill in reading human nature, and I should have been disappointed in you had you failed me."

Uncle Peabody was late in returning to the villa, and the family had already seated themselves at dinner.

"We are all going for a moonlight ride," announced Armstrong as Mr. Cartwright apologized for his tardy appearance, "and we felt sure you would soon be here. Did you ever see such a perfect evening?"

Uncle Peabody resolved to try an experiment. "May I venture to suggest an amendment?" he asked.

"What improvement can you possibly make on my plan?" Armstrong was incredulous.

"Simply that Miss Thayer and I give you and Helen a chance to enjoy the ride by yourselves, after the style of true honeymooners."

Helen's face flushed with pleasure, but Armstrong resented any change in his original arrangement.

"Nonsense!" he exclaimed. "Helen and I are not so sentimental, I trust, as to wish to keep you and Miss Thayer from enjoying the ride with us on such a night as this."

"I think Mr. Cartwright's amendment an excellent one," said Inez. "It will be much better for you and Helen to go by yourselves."

"Now you have broken up the whole party!" Armstrong turned petulantly on Uncle Peabody. "Miss Thayer has been working all the afternoon in the library, and needs the refreshment of the air even more than Helen."

"If Miss Thayer will permit," replied Uncle Peabody, maintaining his ground stoutly, "I will do my best to make her evening an agreeable one."

Armstrong was not appeased, but could hardly do other than accept the situation. After seeing the car depart from the court-yard, Uncle Peabody and Miss Thayer strolled out to the garden, where he arranged their chairs so that they might gain the choicest view of the moon-illumined city and the winding river, silver in the soft, pale light.

"I have kept you from an interesting experience," Uncle Peabody began, "but I know how much it will mean to Helen to have her husband all to herself. You understand, I am sure."

"I do understand, perfectly," replied Inez, heartily. "I am only ashamed that I did not think of it myself; but it is difficult to oppose Mr. Armstrong in anything he has his heart set on, and I confess that I do not possess your courage."

"I doubt if I should have been so courageous had I realized how disagreeable he would be. Armstrong has changed much in the few weeks I have known him."

Uncle Peabody made his assertion boldly, and then waited for a response. Inez looked up quickly.

"I think it is hard for any one to understand Mr. Armstrong without seeing him at his work. He has changed, as you say, but it is a change which no one—least of all himself—could prevent."

Uncle Peabody expected a defence—that was but natural.

"I don't think I quite follow you," he said, wishing to draw her out. "Would you mind telling me more about the work, and what there is in it to affect him in this way?"

"I wish I could make it clear to you, for unless you understand it you will do him a great injustice." Inez again keyed herself up to her self-appointed task. "Helen asked me the same question last evening, and I realized while talking with her how poorly fitted I myself am to attempt any explanation."

The girl paused. She knew that her companion would analyze what she said much more thoroughly than Helen had done.

"Were you ever under an hypnotic influence?" she asked, suddenly.

"Yes," replied Uncle Peabody, calmly. "But you don't mean to say that this has happened to Jack?"

"Yes and no," Inez continued. "If I believed in reincarnation I should say without hesitation that Mr. Armstrong was living over again, here in Florence, an existence which he had previously experienced centuries ago. As I don't believe in this, I can simply say that there is a something which comes from an intimate contact with these master-spirits of the past which is so compelling that it takes one out of the present and assumes complete control over him. While we are at the library all else is forgotten. I work there beside him hour after hour, yet he seems entirely unconscious of my presence except to the extent to which it assists his own efforts. All personality is absolutely obliterated. I understand it, because to a lesser degree I have felt it myself. When we leave the library he becomes more like himself again; but as he gets deeper into his work, his absorption is greater, and for that reason alone, I believe, he is less mindful of the usual every-day conventions. I wish I could make it clear to you."

Uncle Peabody did not reply at once. What Inez had said gave him a new viewpoint both of Armstrong and of her.

"How long do you think this will continue?" he asked at length.

"Until his work is finished."

"And when will that be?"

"Another month, at least."

Uncle Peabody was again silent, weighing the situation from the present standpoint. "What is to become of Helen in the mean time?" he asked, abruptly.

Miss Thayer had anticipated this question. "Helen understands the situation perfectly," she said, confidently. "She has talked it over with him and with me. It is a sacrifice on her part to be separated from her husband, especially at this time, but it is one which she is willing to accept for her husband's sake."

"Would you be willing to accept it were the conditions reversed?"

Inez flushed, but stood her ground bravely. "Perhaps not," she admitted; "but Helen is a stronger woman than I."

"She does not think so."

"Helen is a much stronger woman than she herself realizes."

Uncle Peabody was thoughtful. "Let me ask you one more question. Do you think that this spell, or influence, or whatever you may call it, in any way affects Armstrong's affection for his wife?"

"I am sure that it does not," replied Inez, with decision. "His devotion to Helen must be even stronger, because he can but appreciate the splendid generosity she is showing."

"He certainly adopts curious methods of demonstrating it."

"But consider the influences he is under!" Inez urged.

Uncle Peabody admired the girl's handling of the catechising he had given her. He looked steadily into her face before replying.

"You are a noble champion, Miss Thayer," he said, at length.

"That is because I have faith in the cause," responded Inez, smiling. "I have been brought up to believe that every married woman must at some time in her life make a supreme sacrifice for her husband. I only hope that when my turn comes the sacrifice may be made for so good a cause."

"This is another version of the chastening of the spirit," added Uncle Peabody; "but I am thinking of a certain spirit which received so much chastening that it never revived. I sincerely trust that history may not repeat itself."

XIV

Uncle Peabody was entirely right when he stated that Armstrong had become a changed man since he first came to Florence; Miss Thayer was right when she attributed this change to the associations into which he had thrown himself—yet both were wrong in thinking him unconscious of his own altered condition. As he told Helen, he had ever felt some irresistible influence drawing him back to Florence, even while engrossed in the duties of his profession. Just what the craving was he could not have explained even to himself. What he should find in Florence had taken no definite form in his mind, yet the longing possessed him in spite of all he could do to reason with himself against it.

After his arrival in Florence, even, it was not until Cerini suggested the Michelangelo letters that he formulated any plan to gratify his long-anticipated expectations. His arguments with himself had prepared him for a disappointment. It had been a boyish fancy, he said, inwardly; he had felt the influences of his environment simply because he had been young and impressionable, and it was quite impossible that he should now, man-grown, prove susceptible to anything so inexplicable as what he had felt in his earlier days.

Then came the experience with Cerini and Miss Thayer. She was a woman, truly, and subject to a woman's physical frailties, yet she was intellectually strong, and could not so have yielded to anything but a controlling power. Here, then, was a second personality affected in a like manner as himself by the same influences. He did not try to explain it; he accepted it as an evidence that this influence, whatever it was, existed and made itself manifest. From that moment he merged his own individuality into those to whom Cerini with gentle suasion introduced him. The librarian incited him by his own enthusiasm, and then directed him along the paths which he himself so loved to tread.

But Cerini did not foresee the extremes to which his pupil's devotion would carry him. Day by day Armstrong felt himself becoming more and more separated from all about him, and more and more amalgamated with those forces which had preceded him. The society of any save those who acted and thought as he did failed to appeal to him. His affection for Helen suffered no change, except that she became less necessary to him. As the work progressed the intervals away from the library seemed longer, and he found it more difficult to enter into the life about him. Then came an irritability, entirely foreign to his nature, which he could not curb.

Yet through it all he was entirely conscious of what was happening. He compared himself more than once to a man in a trance, painfully alive to all the preparations going on about him for his own entombment, yet unable to cry out and put a stop to it all. He wished that Helen would object to his absences and force him to become a part of her life again. He wished that Miss Thayer would tire of the work and leave him alone in it. In contemplating either event he suffered at the mere thought of what such an interruption would mean to him, he knew that he would interpose strenuous objections—yet in a way he longed for the break to come.

Armstrong had been in one of these inexplicably irritable moods when Uncle Peabody crossed him in his plan for the moonlight ride to San Miniato. As a matter of fact, it was only because Miss Thayer had complained of a headache as they left the library that the idea of a ride had occurred to him at all; and to have Mr. Cartwright calmly propose that she drop out of the planned excursion struck him as a distinct intrusion upon his own prerogatives. The automobile fever was out of his blood now; the motor-car had become to him merely a convenience, and no longer an exhilaration. It was quite inevitable that Miss Thayer should acquiesce in Uncle Peabody's suggestion—in fact, she could do nothing else; yet at the library she accepted even his slightest suggestion without question, and Armstrong preferred this latter responsive attitude. All in all, he would have been glad to find some excuse for giving up the ride altogether; but none offered itself, so, with every movement an obvious protest, he had helped Helen into the tonneau and stepped in after her.

Helen was hardly in a happier frame of mind, yet she found herself so eager for this time alone with her husband that she raised none of the obstacles which she would have done a month earlier. It was a perfect June evening, with the air cooled enough by the light wind to make the breeze raised by the speed of the car agreeable to the face. The moon was just high enough to cause deep shadows to fall across the roadway and merge into fantastic shapes as the machine approached and passed over them. The peasants were out-of-doors, and expressed their contentment by snatches of song, rendered in the rich, melodious voices which are the natural heritage of this light-hearted people. The toil of the day was over, and they were entering into a well-earned *riposo* before the duties of the next sunrise claimed their strength.

"How peaceful this is!" Helen exclaimed, turning to her husband. The breeze had blown back the lace scarf from her head, and the moon fell full upon her luxuriant hair, lighting her upturned face. "All nature is at rest and peace, and the people reflect the contentment of the land."

"Your uncle is becoming very dictatorial," replied Armstrong, quite at variance with her mood.

"Why, Jack!"

Helen was mildly reproachful, yet she instinctively felt the necessity of being cautious. Perhaps she could make him forget his resentment.

"Uncle Peabody only meant to give us an opportunity to be by ourselves. We have had so few."

"He should have understood that I had some good reason for planning matters just as I did or I should not have done it."

"Do you regret being alone with me?"

Helen struggled to keep the tears out of her voice.

"Don't be absurd, Helen," replied Armstrong, impatiently. "That is not the point at all. Miss Thayer is tired and needed this relaxation. Mr. Cartwright had no right to interfere."

There was a long silence, during which Armstrong relapsed into a profound taciturnity, while Helen found it hard to know what tack to take. She glanced occasionally at her husband, but could gain no inspiration from his grim, set features.

"Tell me, Jack," she said, at length, "is it not possible for you to pursue your work at the library without having it make you so indifferent to everything else?"

He shifted his position uneasily. "I am not indifferent to everything else. The fact that I proposed this ride is an evidence of that."

"Has something happened to make my companionship distasteful to you?"

Armstrong became more and more irritated. "I don't see why you are so possessed to make me uncomfortable, Helen. But I understand what you are driving at."

"What am I driving at?" she asked, quietly.

"You are taking this method to force me to put an end to my work."

Helen winced. "Is that fair, Jack? What have I said to you every time the subject has been mentioned?"

"You have told me to go ahead, and then you have shown quite plainly by every action that you did not mean it."

"Jack Armstrong!" She was indignant at his gross injustice.

"What have I said each time the subject has come up?" continued Armstrong. "You have had every opportunity to have your own way in this as in all other matters. I repeat it now—is it your wish that I stop my work? Say but the word and I will never enter that library again."

Helen was hurt through and through. To what avail was her sacrifice if it be so little understood, so little appreciated?

"I don't wish to be misunderstood in this," added Armstrong, as if in answer to her thoughts. "I quite realize that I have asked much of you who can understand so little of what my book means to me. I have been entirely frank, and have accepted from you the time which rightfully belongs to you in the spirit, as I supposed, in which you gave it to me. If you did not mean what you said, you have but to tell me so and it shall be exactly as you wish."

"I have meant every word I have said, Jack," replied Helen, in a low, strained voice. "I have been glad to contribute in the only way I could to anything which means so much to you. I simply ask you now whether it is necessary for this absorption to include all of yourself even when you are away from it. I did not suppose that this was essential."

"You are exaggerating the situation out of all proportion."

"I wish I were, Jack."

Helen's voice had a tired note in it which Armstrong could not fail to perceive. He was amazed by his own apathy. Why did it mean so little to him? Why did he sit there beside her as if he had not noticed it when in reality he felt the pain as keenly as she did? He turned and looked at her for the first time since they had started. Helen gave no sign that she was conscious of his scrutiny, lying back with her cheek resting upon her hand, her eyes closed, her lips quivering now and then in spite of her supreme effort to control herself. Always, before, Armstrong would have folded her in his arms and brushed away the heart-pains, real or imaginary as they might have been. Now he sat watching her suffer without making any effort to relieve her.

He despised himself for his attitude. What wretched thing had come between him and this girl whom he had idolized, and prevented him from extending even the common sympathy which belonged to any one who needed it? What malevolent power forced him to be the cause of this sorrow and yet forbade him the privilege of assuaging it? This was not the lesson learned from the humanists. Why should not he be able to give out to those around him the reflection of that true happiness which their work first taught the world?

Helen opened her eyes suddenly and looked full into his. Startled at the expression on his face, she sat upright, keenly anxious and forgetful of her own troubles.

"Jack dear," she cried, "you are not well! You are unhappy, too! Tell me what it all means, and let us understand it together!"

Her voice brought back the old condition. His eyes lowered and he withdrew his hand from Helen's impulsive grasp. With a heart heavy for the explanation which lay close at hand, his voice refused to obey.

"I am perfectly well, Helen," he replied. "Why should you think me otherwise?"

The reaction was great, yet Helen succeeded in retaining her control. While conscious, during the weeks past, of the change in her husband's bearing toward her, she was unprepared for his present attitude. Yet the look in his face when she had surprised him by opening her eyes was the old expression by which in the past she had known that something had touched him deeply—but it was intensified beyond anything she had ever seen. It had always been her privilege to comfort him under these conditions, and instinctively her heart sprang forward to meet his. Then she saw the expression change and she grew cold with apprehension.

"Ask Alfonse to turn back, please," she begged. "The air is getting chilly and I think I would rather be home."

In response to her desire the chauffeur turned the car, and the ride back to the villa was accomplished in silence. Helen's thoughts ran rampant, but further conversation was impossible. Her pain was now tempered by her anxiety. Jack was not well, in spite of his disclaimers. His close application to his work in the poorly ventilated library had undoubtedly affected him, and this was the explanation of his otherwise inexplicable attitude toward her. It was with positive relief that she discovered any explanation, and as she thought things over this relief lightened the burden she had been carrying all these weeks more than anything which had happened since the cloud began to gather. In some way she must plan to relieve the pressure and bring her husband back to her and to himself again.

Inez and Uncle Peabody met them at the doorway.

"The ride has done you good," said the latter, giving his hand to Helen and noting the light in the girl's eyes as they walked toward the hall.

"I have left my scarf in the car," said Helen, turning back so quickly that Mr. Cartwright had no opportunity to offer his services.

Armstrong and Inez were standing together on the step, and as Helen approached she could not help overhearing her husband's reply to Miss Thayer's inquiring looks.

"You are the only one who understands me," Armstrong was saying—"you are the only one!"

XV

The next afternoon was a warm one, and Annetta searched for some little time before she discovered Uncle Peabody half concealed within a natural arbor formed by the falling branches of an ancient tree. Here, in the cooling shade, he was reading over a budget of letters just received from America. Emory followed close behind the maid, and laughed heartily at Mr. Cartwright's jump of startled surprise when Annetta broke into his absorption with the announcement of "Signor Emori."

"Hello, Emory!" he cried, looking up genially from the letter in his hand. "I was thousands of miles away, and two words from the lips of the gentle serving-maid brought me back to Florence. Marconigrams are nothing compared with the marvellous exhibition you have just witnessed."

"It is a shame to interrupt you," Emory apologized. "I came up early hoping to have a little chat with you before Professor Tesso and tea-time arrived."

"Don't apologize, I beg of you," protested Uncle Peabody, gathering up his letters and making room for Emory to sit beside him. "I was just on the point of returning, anyway, and you have saved me the necessity of packing up. In fact, you are very welcome."

"I judge your news is of an agreeable nature?"

Emory saw that Uncle Peabody was eager to be questioned.

"Things are advancing famously," replied Mr. Cartwright, enthusiastically. "These letters are from America, and report the fullest success attending the experiments there with which I am so vitally concerned. But what are you carrying so carefully at arm's-length?"

Uncle Peabody peered into the little wicker cage Emory was holding.

"Ah, a *grillo!*" he said. "Then to-day must be Ascension Day and the *Festa dei Grilli.* I had forgotten the date."

"So that explains why they are selling these little cages with crickets inside of them all over the city. The old woman I bought this of told me it was a token of good luck, so I brought it to Helen."

"She will be interested in it," replied Uncle Peabody. "The little *grillo* brought luck once upon a time, if the legend be true, and it may do so again."

"Is this *Festa dei Grilli*, as you call it, an annual festival?"

"Yes; and as firmly established as the Feast of the Dove on Easter eve. The story goes that an attempt was once made upon the life of Lorenzo de' Medici in his own garden by the familiar means of a goblet of poisoned wine. As the would-be assassin handed the goblet to Lorenzo a cricket alighted on the surface of the wine and immediately expired. Thus, as in modern melodrama, the villain was foiled. Since then, a Florentine would harm a human being as soon as he would a *grillo*. Each year these cages are taken into the homes, and as long as the little crickets can be kept alive good luck attends the household."

"Speaking of conspiracies," remarked Emory, who lost no time in finding an opening, "how advances our present one? I have been thinking of nothing else since our talk about Helen."

Uncle Peabody rose and glanced around the garden from his point of vantage. "Careful!" he said, drawing back. "Helen is coming, and I can only say that we must move very cautiously—even more so than I supposed. I will tell you more later."

"Here we are, Helen," he answered, in response to his niece's call, and both men advanced to meet her.

"Oh, you have found my 'snuggery'!" cried Helen, seeing them emerge from the arbor. "I intended to keep that entirely for myself, but I will be generous and share it with you."

"Mr. Emory has brought you a talisman," said Uncle Peabody, pointing to the wicker cage. "Perhaps you will permit this to appease your displeasure."

Helen examined with interest the cage Emory placed in her hand.

"Why, it is a cricket!" she exclaimed, as she discovered the occupant beneath the green leaves.

The story of the origin of the *festa* was retold and the *grillo* placed under her special protection.

"It is an emblem of good luck, Helen," added Emory—"like the swastika, only a great deal less commonplace."

"Thank you, Phil," replied Helen. Then she looked up at him suddenly. "Why did you bring it to me?" she asked, suspiciously. "Do you think I need it?"

"I think we all need all the good luck we can get," replied Emory, guardedly.

"Tesso is late," remarked Uncle Peabody, opportunely, looking at his watch. "He will be greatly interested in the reports of these American experiments."

Another half-hour passed by before the professor from Turin arrived. Helen strolled about the garden with Emory, pointing out the unusual flowers and shrubs, while Uncle Peabody collected his letters and arranged them in proper sequence. Annetta brought out the tea-table and laid everything in readiness, returning to the house just in time to usher the dignified figure into the hall.

"I hope I have not disarranged your plans," apologized the professor, pleased with the cordiality of his reception. "I had a little experience which delayed me."

"My uncle is so anxious to tell you of some good tidings, professor, that he has almost become impatient," replied Helen, smiling. "You observe that I say 'almost,' do you not?"

"It would never do for him to become impatient, would it?" replied Tesso, turning to his friend—"you the disciple of Cornaro and the example to us all! But I myself am weaker—I admit my impatience."

Uncle Peabody and Emory drew up the chairs, and Tesso seated himself next to Mr. Cartwright with obvious expectancy.

"You recall the results of my own experiments in attempting to show increased muscular and mental endurance as a result of eating in right manner what the appetite selects instead of eating in wrong manner what the doctors advise?" began Uncle Peabody.

"And incidentally demonstrating that the existing standard of minimum nutrition for man was three times too large?" queried Tesso.

"Yes. You all were very generous, but I know you attributed the results in a measure to my own personal peculiarities."

"You are right to a certain extent," admitted Tesso, "yet, so far as the experiment went, it proved that your theory was correct."

"Now I have further evidence to add which is overwhelming," continued Uncle Peabody, triumphantly. "For the last six months experiments have been in progress in America, taking as subjects groups of men in different walks of life—college professors, athletes, and soldiers. To-day I have received a report of the results. In every instance, on an intake of less than the recognized minimum standard, the subjects improved in physical condition and increased their strength efficiency from twenty-five to one hundred per cent. Think of that, Tesso—from twenty-five to one hundred per cent.!"

"I congratulate you heartily, my dear friend," replied the professor, warmly. "The effects of this will be most far-reaching. I foresaw that you might demonstrate a new minimum, but I had not expected that an increased efficiency would accompany it."

"I wish you would introduce this discovery of yours to the Harvard football team," remarked Emory, feelingly. "Perhaps it would result in a few more victories on the right side."

"It certainly would help matters," assented Uncle Peabody, with confidence. "All this so-called training is necessary only because of the abuse which the average man's stomach suffers from its owner. My theory is that any man, college athlete or otherwise, can keep in perfect condition all the time, simply by following a few easy rules and by knowing how to take care of himself. It is just as important to be in training for his every-day life as for an athletic contest."

"How did the experiments result with the athletes?" Emory inquired.

"These records are the most interesting of all," replied Uncle Peabody, referring to his letter. "This group included track athletes, football players, the intercollegiate all-around champion, and several others—all at full training. They had already increased their strength and endurance efficiency at least twenty-five per cent during the training period before taking up the new system. In four months, eating whatever they craved, but using only the amount demanded by their appetites and giving it careful treatment in the mouth, these athletes reduced the amount of their food from one-third to one-half, and increased their strength and endurance records from twenty-five to one hundred per cent."

"You ought to feel pretty well satisfied with that," said Emory.

"I am satisfied," replied Uncle Peabody, "as far as it goes, but I hope for far more important results than these."

"Indeed?" queried Professor Tesso. "I shared the thought expressed by Mr. Emory that your ambition ought now to be satisfied."

Uncle Peabody was silent for a moment. "I wonder if I dare tell you what my whole scheme really is," he said, at length.

"You can't startle me any more than you did with your original proposition three years ago," encouraged the professor, smiling. "At that time I could but consider you a physiological heretic."

"Tesso," said Uncle Peabody, deliberately, "the results of these experiments confirm me absolutely that I am on the right track. These revelations on the subject of nutrition are but the spokes of the great movement I have at heart—or perhaps, more properly speaking, they are the hub into which the spokes are being fitted. What I really hope and expect to do is to put education on a physiological basis, and to demonstrate that it is possible to cultivate progressive efficiency—that a man of sixty ought to be more powerful, physically and intellectually, than a man of forty. I can see no reason, logically, for one to retrograde as rapidly as men do now, but this depends upon his knowing how to run the human engine intelligently and economically and thus keeping it always in repair."

"You astonish me, truly," said Tesso, thoughtfully, "yet I can advance no argument except faulty human experience to refute your theory. In fact, you yourself are a living demonstration of its truth."

"Then there would be no old age?" queried Helen.

"There would be age just the same," replied Uncle Peabody, "but it would be ripe and natural age, with only such infirmities as come from accident; and less of these, since disease would find fewer opportunities to fasten itself upon its victims. If all the world knew what some know the death-rate could be cut in two, the average of human efficiency doubled, and the cost of necessary sustenance halved."

"Mr. Cartwright," said Professor Tesso, impressively, "if you succeed in carrying through this great reform of yours, even in part, you will be the greatest benefactor of mankind the world has known."

"It is too large a contract to be carried through by any single one, but my confidence in the final outcome is based on the intelligent interest which others are taking in my work. I am glad you do not think the idea chimerical. It encourages me to keep at it with tireless application."

"Dare I interrupt with so prosaic a suggestion as a cup of tea?" asked Helen, as there came a lull in the conversation.

"Mr. Cartwright has given me so much to think about that a little relaxation will be grateful," replied the professor. "Perhaps you would be interested if I gave you an account of the experience which delayed me this afternoon?"

"By all means," said Helen, as she prepared the tea. "I am sure it was an interesting one."

"You may not know that I have a great love for the romantic," confessed Professor Tesso. "It seems a far cry from my every-day life, but sometime I mean to prepare an essay upon the subject of the relation between science and romance. In fact, I believe them to be very closely allied."

"What a clever idea!" cried Helen. "If you ever prove that to be true it will explain a lot of things."

"Perhaps I can do it sometime," continued the scientist, complacently, "and in the mean time I gratify my whim by taking observations whenever the opportunity offers. To-day I had a most charming illustration, and I became so much interested that it made me late in coming to you."

"You certainly have an admirable excuse," assented his hostess.

"I suspect that the objects of my observation are fellow-patriots of yours, but I am not certain. The man was a strong, fine-looking fellow with ability and determination written clearly in his face. He was evidently a deep student—perhaps a professor in some one of your American colleges. His companion, the heroine of my story, was a small woman, but so intense! I think it was her intensity which first attracted my attention."

"I am sure they could not have been Americans, professor," interrupted Helen. "No American woman would display her emotion like that, I am sure.—Do you take cream, and how many lumps of sugar, please?"

"You may be right, of course," continued Tesso, giving her the necessary information. "In fact, my whole story is based upon supposition. However, as they sat there together, first he would say something to her, and they would look into each other's faces, and then she would say something to him, and the operation would be repeated. They spoke little, but the silent communion of their hearts as they looked at each other spoke more eloquently than words. It was beautiful to behold. 'There,' I said to myself, 'is a perfect union of well-mated souls. What a pity that they must ever go out into the world and run the risk of having something commonplace come between them and their devotion!'"

"Splendid!" cried Helen. "How I wish I might have been with you!"

"The whole episode could not have failed to interest you as it did me." The professor was ingenuously sincere in his narrative. "In these days one so seldom sees husbands and wives properly matched up. Of course, it is quite possible that when this pair I speak of are actually married they will quarrel like cats and dogs. But for the present their devotion was so natural, so untainted by the world's actualities, that I confess myself guilty of having deliberately watched them far beyond the bounds of common decency."

"You should certainly pursue your investigations further," said Uncle Peabody. "After having discovered psychological subjects in a man and a woman perfectly adapted to each other, it would be a pity not to continue your researches that their perfections might be recorded for the benefit of others less fortunate."

"Have you no idea who they were?" asked Emory.

"Not the slightest. I might have found out, as my friend, whom I went to see, must know them; but I was aghast when I discovered the hour, and ran away without so much as leaving my name."

"Where did all this happen?" asked Helen.

"At the Laurenziana," replied Tesso. "I went to call on my old friend Cerini." The professor laughed guiltily. "I hope he never learns the reason why I failed to keep my appointment!"

Helen placed her cup abruptly upon the table and stared stonily at Tesso. Uncle Peabody and Emory glanced quickly at each other in absolute helplessness. The professor, however, failed to notice the effect of his words upon his auditors; he was too much amused by the mental picture of Cerini waiting for him while he, only a few feet away from the librarian's study, was gratifying his love for the romantic.

"May I join you?" cried a voice behind Helen, as Inez Thayer approached unnoticed in the dim light. "Mr. Armstrong went down to the station to send a cable, so I came back alone."

"Inez—Miss Thayer, let me present Professor Tesso," said Helen, mechanically.

The professor held out his hand and stepped toward her. As the features of her face became clear a great joy overwhelmed him.

"My heroine!" he cried, turning to the others. "This is the heroine of my story! Now, my dear Mr. Cartwright, I can record these perfections for the benefit of others less fortunate!"

XVI

What happened after Inez arrived, how she herself had acted, and how Professor Tesso's departure had been accomplished remained a blank to Helen. All that was clear to her was the pain—the sharp, aching pain—which came to her with a realization of the true significance of the story Tesso told. The crisis was coming fast, Helen was conscious of that; she even wondered if it was not at hand already.

Throughout the long, sleepless night Helen reviewed the events of the brief months of her married life. She even began earlier than that, and recalled those days in Boston when Jack Armstrong had appeared before her first as an acquaintance, then as a friend—sympathetic, helpful, congenial—and finally as a suitor for her hand. As she looked back now the period of friendship was recalled with the greatest happiness. Perhaps this was because he had then been more thoughtful of her and less masterful, perhaps it was because the friendship entailed less responsibility—she could not tell. Even during their engagement she had laughed at those moods which she had not understood, and he had accepted her attitude good-naturedly and become himself again. Now she wondered how she had dared to laugh at him!

Then her mind dwelt upon the ocean voyage—those days of cloudless happiness, of unalloyed joy. The visit in Paris, where the sights, although not new, seemed so different because of the companionship of her husband. The trip to Florence, the first glimpse of the Villa Godilombra—which was to be their earliest home together—all came back to her with vivid distinctness. And the day at Fiesole—that day when her husband had become a boy again, and had shown her a side of his nature so unreserved, so natural that she had felt a new world opening before her, a new happiness, the like of which she had never known.

"Oh, Jack!" she cried, aloud, "why could not that day at Fiesole have lasted forever!"

Still the panorama of reminiscence continued. That evening when De Peyster, all unconsciously, repeated to her those words of Inez' which first altered the aspect of her entire world was clearly recalled. Perhaps she might have prevented the present crisis had she recognized the danger then and acted upon the information she had unintentionally received. Perhaps if she had in some way interfered with the work at the library, and thus prevented the constant companionship of her husband and Inez, the trouble might have been averted. But she would have despised herself had she done that. If she could hold her husband's love only by preventing him from meeting other women her happiness had indeed never been secure.

And she had tried to enter into his life, to understand this phase of his nature which, after all her efforts, had baffled her intentions. She had gone to the library with him, expecting to apply herself to her self-appointed task until she succeeded in satisfying even so exacting a master as she knew her husband to be. He would have been patient with her; he would have appreciated the love which prompted her efforts, and all would have been well. But Cerini had interfered. She could hear his voice now; she could see the expression on his face as he spoke the words, "By not interfering with this character-building, you, his wife, will later reap rich returns." Helen laughed bitterly to herself. She was reaping the rich returns now—rich in sorrow and pain and suffering.

Perhaps she could have forced the crisis to come when Inez' confession to De Peyster had been disclosed by Emory. Jack's conduct at that time had almost brought Helen's resentment to the breaking-point; but what Inez had told her afterward had made her feel more in sympathy with him, even though she understood him no better than before. "Your husband is a god among them all," Inez had said; "you will be so proud of him—so proud that he belongs to you." She was proud of him, but her pride could in no way make up to her for the loss of his affection. In her mind's eye she could see him, with his masterpiece completed, receiving the world's plaudits, but entirely unmindful of her, his wife, who had stood aside and made it possible for him to accomplish it all. Oh, it was too cruel, too unfair! Helen buried her head in the pillows and moaned piteously.

She lived over again that one moment in the automobile, that one look in her husband's face which had given her relief. It had, indeed, been a brief respite! At that moment she felt that Jack's love for her still existed, strong and deathless, in the face of temporary abstraction. With this certainty she could endure in patience whatever sacrifices were necessary to win him back to herself. But Jack's words to Inez on the steps, "You are the only one who understands me"—there could be no mistake there. It was to Inez and not to her that he turned for understanding and for comfort.

All through the day she had tried to deceive herself into believing that even this was the result of some mental illness from which Jack was suffering, but Tesso had added just the necessary detail to destroy even the semblance of comfort to which she had so tenaciously clung. "A perfect union of well-mated souls," the professor had called them. "What a pity to have something commonplace come between them and their devotion!" And she was that "commonplace something"!

At all events, the main point had been definitely settled. For weeks she had known that Inez loved Jack; now she felt sure that this affection must be reciprocated. She should have known it sooner, she told herself. "I have been such a coward," she said, inwardly—"I could not bear to know for a certainty what I feared to be true." Now the worst that could happen had happened. Jack would in all probability be the last one to suggest any break. He would keep on as at present with his book—perhaps he might extend the work somewhat, in order to be with Inez a little longer; but when this was completed he would come back to her again, his obsession would disappear, and outwardly there would be no change. They would return to Boston and be received by their friends with glad acclaim, and with congratulations upon the happy months of the honey-moon passed under such congenial conditions! Jack would be an exemplary husband, she knew that. With the book completed and away from the overpowering influences which had controlled him in Florence he would again be to her, perhaps, all he had ever been. But what an irony it would be!

Not for a moment did she accuse him of having married her without believing that he loved her. Armstrong's sincerity was a characteristic which could never be denied. He had not known Inez then. Any one could see that he and Inez were meant for each other; Cerini saw it and said so; Tesso saw it and said so; she herself felt it without a question. Her marriage to Jack had been a mistake, an awful mistake. If only he and Inez had met earlier! Her own life was ruined, but was there any reason why the tragedy should include the others? If it would help matters Helen might be selfish enough to let them share the pain, but as there was nothing to be gained it would be worse than selfish. Jack had no idea that she was aware of the true conditions. He would oppose her if she attempted to take it all into her own life, yet this was the only course to pursue which could minimize the suffering.

Helen shut her eyes, but sleep was still far distant. The first agony had not run its course, and it would have been a misdirected mercy to stem its flow. There was no resentment in Helen's heart, and at this she herself wondered. Inez was not to blame for loving Jack—it was the most natural thing in the world. She had tried her best to keep the knowledge of her affection to herself, and but for the double accident she might have succeeded. Jack was not to blame. He himself had not known the strength of the power which drew him back to Florence, nor could he have foreseen how wholly it would possess him when once he yielded himself to it. He had not sought Inez; Helen herself had brought them together. He had found her useful to him in his work; he had found her agreeable as a friend; all beyond that had been a natural growth which could not and perhaps should not have been checked. The more the pity of it!

At first Helen felt that if Jack could return to his old self inwardly it would be worth the struggle. Then she realized that this could never be. The intellectual strength of her husband had won Helen's profoundest admiration, even though it was beyond her understanding. She longed to be able to enter into it and respond to it as Inez did, yet she felt her limitations. But her love had increased in its intensity by passing through the fire. The man she knew now was infinitely stronger and grander than ever before, and in the light of this new development of character she questioned whether her affection would not suffer a shock if Jack were to become again the man she had known in Boston. This new self was his real self, and the self which he must be in order to express his own individuality. It was even as Cerini had said—character-building had been in process, bringing to the surface qualities which had lain dormant perhaps for centuries; but—and here was where Cerini's wisdom had been at fault— this development had not been for her but for another.

The faint rays of dawn crept in through the lattice windows of Helen's room before she sank into a restless sleep. A few hours later Armstrong softly entered the room before leaving for the library and stood for several moments looking at his wife's face, in which the lines of her struggle still left their mark. When he returned to the hall he met Uncle Peabody.

"May I have a word with you?" Armstrong asked, leading the way to the library.

Uncle Peabody acquiesced.

"Helen is still asleep," said Armstrong by way of preliminaries. "The girl is overdoing somehow, and she acts very tired. As I looked at her just now she seemed ten years older than when we left Boston. Don't you think she is taking on too many of these social functions?"

Uncle Peabody glanced at Armstrong to make sure that he was quite sincere. "I am glad that you have noticed it at last," he replied, quietly. "I have wondered that you did not perceive the change."

"I must speak to her about it."

"But you have not hit on the cause of the change yet," continued Uncle Peabody, suggestively.

"What else can it be?"

"I wish I knew you well enough to talk frankly with you, Jack."

Uncle Peabody was bidding for an opening.

"I suppose that means that I have done something which has not met with your approval."

"That answers my question, Jack. I don't know you well enough, so I will refrain."

"Has it to do with Helen?" insisted Armstrong.

"It has," replied Uncle Peabody. "But what I have to say is not intended as a reproach. I simply feel that if you have not already discovered that Helen is a very unhappy girl it is time some one called your attention to it."

Armstrong was thoughtful. "Do you mean that Helen is really unhappy, or simply upset over some specific thing?"

"I mean that she is suffering, day after day, without relief."

"You must be wrong," replied Armstrong, decisively. "She was a little hurt over something I said to her night before last, and I mean to straighten that out; but if there was anything beyond that, I should surely have known of it."

"You are the last one she would speak to about it," Uncle Peabody said, gravely.

"Why are you so mysterious? Perhaps you are referring to my work at the library. Has Helen been talking to you about that?" Armstrong demanded, suspiciously.

"Helen has said nothing to me, and does not even know that I have noticed anything," said Uncle Peabody, emphatically.

"Which shows you how little there is to your fears," retorted Armstrong, relieved.

"I have no wish to prove anything, Jack," continued Uncle Peabody. "The fact remains, whatever the cause, that Helen is fast getting herself into a condition where she will be an easy victim for this accursed Italian malarial fever. I sound the warning note; I can do no more."

Armstrong was unconvinced. "I never looked upon you as an alarmist before," he replied, glancing at his watch. "I am late for my work this morning, but when I return I will question Helen carefully and arrive at the root of the difficulty."

"I hope you succeed," replied Uncle Peabody, feelingly.

Helen came down-stairs in the afternoon and found the villa deserted. Instinctively she sought the garden, walking out upon the terrace, where she leaned against one of the ancient pillars, her gaze extending to the familiar view of the river and the city beyond. She thought of the dramas which had been enacted within the walls of the weather-stained palaces whose roofs identified their location. These had been more spectacular, and had won their place in history, but she questioned whether they could have been more tragical than the one she was now passing through. Surely it was as easy, she told herself, to meet intrigue and opposition, as to be confronted with the necessity of decreeing one's own sentence and then carrying it into execution.

"Oh, Jack!—my husband!" her heart again cried out in its pain. "Why did you come into my life, since I never belonged in yours, only to give me a taste of what might have been!"

Her reveries were interrupted by Annetta's announcement that the Contessa Morelli was at the door, in her motor-car. Glad of any diversion, Helen hastened to welcome her, and returned with her to the garden.

"I am so glad to find you in," the contessa remarked, with evident sincerity, as they seated themselves in the shade. "In the first place, I really wanted to see you, and, in the second, my dear Morelli is in his most aggravating mood to-day, and we should have come to blows if I had not run away."

"How unfortunate that your husband suffers so!" Helen replied, sympathetically.

"It certainly is unfortunate for me."

"And for him, too, I imagine," insisted Helen, smiling.

The contessa was unwilling to yield the point. "I claim all the sympathy," she said, with finality. "When a man has had sixty years of fun in getting the gout, he has no right to complain."

"Sixty years—" began Helen, in surprise.

"Yes, my dear," replied the contessa, complacently. "I belong to the second crop. He was a widower with a title and position, and I had money; but I must admit that we were both moderately disappointed. However, marriage is always a disappointment, and I consider myself fortunate that things are no worse."

Helen felt the color come to her face as the contessa's words recalled her own sorrow, which for the moment she had forgotten. The freedom with which her guest spoke of her personal affairs repelled her, yet there was a subtle attraction which Helen could not help feeling.

"You are very pessimistic on the subject of marriage," she ventured.

"Not at all," the contessa insisted, calmly. "Husbands are selfish brutes, all of them; but they are absolutely necessary to give one respectability. Perhaps your husband is an exception, but I doubt it. Where is he now?"

"He is at the library," Helen faltered, resenting the contessa's question, but forced to an answer by the suddenness with which it was put.

"At the library?" repeated the contessa, interrogatively. "That is where he was on the afternoon of the Londi reception. Is he there all the time?"

"A good deal of the time," admitted Helen. "He is engaged upon an important literary work."

"In which he takes a great interest and you none at all. There you have it—selfishness, the chief attribute of man!"

"It does look like it," Helen answered, concluding that she had better move in the line of the least resistance. "But in this particular case I am very much interested in my husband's work, even though I am unable to enter into it."

"That is not interest," corrected the contessa—"it is sacrifice; and that is woman's chief attribute."

"I see you are determined to include my husband in your general category."

"I must, because he is a man. But my reason for doing this is to convince you that it is the thing to be expected. Unless you learn that lesson early in your married life, my dear, you will be miserably unhappy. I am certain that the old Persian proverb, 'Blessed is he who expecteth nothing, for he shall not be disappointed,' was written by a woman—and a married woman at that."

Helen's duties at the tea-table aided her to preserve her composure, but the contessa's matter-of-fact expressions were not reassuring in the present crisis she was passing through. She felt herself in no position to combat her theories, yet not to do so seemed a tacit admission of all which she strove to conceal.

"I could not live with a man such as you describe," she said, quietly.

"Oh yes, you could!" The contessa laughed at Helen's innocence and inexperience. "That is the way we all feel when we are first married; but we soon get over it—unless there is another woman in the case; then it is different."

"What do we do in that case?" asked Helen, looking up at her guest with a smile. "You may as well prepare me for any emergency."

"In that case," the contessa replied, seriously, resting her elbow upon the little table and returning Helen's glance—"in that case we try to arouse our husband's jealousy; but we must do it discreetly, as they are not so long-suffering as we."

"Why not leave one's husband?"

"You dear, simple little bride!" cried the contessa, indulgently—"and let him have a clear field? What an original idea! But how our conversation has run on!" The contessa rose and held out her hand graciously. "I really must be going now; but I wish you and Mr. Armstrong would take tea with me— say day after to-morrow. I want to see this exceptional husband of yours, and if my dear Morelli is not too impossible I will show him off to you."

"I doubt if Mr. Armstrong will feel that he can spare the time away from his book—" began Helen.

"In that case, then, come alone. Perhaps we can have all the better visit by ourselves. I shall expect you. Good-bye!"

Before Helen could make any further remonstrance the contessa had vanished through the hall-door, and a moment later the car could be heard moving out of the court-yard. She again leaned against her favorite pillar, trying to comprehend this new phase of life. Uncle Peabody found her standing there a few moments later when he returned from the city. Helen pulled herself together when she saw him coming, even though she made no attempt to change her position. Mr. Cartwright longed to comfort her, but something in the girl's face told him that the time had not yet come. So he took his place beside her, and, passing his arm about her waist, gently drew her toward him. Helen accepted the caress with the smile which she had learned to use to conceal the ruffled surface of her heart.

"The Contessa Morelli has just been here," she observed.

"Ah! Did you find her entertaining?"

"Yes; I think that just expresses it."

"And—worldly?"

Helen laughed. "She is certainly worldly. Yet there is something beneath it all which attracts me."

"She is a splendid example of a woman who takes the world as she finds it," Uncle Peabody continued, seriously. "Most women consider their husbands as material for idealizing. Then they rub their Aladdin's lamp, set a train of wishing in operation, and expect their selected material to live up to the ideals. When the material proves unworthy, they lose faith in everything instead of letting their experience educate their ideals. The contessa has risen above this."

"Yet, I judge, her husband has given her plenty of opportunity to lose her faith," Helen added.

"Yes," Uncle Peabody acquiesced. He looked affectionately at her, and fastened behind her ear a little strand of hair which had become loose. Then he continued, half-jocosely, "The men I know whom I would marry if I were a woman are so precious few that I would certainly be a bachelor maid."

Helen smiled at the expression on Uncle Peabody's face. "Is it not good to be here together?" she said, simply. "Your visit has meant so much to me, and now I have been considering a lot of plans which you must help me to work out. I have been waiting for just the right time, and now I believe it has come."

Uncle Peabody was genuinely surprised by Helen's manner as well as by her words.

"How much longer are you going to stay in Florence, Helen?" he asked, pointedly.

"I don't really know," she replied, frankly. "Our original plan was to leave early in July; but that is only about a month from now, and I presume Jack will require a longer time to complete his work."

"He has not made any definite plans, then?"

"No, and I hope we shall stay at least as long as that. The things which I have in mind may require even more time than I suspect."

"And these things are—"

"You inquisitive old Uncle Peabody!" Helen took his face between her hands as she kissed him affectionately. "I will tell you all in good time, and you shall be the first to know!"

XVII

Helen debated with herself long and seriously regarding the contessa's invitation. As she had said to Uncle Peabody, her new acquaintance both repelled and attracted her. Here was a woman who had undoubtedly passed through far more bitter experiences than she herself would ever be called upon to endure, yet was able to rise supremely above them and force from the world that which she still considered to be her just due. Helen could not help admiring her for this quality, and she tried to draw from her example some lessons which might be applicable to the present situation. At first she thought of insisting that her husband accompany her. She felt certain that he would not refuse her if he really understood that she expected and wished it, yet she knew without his telling her how distasteful it would be to him. If they were planning to live in Florence, it would, of course, be necessary for him to place himself in evidence, as the contessa had said, for the "respectability" of it; but as their life in Italy was so nearly ended—as their life together was so nearly ended—she felt that there was nothing to be gained in asking him to make this sacrifice. So Helen decided to return the contessa's call alone.

Alfonse was waiting for her in the motor-car when Emory drove into the court-yard. Seeing the machine, he alighted and stepped through the open door into the hall, where he intercepted her a few moments later when she came down-stairs.

"So you are just going out?" he said, by way of greeting.

"Why, Phil—where did you come from?"

"Out of that old picture there," he replied, pointing to the wall. "Don't I look funny without my ruffles and knee-breeches?"

"Do be serious, Phil," Helen laughed.

"I am serious. How could I be otherwise when I see you just going out when I have come all the way up here to have a quiet little chat?"

Helen was clearly disturbed. "This is really too bad," she said, trying to think of some plan out of it. "I promised the Contessa Morelli to take tea with her this afternoon, or I would stay home."

"The Contessa Morelli!" exclaimed Emory. "That simplifies everything."

"I don't see how," Helen remarked, frankly.

"Why, you can take me with you. What could be easier?"

"That is true," admitted Helen, meditatively. "Why not?"

"I don't see any 'why not,'" Emory asserted.

The contessa welcomed Helen with open arms. "But this is not your husband!" she exclaimed, turning to Emory before Helen had an opportunity to explain. "I had the pleasure of meeting you at the Londi reception, did I not?"

"Mr. Emory came to call just as I was starting out," Helen hastened to say, "and he begged so hard to be allowed to see you again that I could not refuse him."

"So you could not pull your learned husband away from his books?" the contessa queried, after smilingly accepting Emory's presence.

"I did not try, contessa," Helen answered, promptly. "He has reached a crisis in his work, and I was unwilling to suggest anything which might divert his mind."

"What an exemplary wife you are! If we all treated our husbands with such consideration they would become even more uncontrollable than at present. Don't you think so, Mr. Emory?"

"The suggestion is so impossible that I can think of no reply," Emory answered. "Mrs. Armstrong is such an unusual wife as to warrant considering her as an isolated exception."

Emory spoke with such sincerity that the contessa looked at him with renewed interest.

"I knew that to be the case," she said at length, "but I am glad to hear you say it. One so seldom hears a married woman championed so freely by a friend of the opposite sex."

"Mrs. Armstrong needs no champion," Emory hastened to add, feeling somewhat uncomfortable, for Helen's sake, over the turn the conversation had taken. "But why should I not be permitted to express my admiration for you or for her just as I would for a beautiful painting or any other creation of a lesser artist?"

"Because 'beautiful paintings' do not have husbands," replied the contessa, sagely, smiling at Emory's compliment.

"BECAUSE 'BEAUTIFUL PAINTINGS' DO NOT POSSESS HUSBANDS," REPLIED THE CONTESSA, SAGELY

"Since we are speaking of husbands," Helen interrupted, thinking it time to make her hostess exchange places with her, "you promised me that I should meet yours this afternoon."

"Oh no, my dear," the contessa corrected. "I said 'unless he was impossible,' and that is just what he is to-day. Be thankful that your husband's infirmity takes the form it does rather than the gout."

"Tell me something about your villa," suggested Helen, glancing around her. "All these places have romantic histories, and I am sure that this is no exception."

"All one has to do in order to forget the romance with which old Italian houses are invested is to live in one," the contessa replied. "As a matter of fact, they contain more rheumatism than romance. This one is fairly livable now, but I wish you could have seen it when Morelli first brought me here as a bride! Words can't express it. An old-fashioned house-cleaning and some good American dollars make the best antidote I know. The first point of interest I was shown here was the room in which the previous Contessa Morelli died. My ambitions were along different lines, so I added some modern improvements, much to the consternation of my husband and the servants. And the present Contessa Morelli, you may have observed, is still very much alive."

By the time the call came to an end Helen and Emory had learned much regarding Italian life from an American woman's standpoint, but in the mean time the contessa's active brain had not been idle. The situation in which she found her new friends puzzled her somewhat and interested her more. She had discovered the indifferent husband and the passive wife— two necessary elements in every domestic drama. Emory answered well enough for the admiring friend of the wife, so all that was necessary was to find the second woman and the *dramatis personæ* would be complete. This would explain the husband's indifference and the wife's passivity. It was an interesting problem, and the contessa saw definite possibilities in it.

As Emory and Helen took their leave Phil suggested that they run down to the library in the motor-car to pick up Armstrong and Miss Thayer.

"Miss Thayer?" queried the contessa.

"My friend, whom you must meet," Helen explained. "She has been with us almost since our arrival, and is assisting Mr. Armstrong in his literary work."

"Ah!" exclaimed the contessa, beaming as the completeness of her intuition came to her. "How very interesting! I shall look forward to meeting these two other members of your family."

The machine reached the foot of the hill and slowed down to pass through the city streets before either Emory or Helen broke the silence, yet it was evident that their minds found full employment. The call upon the contessa left them both with an intangibly unpleasant sensation.

"I am sorry I went with you, Helen," Emory remarked, after the long pause.

"I am sorry you did," admitted Helen, frankly, his words fitting in exactly with her own thoughts.

"It is too bad that one can't do or say the natural thing without having it misunderstood. The contessa is determined to find something upon which she may seize as material for gossip."

"That is usually not difficult when one tries hard enough," Helen agreed; "especially when one is living in such an atmosphere as she is."

"Jack will have to sacrifice himself temporarily or he will leave you in an uncomfortable position."

Emory spoke guardedly and watched the effect of his words.

"He would have come this afternoon if I had asked him," Helen asserted, confidently, "but his book is nearly finished and he is not in a mood to be interrupted. I don't want anything to interfere with its completion."

"It will be a relief, though, to have it finished, won't it?"

Helen looked up quickly at Emory's question and as quickly dropped her eyes as they met his. "Why—yes," she admitted, slowly. "I shall be glad to have him take a little rest. I am sure he has been overdoing."

The girl felt Emory's questioning glance upon her, and it added to her discomfiture.

"Don't you think it is time to let me help you, Helen?" he asked, pointedly. "You know perfectly well that I feel toward you just as I always have. No"—he stopped the restraining words upon her lips—"I am going to say nothing which I ought not to say, nothing which you ought not to hear. But I want you to be happy, Helen, and sometimes a man can help. Don't be afraid to ask me; don't let your pride stand between us. You know that I shall take no advantage of anything you tell me."

Helen's lips quivered slightly as she listened, but her voice was natural though restrained. "Something is misleading you, Phil," she answered, calmly. "Nothing has happened to make it necessary for me to ask help from any one. If there had I should be glad to have so good a friend to fall back upon."

"You are deceiving no one but yourself, Helen."

"What do you mean?"

She turned quickly toward him.

"Every one knows how much you are suffering in spite of your brave attempt to keep it to yourself. Why won't you let me help you, Helen?"

"Who is 'every one'?" she demanded.

"Why—your uncle Peabody and I and—the contessa," stammered Emory.

"You and Uncle Peabody think I am suffering?"

"We know it!"

Helen held her head very high in the air, and spoke in a superior tone so obviously assumed as a cloak to disguise her real feelings, that Emory regretted that he had forced the subject upon her; but now it had gone too far to draw back.

"If you know that, perhaps you know the cause of it as well?"

"We do. Jack—"

"Stop!" Helen commanded. The motor-car turned into the Piazza San Lorenzo. "If you have anything to say about my husband," she continued, "you had better say it direct to him."

"May I?" cried Emory, leaning forward eagerly. He looked at Helen steadily for a moment, like a runner waiting for the pistol-shot to release him from his strained position at "set." The girl returned his look with equal steadiness for only an instant before she read what was in his mind. Armstrong and Inez were just coming out through the cloister gates.

"May I?" Emory repeated.

"No!" Helen replied, quickly, sinking back against the cushions.

XVIII

Armstrong was most enthusiastic when he returned late the next afternoon, and Miss Thayer's face reflected his own great satisfaction. The book was beginning to round into completeness, Cerini had placed upon it the stamp of his unqualified approval, and the author himself had reason to feel well pleased with the results of his tireless application. Helen watched the two as they came out into the garden where she and Uncle Peabody had been visiting. Yes, they were meant for each other. Helen could see this more plainly now even than before. Her husband had lost in weight and in color since he began his work at the library, but the slighter frame and paler face seemed more in keeping with the man whom she now knew. Inez had also changed. The individuality which Helen had always considered a striking characteristic of her friend while at school and later was now completely merged into that of the man beside her. They thought alike, talked alike, acted alike. That was what Jack preferred and what he needed, Helen admitted, and she felt a certain satisfaction that she was at least strong enough to see and to admit it.

"You seem to be very happy to-night, Jack." Helen tried hard to be natural. "What pleasant thing has happened to you to-day?"

Armstrong drew up a chair for Inez and seated himself beside Helen. "Nothing in particular," he replied, "except that I begin to see the end of my book in sight."

"I am very glad," Helen answered, simply.

"Yes, I suppose you are." Armstrong spoke pointedly, looking at Helen with a curious expression on his face. "Yes, I suppose you are."

Helen flushed. "I don't mean it as you have taken it, Jack," she replied, quietly. "It has been a hard strain on you, and I am glad to know that you can soon get a change. I think you need it."

Armstrong still looked at Helen intently. "It has been a strain," he admitted, at length—"a strain on all of us." Then his face lighted up as of old. "Cerini says the book is a masterpiece, Helen—do you understand, a masterpiece. He says it is better than he believed it possible for me to do; in fact, the best work on the period which has ever been written. Can you wonder that I am happy?" He turned from Helen to Inez. "And I could never have accomplished it except for the help of our friend here, who has so unselfishly changed her plans at my request. You must thank her for me—for both of us."

"Does it mean that your visit to Florence is about at an end, Jack?" asked Uncle Peabody.

"Oh, there is much to be done yet," replied Armstrong. "The first draft is nearly finished, and the material has all been sifted through; but I must go over the manuscript once more at least, here in this atmosphere, before returning to Boston."

"Even the Old South Church and Bunker Hill Monument will seem very modern when you get back home, won't they?"

"Everything will seem modern," Armstrong assented. "I hate to think of leaving Florence, but there is one thought which makes it easier. Miss Thayer will, of course, visit us in Boston next winter, and she and I will then have a chance to do some other work like this together."

"Why, Mr. Armstrong!" cried Inez, aghast. "I should not think of that for a moment. Believe me, Helen, this is the first I have heard of it. It could not be, of course."

"Why could it not be?" insisted Armstrong, stoutly.

"You will understand when you take time to think it over," said Inez, picking up her gloves and starting for the hall. "He does not mean it, Helen—truly he does not!"

"I do mean it," urged Armstrong, as Inez disappeared. "I mean every word of it. She is your most intimate friend, and what could be more natural than for her to visit us? Why could it not be?"

Uncle Peabody answered:

"There are some things in Boston which are as old as anything you will find in Florence, Jack."

Armstrong failed to catch the drift of Mr. Cartwright's remarks.

"You are trying to avoid answering my question," he replied. "To what do you refer that bears at all upon the present discussion?"

"Conventions," said Uncle Peabody, calmly.

"Conventions!" Armstrong repeated the word with emphasis. "You don't imagine that I am going to let local conventions tell me what to do when I get home?"

"I don't imagine anything," replied Uncle Peabody. "I was merely stating a fact."

Helen saw the hot retort upon her husband's lips. "I would not discuss this any more until after dinner," she said, quietly, as she rose. "As Jack says, it is a perfectly natural thing for Inez to visit me. It is possible that it can be arranged in some way."

"Good!" cried Armstrong. "I am glad that there is one sensible person in the party!"

He tried to slip his arm around Helen's waist, but she gently avoided him.

"Come," she urged, "we shall be late if we don't get ready now. We have too little time as it is."

After dinner Uncle Peabody and Inez announced their intention of devoting the evening to letter-writing, so Helen and Jack found themselves alone together in the garden. Helen wrapped her shawl closely about her, wondering at the chill which came over her when she realized that she was alone with her husband and that the opportunity for which she had waited was at hand. She was silent, trying to decide how best to open the conversation. Her mind was made up at last. If others had begun to notice the estrangement, it was time that Jack knew of it, and from her. All doubt, all uncertainty had vanished.

She looked long at her husband in the dim starlight. He was so near her, yet how far away he really was! Even he did not realize how far. She could see the lines of his face lighted by his cigar as he silently smoked it, his eyes fixed upon the lights of the city beyond. How strong it was, Helen thought, how strong he was compared with her own weak self! She wondered what his thoughts were centred upon—whether on his masterpiece or upon Inez! Upon Inez! That brought her back to the task before her.

It was a difficult task; she realized that. There could be no immediate separation, for that would mean an interruption to the work. She must stay in Florence until the manuscript was completed or Inez could not remain. No, there must not be any break between Jack and herself for the present, or his mind would be taken from his book and another failure added to the great one in which she felt herself to be the most concerned. Yet she must make him understand that she was not dull to the signs which she and the others could but read. To continue to act as if ignorant of them would be the worst of all. She must remain his wife until his supreme effort was accomplished, then the living lie could be ended and the new and separate life begun.

Armstrong interrupted her reverie before it had quite come to an end.

"You are not looking like yourself lately, Helen," he said, abruptly. "I meant to have spoken of it before."

Helen started at the suddenness of his remark. "Not looking like myself?" she repeated, mechanically. "How do you mean?"

"You look tired and worn out."

"I am getting older, Jack," Helen smiled, sadly. "Perhaps that is what you have noticed."

"Nonsense," replied Armstrong. "You used to be so bright and vivacious, and now you sit around and hardly say a word."

She could not answer for a moment. "I did not realize that I had become such poor company, Jack. You have not seemed interested lately in the things I would naturally talk about, and of course a great deal of your conversation is upon subjects with which I am unfamiliar."

"You are quite sure that you are not getting too tired going to all these social functions?"

"Quite sure. If you stop to think a moment, these are really the only entertainment I get. Would you prefer that I stayed here at the villa alone?"

"Why, no; unless you are doing too much of that sort of thing. Are you feeling perfectly well?"

Helen hardly knew what to reply. "Yes," she said, at length, "I am feeling perfectly well."

Armstrong showed his relief. "I told Uncle Peabody he was an alarmist," he said.

"What did Uncle Peabody say?" queried Helen, straightening up, Emory's remarks coming back to her. "I did not know that you and he had been discussing me."

"He said that you were unhappy, and fast becoming a fit subject for Italian malaria. He had better stick to his specialty, and not try to become a general practitioner."

"Oh," said Helen, relieved that she had not been anticipated, and resuming her former position.

"Of course he was as mistaken about your being unhappy as he was about your being ill," Armstrong continued, his remark being half assertion and half question.

Helen made no response. He waited a moment or two, glancing at her furtively, and then put his question more directly.

"You are not unhappy, are you?"

Helen tried to fathom the motive which underlay this question. At last Jack had become conscious of the fact that he had hurt her and was endeavoring to make amends. This was like him; what he had said and done during the weeks past was not like him. Now something which Uncle Peabody had said had brought him to himself again. He saw a duty to perform, and he assumed it conscientiously; but it was an act of duty rather than an act of love—she felt that in every word he spoke.

"Yes, Jack," she finally admitted, "I am very unhappy."

Armstrong was annoyed. "I really thought you were stronger, Helen," he said, petulantly. "It is all over this library work, I suppose."

"I am not strong," replied Helen, quietly. "That is where the whole trouble lies. I am wofully weak, and I only wish that you and I had discovered it sooner."

"How would that have helped matters any?"

"If we had discovered it before we were married it would have helped matters a great deal," said Helen, with decision. "As we did not do that we must accept things as they are until we can find a solution of the problem."

"I have offered time and again to give up my work; now it has reached a point where I simply must finish it."

"Of course you must; I should be the first to oppose you were you to suggest anything different."

"Then why are you unhappy? I don't understand you at all."

"I know you don't, and you understand yourself just as little. The work you are doing is simply an incident; the results of that work in making you an entirely different man is the main point. Do you not feel that yourself?"

"So that is it," replied Armstrong. "The work has made a different man of me, and you object to the change."

"No, it is not the change which has made me unhappy. During these weeks you have become infinitely bigger and stronger and grander, and I admire you just that much the more."

"Then why are you unhappy?"

"Because"—Helen choked down a little sob—"because, as you say, I am so weak. Because it has left me just that much behind, and has shown me how little suited I am to be your wife."

"How you do magnify things!" exclaimed Armstrong. "It is not an uncommon thing for a husband to have interests apart from his wife; it is no reflection on the wife."

"But how much better—how much more helpful—if the husband and the wife can share the same interests?"

"Granted. But why suggest a modern miracle?"

"It has shown me another thing," Helen continued, fearful lest she should be diverted from her main theme. "Inez is already much more to you than I."

Armstrong sprang to his feet, with difficulty holding back the angry words upon his lips. "This is going too far, Helen," he said, with forced calm. "Do you realize that you are actually making an accusation?"

Helen regarded him calmly but sadly. "I am making no accusation," she said, quietly. "I believe in your loyalty to me and in your sense of what is right, but the fact remains. Inez loves you, and has loved you almost since the day she arrived. Is it possible that you are insensible to this?"

"You must stop!" expostulated Armstrong. "You cannot realize what you are saying!"

"Do you remember what she told Ferdy De Peyster—'I love him better than my life'? Do you remember the scene at the table when Phil Emory spoke of it and her reply? Have you been with her day after day without discovering that she worships the very ground you walk on?"

"It would be useless to try to answer you, Helen," Armstrong replied, forcefully. "The most generous view I can take of what you say is to attribute it to a jealousy as unfounded as it is unworthy of you."

"Ah, Jack, if you only knew!" Helen looked at him reproachfully. "There is no jealousy in my heart even now, my husband, nothing but the greatest admiration and the deepest love. Sometime you will understand. You have a great career before you—greater, perhaps, than I can realize, because I know of your work only through others. This career is one which I must not injure, which I shall not limit. Inez can help you in attaining it, and it is right that she should do so."

Armstrong's curiosity gained the better of his resentment. "What do you propose to do to bring all this about?" he asked, incredulously.

"Whatever may be necessary," Helen replied, looking at him firmly, "even though it breaks my heart."

"Surely you have not suggested any of this nonsense to Miss Thayer?" Armstrong asked, suddenly.

"I have not talked with her about it," replied Helen, quietly.

"That is to be placed to your credit, at all events. Miss Thayer has no more sentiment toward me of the kind you suggest than if she had never met me. She is the best kind of a friend and a most valuable assistant, but that is all. My feelings toward her are exactly the same—no more, no less. I beg of you not to let anything so absurdly improbable stand between us now or later. Come, we had better go in."

"Don't wait for me," Helen answered, wearily. "I will stay here a while longer. The cool air feels very grateful to-night."

Armstrong left her there, alone with the stars and her thoughts. The break was made. They had stood at the parting of the ways, and Helen had pointed out to him the path which she knew she could not travel with him. He, with all his strength of mind, had left her without realizing what had happened. Helen had not expected him to understand her motive—that must come later—but she had thought that he would at least appreciate what she had said. Perhaps it was better so. She had known that he would disclaim the affection which she felt he could but entertain toward Inez; she was certain that he himself did not yet appreciate how firmly installed his "sister worker" had become in his heart. But Helen was no less convinced that she was right. Jack would realize it soon enough, and then he would know what she had really done to make it easier for him. Perhaps this was better, too.

The storm was over, and Helen remained as the weather-beaten evidence that it had taken place. Exhausted both in mind and body, she lay back in her chair, with her eyes wide open, her thoughts rushing madly to and fro seeking a new anchorage. She must keep her strength for the ordeal yet before her. She must play her part through to the end without wavering, or what she had already endured would be of no avail. So at last she bade good-night to the stars which had been her silent companions and entered the house. Mechanically she fastened the veranda shutters and went up-stairs to her room, closing the door to the world outside, with which she felt she must become acquainted anew as she pursued her chosen path—alone.

XIX

The contessa found herself eager to continue her inquiries along the new lines which had so clearly indicated themselves during the conversation with Mrs. Armstrong and Emory. This desire was by no means malicious, for those very attributes which attracted Helen to her would have contradicted anything so really reprehensible, even as a counter-irritant. In the contessa's life, filled as it was with *ennui* in spite of her heroic efforts to enliven it with excitement, gossip and a bit of scandal acted as agreeable and much-needed stimulants. She may never have put this thought into words any more than the man does who depends upon his modest tipple to give zest to his daily routine; yet, like him, she found her dependence upon her stimulant growing slowly yet steadily as the days advanced and the "dear Morelli" became more and more "impossible." In the present instance the interval since the last spicy episode had been longer than usual, and the contessa felt a thrill of enthusiastic delight replace the dull apathy which she had lately experienced, even at the suggestion of the conditions as she thought she saw them. It was a problem which offered her the joy of solution rather than merely a curiosity to learn more of the various factors which entered into it.

She liked Helen from the first moment of their meeting. America often seemed far away to the contessa, and her new acquaintance brought it nearer to her; but beyond this Helen proved in herself to be more than ordinarily interesting. The contessa had known women as beautiful as Mrs. Armstrong, she had known women who carried themselves with equal self-confidence and independence; but never had she seen these combined with such lofty ideals actually maintained. Her early impression that Helen's idealism was the result of innocence was soon corrected. In the school of experience there are taught two branches in which every clever woman of the world must perfect herself—character-reading and the gentle art of self-defence; both are absolutely essential to her success. Men underestimate their importance, and thus develop them to a lesser degree; as a result, the woman's intuitive reading of character is as much more delicate and subtle as is her practise of self-defence, and to a similar extent more effective. Amélie was a medal pupil in both these branches, and her instinctive exercise of the first told her that she had discovered an unusual personality among conditions which under ordinary circumstances would work out along but one line. This solution was not in keeping with what she had read in Helen's character, and she wondered how the conditions themselves had come to exist. The contessa hummed cheerily to herself as she moved about the villa the next morning, and the servants took it for granted that their master's malady had taken a more decided turn for the worse.

In the afternoon the contessa's motor-car drew up before the entrance to the Laurentian Library. The custodian at the gate took her card, and presently returned announcing that the librarian was in his study. The name of Morelli was well known to Cerini, who had assisted the count upon several occasions before his marriage in disposing of some of the rare volumes which had once been a part of his grandfather's splendid collection. The librarian had even casually met the new contessa once or twice, but this was the first time she had honored him with a call, and he wondered what her errand might be. Possibly it was her desire to dispose of other volumes; perhaps it was to protest against further despoliation; at all events he would be guarded in his conversation until her object was disclosed.

"Welcome to the halls of the Medici!" exclaimed Cerini, cordially, rising to greet his visitor as she appeared in the doorway.

The contessa smiled so radiantly in acknowledging his salutation that the librarian was convinced that his first hypothesis must be correct. "You are surprised to see me," she remarked, seating herself with deliberation and looking across at her host with a friendly air. "You may as well admit it, for I can read it in your face."

"Both surprised and pleased, contessa," Cerini answered, maintaining his guarded attitude.

"Your surprise should be that I have not been here before," Amélie continued.

"Ah!" The old man held up his hand with a deprecatory gesture. "You society women have so much to divert you otherwise that I could scarcely expect, even with the wonderful books I have here, to prove a magnet sufficiently strong to draw you away from your customary pursuits. And your husband has so many splendid volumes in your own library that these here can hardly prove a novelty."

"It is about these volumes that I came to see you."

Cerini smiled sagely, feeling pleased at his intuition.

"Yes, we have some splendid old volumes, as you say," the contessa continued. "I have looked them all over and have tried to study them, but beyond my admiration for their beauty I must admit that I can't make much out of them."

"Then you are really interested in the books themselves!" exclaimed the librarian, his pleasure increasing with the prospect of securing a new convert. "This is delightful!"

"Of course." The contessa raised her eyebrows with well-feigned surprise. She was entirely satisfied with her progress thus far. "But I don't need to tell you that my interest is not a very intelligent one. I tried to get Morelli to tell me something about them once, but he doesn't know a book of hours from a missal, so I promised myself the pleasure of learning from you, if you were willing to teach me. Are you?"

The contessa was fond of punctuating her conversation with sharp interrogations, but in the present instance the expression upon Cerini's face made any question unnecessary.

"This is the happiest year I have known since I first made my home among these books, my daughter," he replied, with much feeling. "For a long time I felt as a miser must feel surrounded by his gold, far more in quantity than he can ever count, yet separated by its overwhelming value from the world outside. My loneliness came, of course, from another cause—I craved the opportunity to share my treasures, yet this opportunity came but rarely. Patiently have I waited, marvelling that so few should even know that these treasures exist, and a lesser number should care to partake of what is offered to them freely in as large quantities as they are able to carry away. Year by year I have watched the number increase, I have seen the signs of a veritable renaissance; and as one after another comes to me, as you have this afternoon, my heart fills with an unspeakable joy."

The sincerity of the old man penetrated through even the contessa's worldly armor, but the problem she had set herself to solve was too fascinating to be laid aside. The librarian need never know how much less interest she felt in books than in her present undertaking.

"So this year has crowned your labors," she replied, sympathetically. "I do not wonder that you feel gratified! You have had a greater number of converts, you say, most of whom, I presume, come from the libraries and universities near by."

"Not at all!" contradicted Cerini, eagerly. "They come from England, from France, from Germany—and even from your own far-off country, contessa."

"Indeed!" Amélie smiled at the air of triumph with which the librarian uttered the last words. "From America? Have my countrymen really discovered what rich mines of learning are here in Florence?"

Cerini nodded his head and drew his chair closer to hers. "At this very moment there are two Americans working here in the library who have so assimilated the learning of the past that they have become a part of it themselves. I have had many students here during all these years, but never any one who was able so completely to carry out my ideas of modern intellectual expression. What they have done and are doing has given me courage to believe that I am not so much of a visionary as my colleagues think. If by my influence I can produce two such modern humanists my labors will not have been in vain."

"Are these two wonderful men from some library or university in America?" the contessa asked, with apparent innocence.

"They are not," replied the librarian, with emphasis. "If they were they would have come here, as the others have, with preconceived ideas which centuries could not break down. One of them is a young advocate from Boston, and the other—you will scarcely believe me—is a young woman."

"Really?" The contessa manifested an interest not wholly assumed. "A young woman, you say—his wife, perhaps?"

"No, simply a friend."

"Oh!" Amélie smiled knowingly. "Then perhaps soon to be his wife?"

"You are wrong again, contessa," replied Cerini. "The man is already married, so that could hardly be the case."

"And his wife makes no objections? Come, come, monsignore, that would not be human."

"His wife is as remarkable in her way as he is in his," the old man answered, with confidence. "We have discussed the matter, and she understands the importance of allowing the work to go on."

"Then she has raised some objections? Do tell me that she has or I shall find it difficult to believe your story."

"She did suggest that she would have liked to be able to do this work with her husband, but that was quite out of the question, and she saw it just as I did."

"How very, very interesting!" the contessa remarked, more to herself than to him. "I wish I might see them at work." The librarian hesitated, and Amélie knew that hesitation is consent if promptly followed up. "I will promise not to disturb them," she urged.

"I should not wish them to know that I was exhibiting them to my friends," Cerini said, doubtfully. "Still, I can see no harm unless we disturb them."

"Then come!" Amélie exclaimed, rising quickly lest the old man change his mind. "I will be as still as a mouse."

Cerini led the way to the little alcove which Armstrong and Inez had come to regard as a part of themselves. Motioning to the contessa, he pointed out a place beside an ancient book-shelf where she could observe without herself being seen. Amélie studied the faces before her carefully. Armstrong was so seated that only his profile was visible, but Inez sat so squarely in front of her that had she not been so engrossed in her labors she could hardly have avoided seeing the contessa. It was the girl's face which first held Amélie's attention. In it she read all that Inez had fought so hard to conceal. She had found the second woman! It was not the usual type, she told herself. The passionate devotion to its given object was there, but it was evidently absolutely controlled by the intellectual. How much more interesting, the contessa thought, but how much more dangerous!

Then she turned her attention to Armstrong. He was younger than she had expected and his personality far more attractive. The height of his forehead, the depth of his eye, the strength of his mouth were all carefully noted. The contessa watched every movement, every change in the expression, with the keenest delight. They were an interesting pair, she admitted, but even her astuteness, she was forced to confess, was unequal to the task of understanding their relations without further study. The problem was as new as it was fascinating, and the contessa had no misgivings over her little plot, which had worked out so successfully.

She followed the librarian quietly back to his study, where she made an appointment for him to examine with her the Morelli collection and to point out to her the merits of the various volumes. She expressed her thanks for the charming afternoon he had given her, but through it all, and even after she returned to her villa, the faces of Armstrong and Inez were still before her. Beneath that abstraction which the man's face and manner so clearly portrayed, was there a response to the woman's passionate adoration? Was he capable of affection, or had the intellectual so far claimed the ascendency that the physical had, for the time being at least, become so subdued as practically to be eliminated? Where did the wife, who had so attracted her, come in? These were some of the questions over which the contessa pondered. The problem was more complex than she anticipated, and she found herself even more determined to carry it through to a solution.

XX

A week passed by with little outward change at the Villa Godilombra. For a day or two after their interview in the garden Armstrong watched his wife carefully, but as there was apparently no difference in her attitude toward him or toward Miss Thayer he decided that what she had said at that time was the result merely of a momentary mood which had since passed away. He also watched Miss Thayer, to satisfy himself in regard to the monstrous suggestion Helen had made that she was in love with him, and became convinced that his own explanation of her feelings toward him was correct. Having settled these two important matters to his entire satisfaction, he promptly discarded them from his mind and devoted himself to the single purpose of completing his work.

"Once let me get this finished," he said to himself, "and Helen will see that there is nothing between us."

As a matter of fact, Inez had not been pleased with Armstrong's suggestion to Helen that she should take up with him a similar kind of work in Boston. For the first time since she had known him he had done something which annoyed her. She realized better than any one else the absorption which held him subject to a different code of conventions, but this did not give him a right to assume that she would accept such an arrangement, without at least raising the question with her. Helen and Mr. Cartwright could but think that the matter had already been discussed between them, and it placed her in a false light at a time when she felt that her position was sufficiently untenable without this unfair and unnecessary addition. She also realized, as Armstrong apparently did not even after Uncle Peabody's pointed remarks, that this daily companionship would be entirely impossible.

During those few days, therefore, when Armstrong was observing her, she was in a mood quite at variance with what Helen had described; but what had wounded her in one respect proved to be a salve in another. Had Armstrong been conscious of her affection for him, or had he himself reciprocated it, the request would never have been made. She was quite safe, therefore, to continue on until the book was finished, and the danger lay, as she had told her conscience, only with herself. And even with this annoyance, which, after all, was but an incident, she felt it to be her only happiness to stay beside him as long as she could. She dreaded the time when the break must come, for she saw no light beyond that point.

Helen had herself well in hand. She was conscious of Jack's scrutiny, and was also conscious of the relaxing of his watchfulness. She saw his new interest in Inez, and was equally conscious of her friend's unusual frame of mind. Everything seemed to Helen to be intensified to such a degree that she could read all that was passing in the minds of those about her, and she wondered if some new power had been given her to make her test the harder. She had already felt the force of the blow; the others had it still before them. And it would be a blow, at least to Jack, she was sure—not so hard a one as in her own case, for after the pain of the break there was for him happiness and serenity; but he had cared for her, and when he once came to a realization of what must be he would suffer, too. This was her only consolation.

Naturally, Helen turned to Uncle Peabody. Now that all was settled, it was better that he should know from her how matters stood rather than surmise as he and Emory had done; and besides this, the burden had become too heavy to be borne alone. She waited a few days for the right opportunity, which came during a morning walk along the ancient road above the villa which led to the highest point of Settignano. They had left the frequented part of the path behind them, and were strolling among the rocks and trees of the little plateau commanding a view of the panorama on either side.

"I wish I could find out from Jack how much longer you are to remain in Florence," Uncle Peabody said. "I really need to get back to my work."

"Not yet," exclaimed Helen, quickly. "Don't go yet. I need you so much!"

Uncle Peabody regarded his niece critically. There was a new note in her voice, and it pained him.

"It won't be much longer, uncle," Helen continued. "I need you here, and I may want you to go back home with me."

"I could not do that, Helen; but of course I will stay here as long as you really need me."

"But you would go back with me if I needed that, too, would you not?" insisted Helen.

"If you needed me, yes; but I can't imagine any such necessity."

"It would be so hard to go home alone."

Helen's voice sank almost to a whisper.

"Alone?" echoed Uncle Peabody. "Is Jack going to stay over here and send you back?"

"I don't know what Jack is going to do, but I shall return home as soon as his book is completed; and unless you go with me I shall go alone."

Uncle Peabody understood. "My dear, dear child," he said, taking her hand in his and pressing it sympathetically.

"Don't, please." Helen gently withdrew her hand. "If you do that I shall become completely unnerved. Let us return to the villa; I really want to talk with you about it."

The short walk home was accomplished in silence. As they entered the hallway Uncle Peabody was the first to speak. "Where shall we go?" he asked.

"To my 'snuggery,'" Helen answered. "There we are sure not to be interrupted."

"Now tell me all about it," he urged, as they seated themselves.

"I imagine you know a good deal about the situation without my telling you," began Helen, bravely; "but I want you to know the whole story. Otherwise you can't help me, and without your aid I am absolutely alone."

"You know well that you can depend upon that," he interrupted.

Helen moved nearer and passed her hand through his arm. "We have made a horrible mistake, Jack and I," she said. "We are not at all suited to each other, and never should have married."

"That is a pretty serious statement," replied Uncle Peabody.

"It is," assented Helen; "but the fact itself is even more serious. Tell me, do you not see that Jack is a very different man from the one you first met here?"

"Yes," he replied. "There can be no question about that."

"If this change was but a passing mood it would not be so serious," continued Helen, "but the Jack I know now is the real Jack, and as such our interests are entirely apart."

"But all this may correct itself," suggested Uncle Peabody. "Why not get him away from the influences which have produced this change and see if that will not straighten matters out?"

Helen was thoughtful for a moment. "That would never do," she said, at length. "You see, there is another consideration which enters in. Inez and Jack are in love with each other."

"Has Jack admitted this?" demanded Uncle Peabody.

Helen smiled sadly. "No; he would never admit it, even if he knew it to be true. At present his affection is wholly centered upon his book, and he himself has no real conception of how matters stand."

"Then why do you feel so certain? I think you are right about Miss Thayer, but I have seen nothing to criticise in Jack's conduct except this complete subjugation to his work."

"I have been watching it for weeks, uncle, and I know that I am right. The old Jack—the Jack I married—found in me the response he craved; but to the new Jack—the real Jack—I can give nothing. Inez is his counterpart; Inez is the woman who can talk his language and live his life—not I."

"There is no reason why you could not do this if he gave you the chance," he asserted.

"At first it was my fault that I did not make the effort when he did give me the chance. Then I tried to enter into it—you remember the day I went to the library—but it was too late. Cerini showed me how hopeless it was. Then you remember Professor Tesso's story. He was right; they are absolutely suited to each other. It is useless to fight against it and thus increase the misery."

"If you are not going to fight against it, what are you going to do?"

"I am going to right the wrong in the only way which remains," replied Helen, firmly.

"I don't see it yet." Uncle Peabody showed his perplexity. "What are you going to do?"

"Jack and I must be separated just as soon as it can be arranged."

Uncle Peabody placed his hands upon her shoulders and looked into her eyes. With all the advance signals of the storm which he had noted he was unprepared for this climax. "Surely that point has not yet arrived, Helen," he said, slowly. "'Those whom God hath joined together—'"

"That is just the point," she interrupted. "Those whom God joins together are those who are suited to each other. When it becomes evident that two people have been married who are unsuited, it is also evident that God never joined them together, and that they ought not to stay together. That is the case with Jack and me."

"Have you told Jack your decision?"

"Not in so many words, but in substance. He does not appreciate the situation at all, and he won't until the book is finished."

"Why don't you go home for a while and see what happens?"

"If I went away now Inez would have to leave, and that would interrupt the work."

"I can't follow you, Helen. One moment you speak of the misery this work has brought to you, and the next moment you can't do something because it will interfere with the very work which you would like to stop."

"It seems to be my fate not to be able to make myself understood," Helen replied, wearily. "Let me try again. I have no desire to stop the work. It is a necessary part of Jack's development, and it will open up a great future for him."

"But to continue this means to continue the intimacy between him and Miss Thayer," insisted Uncle Peabody.

"I have no desire to stop that, either." Helen was calm and firm in her replies. "It would be no satisfaction to hold Jack to me when I know perfectly well that duty and marriage vows remain as the only ties. It breaks my heart that all this has happened, but neither the work itself nor even Inez is responsible. The other side of Jack was like an undeveloped negative—these are simply the mediums which have brought out the picture which was already there."

"You are not in a condition to consider this matter as you should, Helen," Uncle Peabody replied, hardly knowing what to say. "The whole affair has been preying on your mind for so long that you are arriving at conclusions which may or may not be justified. Your very calmness shows that you do not appreciate the seriousness of your suggestions."

Helen looked at Uncle Peabody reproachfully. "Don't make me think that men are wilfully obtuse," she said. "When I talked it over with Jack he called it jealousy; now you think I lack an appreciation of the seriousness of it all!" Helen paused for a moment and closed her eyes. When she spoke again all the intensity of her nature burst forth. "Can you not see beneath this calmness the effort I am making to do my duty?" she asked, in a low, tense voice. "Can you not see my heart burned to ashes by the fire it has passed through? Look at me, uncle. Jack says I seem ten years older— twenty would be nearer the truth. Do these changes come to those who fail to appreciate what they are doing? It is not that I don't realize; it is because I can't forget."

"Don't misunderstand me, child," Uncle Peabody hastened to say, appalled by the effect of his words. "My own heart has bled for you all these weeks, and I would be the last to add another burden to the load you bear. It is hard to suffer, but sometimes I think it is almost as hard to see those one loves passing through an ordeal which he is powerless to lighten. I don't want you to take a step which will plunge you into deeper sorrow, that is all. You may be right, but I pray God that you are wrong. Now let me help you, if I can."

Helen smiled through the mist before her eyes. "You can help me," she said, "just by being your own dear self during these hard weeks to come. Stay here until it is over, and then take me home, where you can show me how to use the years I see before me." Helen buried her face in her hands. "Oh, those years!" she cried; "how can I endure them?"

"Come, come, Helen," urged Uncle Peabody, kindly, "I can't believe that the world has all gone wrong, as you think it has. Let us take one step at a time, and see if together we can't find the sun shining through the cypress-trees. Tell me just what you propose to do."

"The programme is a simple one," Helen answered. "Outwardly there will be no change. I shall make Jack's home as attractive as possible to him while we share it together. Inez is my guest, and will be welcome as long as I am here. Other than this it will be as if we all were visitors. Jack will notice no difference while his work lasts. Then when it is completed you and I will go back home. Jack may stay here or return, as he chooses. Inez will decide her own course. Then Jack will at last understand that I meant what I said—that I saw that I stood in the way of his future and stepped aside."

"Do you imagine that he will permit this when once he understands?" asked Uncle Peabody.

"He will try to prevent it," assented Helen. "He will realize that he has neglected me and he will want to atone, but this will be from a sense of duty, even though he does not know it. The actual break will be a blow to him, but then he will turn to Inez and will find that I understood him better than he did himself."

"But he is counting on continuing this work in Boston next winter. He spoke of it again yesterday, and said how splendid it was of you to make it possible for Miss Thayer to work there with him."

Helen rose and stepped out into the garden, looking far away into the distance. Then she turned toward him.

"I am making it possible, am I not?" she said, simply.

And the lump in Uncle Peabody's throat told him that he understood at last.

XXI

The evening had arrived for the reception at Villa Godilombra by which Helen was to acknowledge the many social obligations laid upon her by her friends in Florence. In the details of preparation she had found temporary relief from her ever-present burden, with Uncle Peabody assuming the rôle of general adviser, comforter, and prop. Together they had worked out the list of guests; together they had planned the many little surprises which should make the event unique. Much to old Giuseppe's disgust, his own flowers were found to be inadequate, and to his camellias, lilies, oleanders, and roses was added a profusion of those rare orchids which bear witness that the City of Flowers is well named. Emory was also pressed into service as the day drew near, and his energy was untiring in carrying out the ideas of his superior officers and in suggesting original ones of his own.

Armstrong had expressed his willingness to co-operate, but was obviously relieved to find his services unnecessary. He had reached a crisis in his work, he explained, and if he really was not needed it would hasten the conclusion of his labors if they might be uninterrupted at this particular point. Inez had also offered her aid, but Armstrong insisted that she could not be spared unless her presence at the villa was absolutely demanded. So the work upon the masterpiece had proceeded without a break, while little by little the plans for the reception matured.

The novelty of the preparations consisted principally in the electrical and the floral displays. Uncle Peabody succeeded in having a number of wires run from the trolley-line into the villa and the garden, leaving Emory to plan an arrangement of lights which did credit to the limited number of electrical courses which his college curriculum had contained. The grotto was lighted by fascinating little incandescent lamps, which shed their rays dimly through the guarding cypresses but full upon the varicolored shells and stones. Along the top of the retaining wall, and scattered here and there at uneven distances and heights among the trees and the statues, the lights looked like a swarm of magnificent fire-flies resting, for the time, wherever they happened to alight. But Emory's *pièce de résistance* was the fountain, beneath the spray of which he had helped the electrician to fashion a brilliant fleur-de-lis in compliment to the city of their adoption.

This final triumph was brought to a successful conclusion almost simultaneously with the cessation of Helen's labors in transforming the dining-room, the hallway, and the verandas into veritable flower arbors.

Old Giuseppe and the florist's men had accomplished wonders under Helen's guidance, and they approved the final result as enthusiastically as they had opposed the scheme at first, when Helen had insisted upon a departure from the conventional "set pieces" which they tried to urge upon her. Realizing that the time was approaching for the light repast, and glad of a respite, Helen wandered out to the garden where Emory and Uncle Peabody, hand in hand, were executing an hilarious dance around the fountain.

"What in the world—" began Helen, in amazement.

"It is great, is it not, Mr. Cartwright?" cried Emory, ceasing his evolutions and turning to Uncle Peabody. "This settles it; I am going home on the next steamer and set myself up as an electrical engineer—specialty, decoration of Italian gardens. Watch, Helen—I will turn on the lights."

In an instant the flitting insects were flickering throughout the garden, and the water of the fountain became a living flame. Helen's first exclamation of delight was interrupted by Giuseppe's groan of terror as the old gardener hastily retreated to the house, crossing himself and praying for divine protection against the magic of the evil one which had entered and taken possession of his very domain. The suspicion with which he had viewed the labors of the electricians during the past few days was now fully justified, and he saw his work of thirty years in danger of destruction by the conflagration which he believed must inevitably follow.

"Splendid, Phil!" cried Helen, when Giuseppe was at last quieted. "I had no idea you were carrying out so grand a scheme. What should I have done without you?"

"It was Mr. Cartwright's idea, you know, Helen," insisted Emory.

"To get the light up here—not the arrangement, which is all to your credit," Uncle Peabody hastened to add.

"I owe everything to both of you," said Helen, holding out a hand to each. "Now I want to see every light." Slowly they walked about the garden inspecting the illumination. "It is perfect," exclaimed Helen. "I can't tell you how pleased I am with it. I ought to be jealous that you have so outdone me in your part of the decoration, but I am really proud of you!"

As they were taking an admiring view of the floral arrangements Jack and Inez rode up. Emory started to suggest to them a view of the garden, but a glance from Helen prevented.

"Save it for a surprise, Phil," she whispered. "They have no idea of what you have done."

It was nearly ten o'clock when the first guests arrived, and for an hour Helen, Jack, and Uncle Peabody greeted the brilliant gathering as it assembled. To most of them Armstrong was a complete stranger, and it was quite evident that many of those who had known and admired Helen and Mr. Cartwright possessed no little curiosity concerning this man of whom so little had been seen.

"Then there really is a Mr. Armstrong, after all," exclaimed the Marchesa Castellani, smiling blandly as Helen presented him. "We had almost come to look upon you as one of those American—what shall we say?— conceits."

The color came to Helen's face, but before she could reply Cerini pressed forward from behind.

"Signor Armstrong has been my guest these weeks, marchesa, inhaling the wisdom of the past instead of the sweeter but more transitory grandeur of Florentine society. This has perhaps been his loss, and yours; but, with his great work nearly ready for the press, dare we say that the world will not be the richer for the sacrifice?"

"I shall not be the one to dare," replied the marchesa, again smiling and passing on to make room for others behind her.

Cerini watched his opportunity for another word with Helen. "I came to-night," he said, "expressly to tell you that your reward is near at hand. Another week and your husband's labors will be completed. I have thought often of our conversation, and of your patience; but the result of my advice has been more far-reaching even than I thought. The character-building has extended beyond him and his 'sister-worker'—it has reached you as well."

The arrival of new guests fortunately delayed the necessity of immediate reply, but it also gave Cerini an opportunity to watch the effect of his words. The old man's voice softened as he continued:

"You have suffered, my daughter; I did not know till now how much. Yet suffering is essential. George Eliot was a woman, and she knew a woman's heart when she wrote, 'Deep, unspeakable suffering is a baptism, a regeneration—the initiation into a new state.' Your initiation is passed, my daughter, and your enjoyment of the new state is near at hand. Do you not see now how far-reaching has been the influence?"

"Yes," Helen replied, with a tremor in her voice; "and this time I think I may say that it has been more far-reaching than even you realize."

Cerini's eyes sought hers searchingly. He had already seen more than she had intended.

"Then the book is really coming to its completion?" she continued, calmly. "And you feel well satisfied with my husband's work?"

"It is superb; it is magnificent," cried Cerini, enthusiastically. "He has produced a work which is without an equal in the veracity of its portrayal of the period and in the insight which he has shown in dealing with the characters themselves. It will make your husband famous."

"We shall be very proud of him, shall we not?" replied Helen, forcing a smile. "And he will owe so much to you for the help and the inspiration you have given him."

"And also to you, my daughter," added the librarian, meaningly.

Emory approached as Cerini left her side. "Every one is in the garden now, Helen. May I take you there?"

Helen glanced around for her husband, and saw him somewhat apart from the other guests engaged in a conversation with the Contessa Morelli. Unconsciously her mind went back to what the contessa had said to her about marriage in general and about her husband in particular, and she wondered what her new friend thought of him, now that they had actually met.

"Jack has his hands full for the present," Emory remarked, noting her glance. "You need not worry about him. By Jove, Helen, you are simply stunning to-night!" he continued, in a low voice, as they strolled across the veranda. "I have been anxious about you, but now you are yourself again. You should always wear white."

Helen made no answer. She was recalling to herself the fact that to-night, for the first time, Jack had made no comment upon her appearance, as he had always done before; yet she had tried to wear the very things which he preferred. After all, she thought, it was better so. But what a mockery to stand beside a man, as she stood with Jack this evening, jointly receiving their friends and their friends' congratulations! What deception! What ignominy!

In the mean time, as Emory had surmised, Armstrong had his hands sufficiently full with the contessa. Her mind had been too constantly applied to her interesting problem, during the days which had elapsed since her call upon Cerini, to allow this opportunity to escape her. She had exercised every art she possessed to learn something further from Helen; she even had Emory take tea with her with the same definite object in view; but either consciously or unconsciously both had parried her diplomatic questioning with an air so natural and simple as to convince her that they were not unskilled themselves in the game in which she considered herself an adept. The one thing which remained was the picture she had seen at the library; but this had been so positive in the impression which it had made that she found herself even more keen than ever to follow up the small advantage she had gained.

Watching her opportunity, Amélie found herself beside Armstrong, with the other guests far enough removed to enable her to converse with him without being overheard.

"All Florence owes you a debt of gratitude for bringing your beautiful wife here," she began. "And how generous you have been to let us have so much of her while you have been otherwise engaged!"

"It has been my misfortune not to be able to share her social pleasures," Armstrong replied. "Perhaps she has told you of the serious work upon which I am engaged."

"Yes, indeed," answered the contessa, cheerfully. "I am sure every man in Florence who has had an opportunity to meet your wife has blessed you for your devotion to this 'serious work,' as you call it. Italian husbands are not so generous, especially upon their honeymoon."

Armstrong bowed stiffly. The contessa's manner was far too affable to warrant him in taking offence, yet he felt distinctly annoyed by what she said. Amélie, however, gave him no opportunity to reply.

"Oh, you don't know these Italian husbands," she continued, shrugging her beautiful shoulders. "I have one, so I know all about it. They go into paroxysms of fury even at the thought of having their wives go about without them, receiving the admiration of other men. I have no doubt that at this very moment my dear Morelli is either abusing one of the servants or breaking some of the furniture, just because I happen to be here while he is nursing his gouty foot at home. I am always proud of my countrymen when I see them, as you are, willing to let their wives enjoy themselves without them."

"I do not think I have observed this trait among American husbands developed to the extent you mention," Armstrong observed, with little enthusiasm.

"You haven't?" queried the contessa, innocently. "Perhaps that is because you are such a learned man, with your eyes upon your books instead of upon the world. You must take my word that it is so. But you know enough of the world to recognize admiration when you yourself become the object of it?"

Amélie fastened upon her companion an arch smile so full of meaning that Armstrong was caught entirely off his guard.

"I the object of admiration?" he asked, incredulously. "I wish I might think that you were speaking of your own."

The contessa laughed merrily. "I certainly laid myself open for that, did I not?" she replied. "Now suppose I had said adoration instead of admiration, then you would not have replied as you did."

"I should hardly have so presumed," he said, mystified by the contessa's conversation.

"Yet I have seen you the object of adoration—nothing less. I have seen eyes resting upon your face filled with a devotion which a woman never gives but once. You ought to feel very proud to be able to inspire all that, Mr. Armstrong. I should if I were a man."

"You have evidently mistaken me for some one else, contessa. Otherwise I cannot understand what you are saying."

Amélie looked at him curiously. "I wonder if you are really ignorant of all this?" she asked.

"You say that you have witnessed it, so it cannot be my wife of whom you speak, as you have never seen us together. I certainly know of no other woman who cares two straws about me. It must be that you have taken some one else for me."

"No; I am not mistaken."

Armstrong's curiosity proved stronger than his resentment. "And you have actually seen this?" he asked.

"Yes."

"Where and when?"

The contessa's mood had become serious. She realized that she was playing with dangerous weapons. "If you are sincere in what you say, Mr. Armstrong, you would not thank me for telling you."

"But you have gone so far that now I must insist." Helen's words suddenly came back to him as he spoke. The contessa saw a change of expression come over his face, and she held back her answer.

"Was it at the Laurentian Library?" Armstrong asked, impulsively.

Amélie smiled triumphantly. "It is really better for me not to answer that question, my dear Mr. Armstrong. I only meant to pay you a compliment, and I fear that I have touched on something I should have avoided. You will forgive me, will you not?"

Armstrong was for the moment too occupied with his own thoughts to comprehend fully what she said to him. Mechanically he pressed the hand which was held out to him, and a moment later the contessa entered into a merry conversation with some of her friends in the garden. Too late he realized that he had tacitly accepted the compromising position into which she had led him.

Emory left Helen in the midst of an animated group discussing in enthusiastic tones their appreciation of the many innovations. The musicians were concealed in the "snuggery," playing airs from favorite operas, while waiters from Doney's served *gelati* and *paste* and champagne at little tables scattered throughout the garden. The cool air was grateful to Helen, and she threw herself into the enjoyment of the moment. No one among her guests realized how little the brilliant, happy scene fitted in with the sorrow in her heart. Yet the musicians played on, the guests chatted merrily, and the lights reflected only that side of life which Helen felt was hers no more. The hour-glass filled and emptied, with no change save the departure of the guests.

As the last good-night was spoken Helen sought mechanically the low retaining wall against which she had so often rested. Jack and Uncle Peabody were for the moment inside the house, and she was alone. Yes, alone! How strongly she felt it, now that the stillness replaced the hum of voices which had filled the garden! Her features did not change, but a tear, unchecked as it was unbidden, coursed its way down her cheeks. Emory saw it as he approached, unnoticed, to say good-night.

"Helen!" he whispered, softly.

She turned quickly and brushed the tear away with her hand. "How you startled me!" she said. "I thought every one had gone."

"Helen," Emory repeated, "you are unhappy."

"I am tired," she replied, lightly; "that is all."

"No, that is not all," he insisted. "You are miserably unhappy."

"Don't, Phil," she entreated.

"I must, Helen," Emory kept on. "I should have no respect for myself if I kept silent another moment. All this time I have stood by and seen you suffer without saying a word, when I have longed to take you in my arms in spite of all and comfort you as you needed to be comforted."

"Phil, I beg of you!" Helen cried, beseechingly. "You must not say such things. I am not strong enough to stop you, and every word adds to the pain."

"Then there is pain!" cried Emory, fiercely. "At last I know it from your own lips. And if there is pain it gives me the right to protect you from it."

"Oh, Phil!" Helen sank helplessly into a chair.

"I have the right," Emory repeated. "My love, which you cast aside when you accepted him, now gives it to me; my loyalty in surrendering you to him for what I thought was your happiness now gives it to me; his selfishness and his neglect now give it to me. And I claim my right."

She made no reply. Convulsed with weeping, she sat huddled in the chair, helpless in her sorrow.

"I am going to Jack Armstrong now," continued Emory, savagely. "I am going to tell him what a brute he is and demand you of him. I did not give you up to be tortured by neglect while he devotes himself to his 'affinity.'" Emory's voice grew bitter. "And he calls it his 'masterpiece'! Better men than he have called it by another name."

Helen rose, white and ghostlike in the pale, dim light. She was calm again, and her voice was compelling in its quiet force.

"You have been my friend, Phil—a friend on whom I have felt I could rely always; yet you take this one moment, when I need real, honest friendship more than ever before in all my life, to add another burden. Is it kind, Phil—is it noble? I have suffered—I admit it. Jack is the cause of it—I admit that, too. You have discovered all this by pulling aside the veil which by my friend should have been held sacred; but with my heart laid bare before you, can you not see that it contains no thought except of him?"

"I do not believe it," Emory replied, stubbornly.

"You must believe it," she continued, with finality. "You know that my words are true. Jack Armstrong is my husband and I am his wife. We must forget what you have said and never refer to it again. Come, let us join them in the house."

"I can't, Helen."

"Then we must say good-night here."

Emory took the outstretched hand in his. For a moment their eyes met firmly. Then he raised her fingers to his lips.

"It is not good-night, Helen," he said, his voice breaking as he spoke; "do you understand, it is not good-night—it is good-bye."

Her glance did not falter, though a new sensation of pain passed through her heart. "Good-bye," she replied, faintly, as she gently withdrew her hand.

Armstrong watched Emory's hasty departure and Helen's slow return to the house from his unintentional place of concealment behind the oleanders, where his footsteps had been arrested by the sound of voices. The contessa's remarks had recalled with vivid intensity his conversation with Helen about Inez. She regarded his relations with Miss Thayer to be at least questionable, and he impatiently awaited the departure of the guests to tell Helen what had happened and to set himself right in her eyes. Now he had just heard Emory express himself even more pointedly upon the same subject.

The consciousness that he had been an eavesdropper, even though unwittingly, prevented him from carrying out his purpose. As he saw Helen drag herself rather than walk along the paths, he longed to fold her to his heart and brush away her doubts for all time; but to do this he must disclose his uncomfortable position, and this he could not do. His resentment against Emory faded away in the face of Helen's splendid loyalty. "My heart contains no thought except of him," he had heard her say; and he thanked God that his awakening had not come too late.

After a few moments he returned to the house from the opposite side of the garden.

"Where is Helen?" he asked Uncle Peabody, whom he met at the door.

"She has gone to her room, Jack," Mr. Cartwright replied, without meeting his eyes. "She said she was very tired, and asked particularly not to be disturbed."

Armstrong hesitated. She was hardly strong enough to talk the matter over to-night, anyway. It would be a kindness to leave it until to-morrow.

"Thank God it is not too late!" Uncle Peabody heard him repeat to himself, and the old man wondered if, after all, the sun was going to shine through the cypress-trees.

XXII

Helen did not come down to breakfast the next morning, so Armstrong and Miss Thayer found themselves at the library at their usual hour in spite of the festivities of the night before. The events of the evening impressed upon Jack the necessity of bringing his work to a speedy conclusion. With feverish haste, and forgetful of his companion, he seized his pen and transferred to the blank paper before him the words which came faster than they could be transcribed. Left to her own resources, Inez picked up the bunch of manuscript and settled back in her chair to run it over, glancing from time to time at Armstrong, who seemed consumed by the task before him. Accustomed as she was to his moods while at work, Inez was almost frightened by the present intensity. She hesitated even to move about lest he be disturbed, yet until he gave her something to do she was wholly unemployed.

For over an hour Armstrong's pen ran on. The fever was upon him, the message was in his mind, the spirit must be translated to the more tangible medium of words. At length, utterly exhausted for the moment, he threw aside his pen and leaned back in his chair.

"It is finished!" he cried, looking for the first time into Inez' face; "all is now actually written, and the revision alone remains."

Inez started to speak a word of congratulation, but in a flood of realization she knew that the companionship of the past three months was at an end. For the revision Armstrong would need no assistance; so she faltered for a moment, but the omission was unnoticed.

"I have just written the summary in the last chapter," Armstrong continued. "I have taken Michelangelo's allegorical statues in the Laurentian Chapel as typifying the characteristics and the tendencies of the period. All that I have written seems naturally to lead up to them. Listen."

In a rich, tense voice Armstrong read from the sheets which he gathered together in proper sequence:

"'Michelangelo himself has given us in his marbles the truest interpretation of the times in which he lived. After analyzing his correspondence and deducing from this the customs of the people, we turn to a consideration of the principles which lay beneath. The sculptor was a poet, and the soul of the poet found expression not through his words but through his hands. In the sacristy of San Lorenzo there are the tombs of the Medici, designed by

Michelangelo. They are unfinished, as is typical of the period in which they were designed. At the entrance to these tombs rest allegorical figures, which to the casual observer indicate phases of darkness and of light, of death and of life. They are two women and two men, and tradition names them 'Night' and 'Day,' 'Twilight' and 'Dawning.' To one who analyzes them, however, after a profound study of the times in which they were produced, comes a realization that they typify the character and the religious belief of the people themselves. These statues and their attendant genii are a series of abstractions, symbolizing the sleep and waking of existence, action, and thought, the gloom of death, the lustre of life, and the intermediate states of sadness and of hope that form the borderland of both. Life is a dream between two slumbers; sleep is death's twin-brother; night is the shadow of death, and death is the gate of life.

"'In each of these statues there is a palpitating thought, torn from the artist's soul and crystallized in marble. It has been said that architecture is petrified music; each of these statues becomes for us a passion, fit for musical expression, but turned, like Niobe, to stone. They have the intellectual vagueness, the emotional certainty that belong to the motives of a symphony. In their allegories, left without a key, sculpture has passed beyond her old domain of placid concrete form. The anguish of intolerable emotion, the quickening of the consciousness to a sense of suffering, the acceptance of the inevitable, the strife of the soul with destiny, the burden and the passion of mankind—this is the symbolism of the period as expressed by their cold, chisel-tortured marble.'"

"Splendid, my son!" spoke Cerini's proud voice as the librarian advanced toward them out of the dim recess in which he had been standing; "that is a fitting ending to a magnificent work. Your use of the statues as symbolisms of their period is masterly. I myself have felt it often, but with me the feeling has never found expression."

"What a period that was!" exclaimed Armstrong. "How it seizes one, even now, after four hundred years! Padre," he said to Cerini, after a moment's pause, "you say that this work of mine is good?"

The librarian nodded assent.

"If that is so," continued Armstrong, impressively, "it is no more to my credit than if Machiavelli or Leonardo or the Buonarroti himself had written it. It is they who have held my hand and guided my pen."

"Ah, my son," cried Cerini, with delight, "you are indeed a true humanist— a man in whom the ancients take delight! Too bad that you must drop it all, after your brief experience among this galaxy of greatness, to return to the humdrum of commonplace existence—too bad, too bad!"

"I shall never give it up, padre," Armstrong replied, firmly; "I could not if I tried." He paused as he recalled Helen's wan face and spiritless step. "I have been too intense. I owe it to my wife to share with her interests which lie along other lines, but my life-work has already been plotted out for me. I met these gods years ago, and I did not know them; I felt them calling me back to them, and I obeyed. They have let me sip their cup of wisdom, and he who once tastes that delectable draught runs the risk of becoming no longer his own master. I must leave them for a breathing-spell; I can never wholly give myself to them again; but never fear, I shall ever come back to them. I could not help it if I tried."

The librarian watched the enthusiasm of the younger man with rapture.

"My son, my son!" he cried, joyfully; "my life has not been spent in vain if I have succeeded in joining one such modern intellect to that noble band of sages who, though of the past, are ever in the present. And you, too, my daughter," he continued, turning to Inez—"you, too, have sipped the draught our friend speaks of; you, too, are linked irrevocably to the wisdom of the ages."

Inez bowed her head as if receiving a benediction.

"I have tasted of it, father," she replied, seriously, "but only in degree. This experience is one which can never be forgotten, can never be repeated. I feel as if I were saying good-bye to friends dear and true whom I shall never see again."

Armstrong looked at her curiously.

"I do not understand," he said. "Why should you ever say good-bye?"

Inez tried to smile, but her attempt ended in a pitiful failure.

"There is nothing very strange about it," she continued. "You and I drifted into this work together almost by accident. To me it has been a happy accident, and I like to think that I have helped a little in your splendid achievement. It has been an experience of a lifetime, but, like most experiences which are worth anything, it could never happen again."

Armstrong failed utterly to grasp the significance of her words.

"Of course not, unless you wished it so," he said.

"Not even though I wished it," replied Inez, firmly.

The contessa's words were in Armstrong's mind as he looked into her face. If Helen could hear what she had just said his explanations would be unnecessary. He wished the contessa were there, if she really possessed any such idea as her conversation had suggested. This girl in love with him, yet calmly stating that their association was at an end, and that any continuance was an impossibility!

"It has been a strain, Miss Thayer, as Helen said," he replied, finally; "I feel it myself. With the manuscript actually completed, I shall take my time in putting it into final shape. And now I suggest that we get out into the air. Suppose we take a little run in the motor-car out around San Domenico, and then back home, to surprise them at luncheon?"

Inez saw in Armstrong's suggestion a relaxing of the strained condition which she had brought upon herself.

"Perhaps Monsignor Cerini will join us," she added.

"Never!" replied the librarian, with sudden fervor. "I may indulge myself in air-ships when once they become popular, but never in an automobile! I will have Maritelli telephone for your car."

Inez smiled at Jack as they watched Cerini disappear through the door of his study. Then Armstrong's face grew serious.

"The old man loves me as if I were his son," he said, feelingly. "He is more proud of what I have done than if he had accomplished it himself."

"He has reason to be proud," replied Inez; "and so have we all."

In olden days the bishop who was obliged to visit his diocese at San Domenico or at Fiesole had not spoken so lightly of the trip. Setting out on mule-back, and scattering blessings as he left the Porta a Pinti by the road still called the Via Fiesolana, he hoped to reach the "Riposo dei Vescovi" in time for dinner. There, after a bountiful repast, he discarded his faithful beast of burden, and entered the ox-drawn sledge which the monks of San Domenico were bound to provide, reaching the hill-top, if all went well, about sunset. But this was before the days even of the stage-coaches, and before the modern tramway enabled Mother Florence to reach out and enfold her daughters in her arms.

The chauffeur carefully picked his way through the narrow Borgo San Lorenzo into the more spacious Piazza del Duomo. Passing around the apse of the cathedral, they entered the Via de' Servi.

"Sometime we must stop and take a look at these fine old palaces," said Armstrong, leaning forward and pointing down the street. "The Antinori, for instance, has just been restored, and it has one of the most stunning Renaissance court-yards in all Florence. We shall pass by it in a moment."

The car crossed the square of the SS. Annunziata, where they stopped for a moment again to admire Andrea Della Robbia's swaddled babies on the façade of the Foundling Hospital, and to look up from Tacca's statue of

Duke Ferdinand to the window of the Antinori Palace, hoping for a glimpse of that face from the past, whose history is recorded by Browning in his "Statue and the Bust." From this point the road was clearer, passing up the Via Gino Capponi, where Armstrong again pointed out the house of Andrea del Sarto—"the little house he used to be so gay in"—past the Capponi Palace, and also that of San Clemente, where lived and died the last Stuart Pretender. With increasing speed, they crossed the Viale Principe Amedeo, past the gloomy Piazza Savonarola, around the Cemetery of the Misericordia, to San Gervasio, where the real ascent began.

The sudden change from the close atmosphere of the library to the invigorating air acted as a tonic on Armstrong and his companion; and in addition to this the tension of three months' close application was lightened. The book was actually written! Inez thought she had never seen him in so incomparable a mood, as he called her attention to many little points of interest which, during other rides, had been passed unnoticed. On they went, olive gardens alternating with splendid villas on either side, until, almost before they realized it, San Domenico was reached, and they paused to regard the magnificent panorama spread out before their eyes. Armstrong looked back and saw the Via della Piazzola behind him. Then his glance turned to the steep hill in front. In a flood of memory came back to him the details of the last time he had been there—alone with Helen, so soon after their arrival in Florence.

"I measure everything by that day at Fiesole," she had said to him; "I believe it was the happiest day I ever spent."

How long ago it seemed to him, and how much had happened since! She was not happy now—she had told him so with her own lips; she had even been forced to acknowledge it to Emory. He had been forgetful of her during these weeks of study; but it was over now, and he would make it up to her. When she saw him back in his old semblance again her pain would pass away, her happiness return, and the present misunderstanding be forgotten.

His thoughts of Helen reminded him of his intention to return to the villa in time for luncheon, after which he would tell her how deeply he regretted all that had happened.

"Turn around, Alfonse," he said, looking at his watch, "and run home as fast as you can; we have hardly time to get there."

The return toward Florence was quickly made in spite of the sudden bends and narrow roads. Turning sharply at Ponte a Mensola, Alfonse increased his speed as they approached the hill leading from the Piazza of Settignano to the villa.

"Careful at the next turn, Alfonse; it's a nasty one," cautioned Armstrong, aware that his instructions were being carried out too literally.

The machine was nearer to the corner than Alfonse realized. He saw the danger, and with his hand upon the emergency-brake he threw his weight upon the wheel. Something gave way, and in another moment the car crashed against the masonry wall, the engine made a few convulsive revolutions, and then lay inert and helpless.

Inez was thrown over the low wall, landing without injury in the cornfield on the other side. Alfonse jumped, and found himself torn and bruised upon the road, with no injuries which could not easily be mended. But Armstrong, sitting nearest to the point of contact, lay amid the wreckage of the machine, still and lifeless, with a gash in the side of his head, showing where he had struck the wall.

By the time Inez had found an opening Alfonse had gathered himself up, and together they lifted Armstrong on to the grass by the side of the road. Two frightened women and a boy hurried out from the peasant's cottage near by, the women wringing their hands, the boy stupefied by fear.

"Some water, quick!" commanded Inez; and one of the women hastened to obey.

Wetting her handkerchief and kneeling beside the still figure, Inez bathed Armstrong's face and washed the blood from the ugly cut. She chafed his hands and felt his pulse. There was no response, and she turned her ashen face to the women watching breathless beside her.

"He is dead," she said, in an almost inarticulate voice. The women crossed themselves and burst into tears.

"May we take him in there," she asked, pointing to the cottage, "while the chauffeur brings his wife?"

Between them the body was gently lifted into the cottage and laid upon the bed in the best room. Then Alfonse set out upon his solemn mission.

"Leave me with him," Inez begged rather than commanded the woman who remained. "I will stay with him until they come."

She closed the door. Leaning against it for support, with her hand upon the latch, she gazed at the inanimate form upon the bed. The necessity of action had dulled her realization of the horror, and, sinking upon the floor, she buried her face in her hands, giving way for the first time to the tears which until now had been denied. The first paroxysm over, she raised her head and looked about the room. Every object in it burned itself into her mind: the straw matting on the floor, the cheap prints upon the wall, the rough cross and the crucified Saviour hanging over the bed. Dead—dead!

"Oh, God," she murmured, incoherently, to herself, "is this to be the solution of this awful problem—inexplicable in life, unendurable in death!"

Suddenly she rose from the floor and stood erect. She looked at the closed door—then turned to where the body lay. She rested her hand upon Armstrong's forehead. Then sitting upon the edge of the bed she gently lifted his arm and grasped his hand as her body became convulsed with heart-breaking sobs.

"Jack!" she cried, covering his hands with kisses, "Jack—speak to me! Tell me that you are not dead," she implored. "Oh no, no—that cannot be; you are too grand, too noble to die like this!"

She rose and stood for a moment looking down at him.

"Dead!" she repeated, piteously—"dead!" A hectic glow came into her face. "Then you are mine!" she cried, fiercely. "Jack, my beloved, you are mine, dear—do you hear?—and I am yours. Oh, Jack, how I have loved you all these weeks! Now I can tell you of it, dear—it will do no harm!"

Again she sat upon the bed and placed her hands upon his cheeks.

"My darling, my beloved!" she whispered. "Open your eyes just once and tell me that I may call you mine if only for this one terrible moment. This is our moment, dear—no one can take it from us! Have you not seen how I have loved you, how I have struggled to keep you from knowing it. Jack, Jack! this is the beginning and the end."

The room seemed to spin around, and before her eyes a mist gathered.

"I am dying, too, Jack," she said, frankly—"thank God, I am dying, too."

At last Nature applied her saving balm to the strained nerves, and Inez' sufferings were temporarily assuaged by that sweet insensibility which stands between the human mind and madness. So Helen found her, a few moments later, when pale and trembling she entered the room.

BOOK III

CO-PARTNER WITH NATURE

XXIII

Helen received the heart-breaking news from Alfonse with a degree of control which surprised even Uncle Peabody. Her questions were few, but so vital in their directness that by the time she had learned the nature and the seriousness of the accident, and the location of the cottage where her husband's body lay, she was hurrying to the scene of the calamity.

"Do you know where to reach an American or English surgeon?" she promptly asked Uncle Peabody, and his affirmative reply as he hastened to the telephone was the last word she heard as she left the villa.

Once in the cottage, she followed the guidance of the weeping, awe-struck peasants, who silently pointed out to her the room of death. She opened the door, and crossed the room with a firm step. Sinking to her knees beside the bed, she buried her face for a brief moment in her hands—then she rose quickly to her feet. With the help of the woman who had entered with her, she lifted Inez' inert figure from across her husband's body.

"She has fainted, poor child!" she said, quietly, divining that the girl's insensibility was not serious. "Let us take her into the next room."

Leaving the woman to provide for Inez' necessities, and giving her instructions how to act, Helen turned from the improvised cot to go back to Jack. His hands were still warm, but she could find no perceptible pulsation. She loosened his collar and moved his head a little to one side, discovering the wound for the first time. A cry of pain burst from her as she drew back sick and dizzy, her lips quivering and tears starting to her eyes. Then she leaned over him again, gently washing away the slight flow of blood with a moist cloth which one of the women handed her.

"Look!" she cried, pathetically, to Uncle Peabody, who entered the room a moment later, pointing to the wound and gazing into his eyes with her own distended by her suffering and her sense of helplessness.

Uncle Peabody put his arm about her, and rested his other hand upon Armstrong's wrist. "Dr. Montgomery will be here in a moment, Helen," he said, quietly, feeling instinctively that this was no time for words of sympathy. "I caught him at the Grand Hotel, and there was a motor-car at the door."

"He is dead!" was Helen's response, piteous in its intensity.

"Perhaps not, dear," replied Uncle Peabody, soothingly. "Let us stand by the window until the doctor comes."

Helen refused to suffer herself to be led away from her husband's side.

"I can't," she said, simply, shaking her head; "I must watch over him."

Then she turned back to resume her self-appointed vigil, and suddenly found herself looking into his open eyes.

"Jack!" she cried, seizing his face in her hands as she again sank upon her knees—"oh, Jack!"

She could find no other words in the revulsion which swept over her. Her cry quickly brought Uncle Peabody, and the women drew near to behold the miracle of the dead brought to life; but all except Helen fell back as the doctor entered.

"He lives, doctor!" she exclaimed exultantly, her face radiant with joy.

"Then there is hope," he replied, with a reassuring smile, as he began the examination of his patient.

Helen followed every motion as the doctor proceeded, encouraged by the confidential little nods he made at the conclusion of each process, as if answering in the affirmative certain questions which he put to himself. Armstrong again opened his eyes as the doctor carefully investigated the depth of the wound, and his lips moved slightly. Helen impulsively drew nearer, but the sound was barely articulate.

The doctor drew back the lids and peered intently into his open eyes, nodding again to himself. At length he turned to the silent group about him, who so eagerly waited for the verdict.

"Will he live?" was Helen's tense question as she seized his arm.

Dr. Montgomery looked into the upturned face with a kindly smile. "I hope so, Mrs. Armstrong," he answered, quietly. "It is a severe concussion of the brain, and we must await developments."

"Are there unfavorable signs?" asked Uncle Peabody, anxiously.

"No; quite the contrary so far. There is no fracture of the skull, and the normal size of the pupils shows no serious injury to the brain."

"The unconsciousness is due simply to the concussion?"

"Exactly."

"Then what do you fear?"

"There is always danger of meningitis. We can tell nothing about this until later."

"Will it be safe to move him?" asked Helen.

"Yes; and you had better do so. I must dress and sew up the wound, and then he can be carried home on a stretcher. Suppose you leave me alone with him now, while I make his head a bit more presentable."

Helen's buoyancy was contagious as she and Uncle Peabody started to leave the room, but Jack's voice recalled them.

"It is—the symbolism—of the period," he muttered, incoherently.

"It is all right," the doctor replied to Helen's startled, unspoken interrogation. "He is delirious, and will be so for days."

Satisfied with the explanation, they passed through the door into the next room, where they found Inez sitting weakly in an arm-chair, her hair dishevelled, her face white as marble, supported by the woman in whose care she had been left.

Helen hurried to her. "He is not dead!" she cried, joyfully—"do you hear, Inez? Jack is alive, and the doctor thinks he will recover!"

Inez answered with a fresh flood of tears. "Oh, Helen! Helen!" she murmured, clinging impulsively to her arm.

Helen's recovery came much more spontaneously than did Inez'. With the one the pendulum had made a completed swing, and the depths at one extreme had been offset by the heights at the other. Inez, however, was hopelessly distraught by the accumulated weight of a multitude of emotions: the physical shock of the accident, the horror of the situation as it first burst upon her with unmitigated force, the involuntary tearing from her heart of the mask it had worn for so many months—and now the painful joy of the reaction. She rested in her chair, almost an inert mass, in total collapse of mind and body.

"I could not help it, Helen," she murmured, piteously, as her friend pushed back the dishevelled hair from her hot forehead.

"Of course you could not, dear," Helen cried, smiling through her tears of joy at the obvious relief her words gave. "Oh, I am so happy, Inez!"

Helen's face grew pale again as her thoughts returned to those first awful moments, which now seemed so long ago. "I really thought him dead, Inez," she continued, after a moment's silence. "We could not have endured that, could we, dear? Now we will take him to the villa and nurse him back to health and strength. How strange it will seem to him not to be able to do things for himself!"

"Is he—badly hurt?" ventured Inez.

"The doctor can't tell yet, but he feels encouraged."

"Is he—conscious?"

"Not wholly—and the doctor says he will be delirious for days."

"Oh," replied Inez, again relaxing.

Dr. Montgomery quietly entered the room, carefully closing the door after him. "All goes well," he replied to the questions before they were put to him. "The patient is resting quietly and may be moved as soon as a stretcher can be secured. Your villa is near by, I think Mr. Cartwright said?"

"The stretcher is being prepared," replied Uncle Peabody, answering the doctor's question, "and I have sent for two strong men."

"Good. Have I another patient here?" Dr. Montgomery turned to Inez.

"She is suffering only from the shock," answered Helen.

"Let me take you both home in my motor-car," suggested the doctor.

"Take Miss Thayer," Helen replied, quickly.

"Oh no!" Inez shuddered; "I can never enter one of those awful things again!"

Dr. Montgomery smiled indulgently. "It will really be better, Miss Thayer, and I will personally guarantee your safe arrival."

"I would rather walk beside the stretcher," Helen continued; "there might be something I could do."

The doctor bowed as he acquiesced. "Your husband will require very little to be done for him for some days, Mrs. Armstrong," he said; "but if you prefer to stay near him your suggestion is better than mine."

"Did he speak again, doctor?" asked Helen.

"Yes," he replied, with a professional shrug; "but he said nothing. You must pay no attention to his ramblings. His mind will remain a blank until Nature supplies the connecting link. In the mean time he will require simply quiet and rest."

Uncle Peabody's stretcher was soon ready for service, and the still unconscious burden was gently lifted upon it and carried with utmost tenderness up the hill to the villa, where old Giuseppe and the maids received the party with unaffected joy at the good news that their master would survive the accident that had befallen him. With the aid of the trained nurse they found awaiting them, Armstrong was carefully transferred from the stretcher to his own bed, Inez was made comfortable in her room, and the doctor sat down upon the veranda with Helen and Uncle Peabody, who welcomed a moment's rest after the wearing experience of the past hour.

"Tell us the probabilities of the case, Dr. Montgomery," said Uncle Peabody. "Mr. and Mrs. Armstrong were planning to return to Boston soon, and now it will of course be necessary to rearrange their plans."

"Naturally," assented the doctor. "I will tell you all I can. These cases are somewhat uncertain, but the patient's delirium will surely last for several days. Then comes a slow period of convalescence, during which time the body repairs much more rapidly than the mind. You cannot count on less than two months, even with everything progressing favorably."

Uncle Peabody glanced over to where Helen was sitting.

"I don't care how long it takes," she replied to his implied interrogation, "so long as he gets well."

Dr. Montgomery smiled as he rose to take his leave. "My patient is evidently in good hands," he said. "The nurse will do all that needs to be done until I return in the course of an hour or two."

Helen and Uncle Peabody sat in silence for some moments after the doctor departed. There was nothing further to be done for the present, as both Jack and Inez were resting as comfortably as could be expected under the circumstances, and absolute quiet was the one thing needful.

"Well," said Uncle Peabody, at length, "it is the unexpected which has happened again."

"Yes," Helen assented without looking up; "if it keeps on happening with such startling regularity I shall begin to expect it, and then your theory will lose its point."

Uncle Peabody was in a thoughtful rather than an argumentative mood.

"If I was not afraid you would think me heartless, Helen, I would say that I believe I see the hand of Providence in this."

She looked up quickly.

"Of course, assuming that Jack recovers," he hastened to add.

"I am afraid my philosophy is hardly equal to this test," Helen replied, unsympathetically. "I am supremely happy that the affair is not so serious as it seemed at first, but I can't see anything particularly providential in the injury poor Jack has sustained, nor in the suffering he must pass through at best."

"Is it not just possible that this long period of convalescence, which Dr. Montgomery says is inevitable, may bring him to himself again?"

Helen smiled sadly. "It was the work at the library which brought him to himself, uncle. A separation from those influences which so strongly affected him there may result in a return to the old self I knew before we came here; but that is not his real self."

"If he returns to that condition, no matter what brings it about, will it not simplify matters?"

"I can't see how," replied Helen, seriously. "If I had never known this new development in Jack's nature, I should of course be quite content to have him return to his former self; but having seen him as he really is, I could never accept any condition which allows him no development of his higher and stronger personality. It would not be fair either to him or to me."

Uncle Peabody regarded Helen curiously. "Let me make myself clearer," he said, with considerable emphasis. "Only this very morning you were discussing with me the final outcome of what appeared to be a domestic tragedy. Your husband was controlled by the spell of the old-time learning which had reached out from its antiquity to grasp a modern convert. You were convinced that Miss Thayer's sentiments toward your husband had developed into affection, and you stated in so many words that if Jack did not reciprocate this affection he really ought to do so, because she was the one woman in the world qualified by nature to be his wife. In the presence of this overwhelming condition you very generously planned—and I expressed to you how much I admired your spirit—to eliminate yourself, and to sacrifice your own happiness in order to enable your husband to accomplish his destiny."

"You are making sport of me—it is most unkind!" she cried, reproachfully.

"You know I wouldn't do that," insisted Uncle Peabody. "I am merely presenting a simple statement of the case in order to prove my original assertion. Please let me continue. Just as the crisis seems to be at hand this accident occurs. In a most unexpected manner Jack is instantly divorced from the influences which have drawn him away from you. The break between him and Miss Thayer has been accomplished naturally, and he has been placed in his wife's hands to be nursed back to health—during which experience you both will come to know each other far better than ever before. Again I say—I believe I see the hand of Providence in the whole affair."

Helen waited to make quite sure that Uncle Peabody had finished. "I wonder if it is I who always see things differently," she said, "or if a man's viewpoint is of necessity different from a woman's. I love Jack more than I can ever express—and this accident has brought that devotion nearer to the surface than I have dared to let it come for many weeks. I have suffered in seeing him drawn away from me, and in realizing that I was becoming less and less essential to his life. Yet, through it all, I have understood. I have suffered to think that any other woman could be more to him than I am, but my love has not blinded my eyes to what I have actually seen. These are conditions which cannot be changed, even by this accident. Suppose it does separate him from all those influences which have brought about the crisis, as you call it; suppose that because of this separation, and the physical weakness through which he must pass, Jack turns to me as before, and for the time being believes that I am more to him than all else in the world—will this change the conditions themselves?"

"Do you mean that you would not accept this change in him?"

"I mean that I would not take advantage of it," replied Helen, firmly. "I have seen the development which has taken place in Jack from the moment of our first meeting down to the present time. Even with the sorrow it has cost me I admire that development. Had I possessed equal possibilities, all would have been well. As I did not, it would be the act not of love but of tyranny to stand between him and his grander potentiality."

"But suppose that as Jack recovers he comes to a realization that his obsession has been a mistake—that your love and companionship really mean more to him than anything he can get elsewhere?"

"That would be a retrogression, after what I have seen him pass through. As I just said, if I possessed the ability to rise to him, what you suggest might be a possibility; but I would never consent to have him assume a lower plane than that upon which he belongs simply that I may retain my claim."

Helen rose as she spoke and walked slowly down the veranda. Uncle Peabody watched her retreating figure, and studied her face as she returned and leaned against one of the pillars in silence.

"Why do you think it would force him to take a lower plane?" he asked, pointedly.

Helen turned abruptly and looked at him with an expression of frank surprise. "Why do I think so?" she repeated. "What a foolish question!"

"Still, I ask you for an answer," Uncle Peabody insisted.

"Because he is so far ahead of me in every way," Helen answered, simply.

"Suppose this is not true?"

"But it is."

"Why are you so positive?"

"Because it is quite apparent to every one—to Jack, to Cerini, and even to myself."

Uncle Peabody rose and stood beside her, taking her face between his hands and looking kindly into her eyes.

"You are not so far behind him as you think," he said, firmly. "Whatever the distance between you may have been when you were first married, the trials I have seen you endure have wrought changes at least as great as those you have noticed in Jack. You are a brave, strong woman, Helen, and your development has been from within outward. I wish I could say as much for him."

"You are trying to give me courage, you dear old comforter," Helen replied, unconvinced but with a grateful smile.

"I am trying to show you yourself as you really are, my child," Uncle Peabody replied, "and to help you to recognize an act of Providence when one falls your way."

XXIV

Dr. Montgomery's approximate estimate of the duration of Armstrong's delirium proved to be only a few days shorter than the actual fact. In less than a week all anxiety regarding any possible complications was set at rest by the doctor's report that his patient was progressing normally and as well as could be expected. The skull had sustained no injury, and the brain suffered only from the concussion. The household became accustomed to the still figure, which gave evidence of its returning strength only by the increasing frequency of incoherent ramblings, the voice developing in firmness as the days progressed.

Inez was about again by this time, and with sunken eyes and ashen face shared with Helen the privilege of watching beside the patient during the last week of his unconsciousness. But it was a different Inez from the serious but happy and alert girl who had sat beside Armstrong in the automobile when it had crashed against the wall. The burden of bearing her secret alone, during all these weeks, had been in itself a wearing experience, but this was as nothing compared with the agony of soul through which she had since passed. The very struggle with herself, and the sense of personal sacrifice she experienced, had previously served in her own mind to sanctify her affection and to justify its existence. Now that she had allowed her passion to burst from her control, all justification was at an end. Her womanhood and sense of right seemed to separate themselves from her weaker emotions, and to judge and condemn them without mitigation.

It was natural that Helen should attribute her changed condition to the horror of the accident itself; yet Inez knew that the scene which was enacted in her mind over and over again until it almost drove her mad was that of her own shameless disloyalty. She shuddered as it returned to her even now while sitting beside Armstrong's bed; she shrank from Helen's sympathetic caress and her thoughtful solicitude. If she could only cry out and proclaim to them all the unworthy part she had performed, she would feel some sense of relief in the self-abasement it must bring to her.

Armstrong's delirious wanderings were a sore trial to Inez, but she accepted and bore them with the unflinching courage of an ascetic. The sound of his voice, the undirected, expressionless gaze of his eyes, the uncertainty of what each disconnected sentence might call to mind—all drove fresh barbs into a soul already tortured by self-condemnation. At first his mind had seemed to center itself upon his wife and his enforced separation from her.

"When it is finished," he had murmured, tossing from side to side and finally raising his hand as if reaching out to some one—"when it is finished she will understand."

"She does understand, dear," Helen had cried out, seizing his hand and pressing it to her lips; but instantly he withdrew it, and his words again became incoherent and meaningless.

At another time, when both Helen and Inez were sitting near by, his eyes opened, and he seemed to be looking directly at his wife.

"She refuses to continue the work, Helen," he said, as she sprang to his side, believing that at last his mind had cleared—"you were quite wrong, do you not see?"

Helen looked at Inez quickly, noting the swift color which suffused her pale face, but before a word could be spoken the invalid had relapsed into his former condition. Inez made an excuse to escape from the room for a moment. "You were quite wrong—do you not see?" she repeated Armstrong's words to herself. Was he simply rambling, or had the subject been brought up for previous discussion? Inez' conscience, sensitive from the load already resting upon it, quivered with new apprehensiveness. Yet Helen's attitude toward her had in no way changed—in fact, the awful anxiety of the first suspense, together with the later mutual responsibilities which they had shared, had seemed to Inez to draw them even more closely to each other. She tried to gain an answer to her inward questionings from Helen's face as she re-entered the room, but found there nothing but cordiality and friendliness.

"He must be getting nearer and nearer to a return of consciousness," Helen had said, quite naturally; "but how he wanders!" She looked over affectionately to her husband, still and helpless, but breathing with the steady regularity of convalescence. "Sometimes it is about his work at the library—sometimes it is about me. What agony of spirit he must be passing through if he realizes any of it!"

"He loves you, Helen," Inez cried, impulsively—"he loves you now, just as he always has!"

"Of course." Helen looked up questioningly from her fancy work. She was not yet ready to take Inez into her confidence. "What a strange remark, dear! Is it not quite natural that my husband should love me?"

Helen's smiling face, as she asked her simple but disconcerting question, completely unnerved Inez.

"He has been so worried about the time which his work compelled him to be away from you," Inez replied, at length, trying to conceal her confusion. "He finished the first draft of the book the day of the accident. His first thought, after he put down his pen, was to return to the villa, that he might surprise you at lunch."

"Cerini!" called Armstrong.

Helen placed her hand upon his forehead soothingly.

"I owe it to my wife—" the invalid continued; "but I shall come back— come back."

"Yes, dear, you shall go back," she answered, quietly, resting her cheek against his—"you shall go back."

"When it is finished—" Armstrong murmured, again subsiding into silence.

So the days passed, one by one, differing little, each from the other, yet filled with many and conflicting emotions on the part of the faithful watcher by the bedside. With all its pain, Helen welcomed this period during which she could work out her problem with the unconscious help of the rambling, disconnected sentences which escaped from her husband's lips. Sometimes they were full of tenderness for her; again they were reproaches, levelled at himself for his neglect; but most frequently they made reference to his work in some of its various stages. Alternately her heart was touched by his apparent affection for her, and the wound again torn open by his appeal to or dependence upon Inez. But through it all came the one conviction, which needed but this strengthening reassurance to make her determined path seem certain—that whatever drew him away from his work and back to her was a sense of duty, and that alone.

Helen questioned Dr. Montgomery upon the ordinary phenomena in cases such as this.

"His mutterings may be absolutely meaningless," he replied to her questions, "or they may be thoughts or actual repetitions of conversations which he has previously had."

"In the latter case, would he be likely to repeat them correctly?"

"Yes, provided he repeats them at all."

"And these thoughts or conversations, if correctly repeated, would presumably indicate his convictions at the time they occurred?"

"His convictions at the time they occurred," Dr. Montgomery assented; "but their reliability as normal expressions would depend upon his mental condition at the time the thoughts occurred or the words were spoken."

Armstrong's recovery came unexpectedly, even after the long days of waiting. The perfect July day was drawing to a close, and Helen had watched the sinking sun from the window beside his bed. It was all so beautiful! The world seemed full of glorious hopefulness and promise, and her heart filled to overflowing at the thought that for her, who loved it so, that promise no longer held good. She turned to the silent figure lying upon the bed. Would he ever realize what she had gone through and must still endure for him? She sank upon her knees, burying her face in the counterpane, as if to shut out the overpowering grandeur, which produced so sad a contrast. Suddenly she felt a hand resting upon her head, and a voice spoke her name.

She looked up quickly straight into her husband's eyes, now wide open and filled with an expression so full of love and devotion that her heart sprang forth in eager response. It was the expression which his face had worn when she had first confessed her love for him, and the intervening months, with their brief joy and their long sorrow, were obliterated on the instant. Once more he was the devoted, thoughtful, irresistible lover, and Helen felt the weight of years roll off her tired shoulders, leaving her the happy, buoyant girl, proud of having won this strong man's affection. She gazed at him silently, fearing lest the eyes close again, and unwilling to lose a moment of their present significance; but they remained open.

"Helen," Armstrong repeated, still looking intently at her, "be patient, dear. I know how shamefully I have neglected you, I know how much I have hurt you; but my work is nearly finished now. Then, believe me, all will be as before."

The voice was calm and sustained. There was no hesitation, no rambling. Still, she did not fully comprehend that he was himself again.

"Yes, dear," she replied, humoring him; "then all will be as before."

He could not see the sharp pain which showed in her face as she spoke, nor did he realize how her heart wished that it might be so.

"I must get up," he continued, after a moment's silence. "What time is it? I shall be late at the library."

"You have finished your work for to-day, Jack," she answered, quietly.

"Have I?" he asked, simply.

His glance slowly wandered about the room. "Is it not morning?" he queried, at length.

"It is afternoon," she replied, turning toward the window. "See—the sun is just sinking behind San Miniato."

"Afternoon?" he queried, vaguely—"afternoon, and I still in bed?"

"You have not been well," she volunteered, guardedly, carefully following the doctor's injunctions. "Don't bother now; you will be feeling much better in the morning."

"Not well?" Armstrong's mind was groping around for some familiar landmark upon which to fasten. "I was at the library—was it this morning?—Cerini was there, Miss Thayer was there—where is Miss Thayer?"

"She went out only a moment ago. But don't try to think about it now. It will be much better for you to do that later."

He weakly acquiesced and closed his eyes, still holding her hand firmly grasped in his own. The doctor found him gently sleeping, with Helen watching patiently beside him, when he entered the room an hour later.

She held up her disengaged hand warningly. "He is himself again," she whispered.

"Good!" replied Dr. Montgomery, with satisfaction. "Tell me about it."

"That is splendid," he said, when she had recounted the details; "he is progressing famously. You won't be able to keep him from questioning, but try to let the awakening come as gradually as possible."

The morning brought renewed strength to the invalid. The nurse called Helen as soon as Armstrong wakened, and he plied her with countless interrogations. Uncle Peabody came in to see him immediately after a light breakfast had been served, but Inez, upon one pretext or another, delayed entering the sick-room.

"It will be better for him to become accustomed to his new conditions," she urged, when Helen suggested her going to see him. "You and Mr. Cartwright should have these first moments with him. Later I shall be only too glad to help in any way I can."

But Armstrong himself was not to be denied.

"There is more to all this than you are telling me," he said, petulantly, at last, after learning from Helen and Uncle Peabody such details as he could draw forth regarding the duration of his illness and its general nature. "I remember now leaving the library in the motor-car with Miss Thayer. We went—where did we go? Oh yes; to San Domenico. Then we came home. Did we come home?" he asked, with uncertainty in his voice; but before an answer could be given he had himself supplied the connecting link.

"I have it!" he cried, raising himself upon his elbow—"there was an accident. Alfonse tried to take that turn at the foot of the hill, and we smashed against the wall."

"Yes," Helen assented, trying to calm his rising excitement, "there was an accident, and you were badly hurt; but you are nearly well now. Please go slowly, Jack, or you will undo all that your long rest has accomplished. There is plenty of time."

"But Miss Thayer," he replied, not heeding her admonition and glancing about searchingly. "Where is Miss Thayer? She was injured, too?"

"Not seriously," Helen reassured him.

"Then where is she?"

"I don't know exactly, but she is not far away."

"You have not sent her away while I have been ill?" he asked, with a touch of his former suspicion.

"No, Jack." All of the tired, strained tone came back in Helen's voice as she turned away from the bed to conceal her disappointment.

Armstrong sensed it all as he had failed to do at other times since the gap had begun to widen.

"I did not mean that, Helen," he said, and reaching over he took her hand and drew her to him; "I really did not mean it."

"It is all right, Jack," Helen replied, withdrawing her hand and trying to smile; "I will find Inez and send her to you." And before he could remonstrate she had left the room.

While he waited Armstrong had a brief moment of introspection. Again he had wounded her, and for no cause. He had enjoyed the short period since his awakening, particularly on account of the tender and affectionate care Helen had given him, which she had for a long time withheld because of his own self-centred interest. It was with real regret that he found this little visit with his wife so abruptly brought to an end, yet he himself had forced the termination. He must fight against this unfortunate attribute, he told himself, and show Helen his real feelings toward her.

His reveries were interrupted by Inez' entrance. Silently she stood beside him, holding out her hand, which he quietly grasped for a moment and then released. He wondered at the color in her face and at her apparent unwillingness to meet his glance.

"They tell me we have been through an accident together," he said, slowly. "Thank God it was I who was injured and not you."

Inez turned from him, closing her eyes involuntarily. "Don't speak of it!" she cried, impulsively; "it was too awful!"

"But it is all over now."

"All but the memory," she replied, faintly. "Let us forget it, I beg of you."

"I was going to ask you for some of the details," Armstrong continued, "which you alone can give."

"Oh, I beg of you," she repeated; "I could not bear it."

"Then by all means let us forget it," he replied, curiously affected by the girl's emotion. "Perhaps some time later you will feel more like talking about it. You see, I can remember nothing after the crash against the wall."

"Thank God!" cried Inez, passionately, turning away her head.

"I suppose it is better so," Armstrong assented, still wondering at the intensity of her emotion. "But when one has had a whole fortnight of his life blotted out, he naturally feels a bit of curiosity concerning what happened during all that time."

"You must excuse me, Mr. Armstrong. You don't know how this tortures me, and I really cannot bear it."

Armstrong watched the girl as she turned and fairly fled from the room, completely mystified by her extraordinary attitude.

"What in the world can have happened?" he asked himself; and then he settled back on the pillow and tried to answer his own question.

XXV

There is no place like the sick-room for self-examination and introspection. In the still monotony of the slow-passing days, the invalid's mind is freed from the conventions of every-day complexities, and can view its problems with a veracity and a clearness at other times impossible. As Armstrong's convalescence continued, he marshalled before him certain events which had occurred since his arrival in Florence, and examined them with great minuteness. Some of these seemed trivial, and he wondered why they came back at this time and forced themselves upon him with such persistence; some of them were important, and he realized that Helen had much of which she might justly complain.

His eyes followed her as she moved about the room, quick to anticipate each wish or necessity, and sweetly eager to respond; yet he distinctly felt the barrier between them. He was conscious now that this barrier had existed for some time, and he found it difficult to explain to himself why he had only recently become aware of it. Helen's conversations with him came back with renewed force and vital meaning. He had resented it when she had told him that his work at the library had made him indifferent to everything else, yet she had been quite right in what she said. He had wilfully misunderstood her efforts to bring him back to himself, and had openly blamed her for faults which existed only in his own neglect. He had accused her of being jealous of his intimacy with Miss Thayer, yet her attitude toward Inez was a constant refutation. He had treated her even with incivility and unpardonable irritability.

The fault was his, he admitted, yet were there not extenuating circumstances? No one could have foreseen how completely engrossed he was to become in his work, or the extent of the mastery which the spell of this old-time learning was to gain over him. Naturally, he would have avoided it had he foreseen it; but once under its influence he had been carried forward irresistibly, unable to withdraw, unwilling to oppose. And yet he had boasted of his strength!

"You have become infinitely bigger and stronger and grander," Helen had said to him, even when her heart was breaking, "and I admire you just so much the more."

Armstrong winced as these words came home to him. With so much real cause for complaint and upbraiding, Helen had gently tried to show him his shortcomings, tempering her comment with expressions full of loyalty and affection.

But on one point she had been wholly wrong. It was natural that she should have misinterpreted the intimacy which a community of interests had brought about between Miss Thayer and himself. Inez was, of course, much stronger intellectually than Helen, and by reason of this was far better fitted to assist him in his own intellectual expressions. But their intimacy had never extended beyond this even in thought or suggestion. Helen had insisted that Inez was in love with him, and he had tried to show her the absurdity of her suspicion. Here, at least, he had been in the right. Throughout their close association, and even after Helen had spoken, he had never discovered the slightest evidence that any such affection existed. The still unexplained remarks of the contessa's might or might not be significant. Emory, of course, was prejudiced, and his comments did not require serious consideration. Miss Thayer's refusal to continue the work, the comparative infrequency of her visits to his sick-chamber—in fact, everything went to show how far Helen had wandered from the actual facts.

Armstrong found some comfort in this conclusion. With Helen so unquestionably wrong in this hypothesis, it of course went without saying that she was equally wrong in what she had said later. She believed that he had a career before him. Cerini had said the same thing, Miss Thayer had said so—and Armstrong himself believed, in the consciousness of having completed an unusual piece of work, that such a possibility might exist. He felt no conceit, but rather that overpowering sense of hopefulness which comes to a man as a result of successful endeavor—not yet crowned, but completed to his own satisfaction. If this career was to be his, he could not follow Helen's assumption that it must separate them. That was, of course, as ridiculous as her feelings about Inez. Success for him must mean the same to her, his wife. When the right time came he would take up these two points specifically with her and show her the error which had misled her.

This self-examination covered several days. At first Armstrong found himself unable to think long at a time without becoming mentally wearied; but by degrees his mind gained in vigor, and proved fully equal to the demands made upon it. The details of what had happened on the day of the accident came back to him one by one up to the point of the accident itself, but he felt annoyed that he could not learn more of this. From Helen, Uncle Peabody, and the doctor he knew of the early belief that he had been killed and of the excitement caused by his revived respiration. Of his period of delirium, the nurse had given him more information than the others; but of the break between the moment when the car struck the wall, and the time when Helen arrived upon the scene, Miss Thayer alone held the key. Armstrong's curiosity regarding this interval was, perhaps, heightened by the evident aversion which she felt to discussing it. To mention the subject in her presence was certain to drive her from the room, her face blazing with color, her body trembling in every nerve.

The patient was able to move about a little by this time, and at the close of each day he found relief from the monotony of his room and the veranda by short walks in the garden, rich in its midsummer gorgeousness of color. A couch had been placed near the retaining wall, so that he could rest upon it whenever he felt fatigued. Between his solicitude concerning the situation with Helen, and his determination to discover from Miss Thayer the occasion of her remarkable attitude, his thoughts were fully occupied.

On this particular afternoon Armstrong had thrown himself upon the couch, and for a moment closed his eyes. With no warning he saw a scene enacted before his mental vision in which he himself was the central figure. He was lying still and lifeless upon the grass by the roadside at the foot of the hill. Four other figures were in the picture. He recognized Inez, but the other women and the boy he had never seen. The figures moved about, as in a kinetoscope. One of the women ran into the cottage and returned with a basin of water. Inez knelt beside him and bathed his forehead. He could see the tense expression on her face. She seemed to speak to the women, but he could distinguish no words. Then he saw himself lifted and carried into the cottage. At this point the picture disappeared as suddenly as it had come.

Armstrong opened his eyes when he found the picture gone, and sat up, gazing about him excitedly. He saw Inez crossing the veranda and called to her abruptly.

"Tell me," he cried, as she hastened to obey the summons and before she reached him, "who carried me into the cottage after the accident?"

The girl paled at the suddenness and intensity of the question. "There were four of us," she said, faintly—"two peasant women, a boy, and myself."

Armstrong passed his hand over his forehead and gazed at Inez intently. So far, then, his vision had been correct. Breathlessly he pursued his interrogations.

"Before that did one of the women bring some water from the cottage, and did you kneel beside me and bathe my face?"

"Yes. Who has told you?"

"Then it all happened just like that?"

"Like what?" Inez was trembling, vaguely apprehensive.

Armstrong rose. "Why, as you have just said," he replied. "You know I have been trying to get you to tell me about it."

"You are unkind," Inez retorted, quickly. "You know how much all mention of this pains me, yet you persist."

"Forgive me." Armstrong controlled himself and held out his hand kindly. "I don't mean to hurt you, believe me, but my mind is ever searching out that connecting link. You won't tell me about it, so I suppose I shall never find it."

She started to reply, but as quickly checked herself. "There is nothing for me to tell," she said, at length, without looking up. "I will send Helen to you," she added, as she hastened away.

Armstrong again threw himself upon the couch, and, trying to assume the same position, closed his eyes in a vain endeavor to summon back the vision he had seen. If it had only continued a little longer he might have learned all! The fugitive nature of his quest proved a fascination, and day after day he exerted every effort to gratify his whim.

Inez clearly avoided him. Whether or not this was apparent to the other members of the family he could not tell, but it was quite obvious to him. There must be some reason beyond what he knew, and he had almost stumbled upon it! Another week passed by, more rapidly than any since his convalescence began because of the determination with which he pursued his baffling problem.

Again he lay upon his couch in the garden, his eyes closed, but with his mind fixed upon its one desire. Suddenly he felt the presence of some one. A thrill of expectation passed through him, but he dared not open his eyes lest the impression should disappear. For what seemed a long time he was conscious of this person standing beside him, and he knew that whoever it might be was gazing at him intently. Then he felt a hand gently take his arm, which was hanging over the side of the couch, and, raising it carefully, place it in a more comfortable position. Then the hand rested for a moment on his forehead.

Opening his eyes a little, as if by intuition, he saw Miss Thayer tiptoeing along the path toward the house. He closed his eyes again, and as he did so he felt a sudden return of the subconscious impression.

Now, in his mind's eye he saw a cheaply furnished room, and Miss Thayer leaning, with ashen face and dishevelled hair, against a closed door. He saw her sink upon the floor and pass through a paroxysm of grief. She murmured some incoherent words, and then stood erect, looking straight at him as he lay upon the bed. Then she lifted his arm, just as she had a moment before, and covered his hand with kisses, sobbing the while with no attempt at control.

"Speak to me!" he seemed to hear her say. "Tell me that you are not dead!" He could feel the intensity of her gaze even as he lay there. "Jack, my beloved; you are mine, dear—do you hear?—and I am yours." Beads of perspiration gathered on his forehead. "How I have loved you all these weeks!... Now I can tell you of it, dear—it will do no harm!"

Held by a force he could not have broken had he wished, Armstrong watched the progress of the tragedy.

"My darling, my beloved!" he heard Inez whisper; "open your eyes just once, and tell me that I may call you mine if only for this one terrible moment.... This is our moment, dear—no one can take it from us!... Have you not seen how I have loved you, how I have struggled to keep you from knowing it?... Jack! Jack! this is the beginning and the end!"

He could endure the scene no longer. With a look of horror on his face, he sprang to his feet and glanced about him. He was alone in the garden. He stumbled rather than walked to the retaining wall, and rested against it for support.

"Great God!" he cried, aloud, "have I regained my mind only to lose it again?"

He glanced toward the house. There was no one in sight, but Helen was playing Debussy's "Claire de Lune" upon the piano in the hall, and the sound of the music soothed him.

"Dreams—hallucinations," he repeated to himself. "God! what an experience!"

XXVI

With Armstrong's convalescence progressing so satisfactorily, Helen returned to her music with a clear conscience. She was determined that the influence upon him of her personal presence should be reduced as nearly as possible to a minimum. Naturally, during the period of his illness and the attendant weakness, she had been with him almost constantly; naturally he had turned to her with what seemed to be his former affection. But the die was cast, and the accident which for the time being interrupted the progress of events predestined to occur could in no way prevent their final accomplishment. Helen thought often of Uncle Peabody's optimistic suggestion that the present condition was bound to straighten matters out, but she refused to be buoyed up by false hopes, only to suffer a harder blow when once again Armstrong became what she believed to be himself. She saw no gain in tuning up the heart-strings to their former pitch, when neither she nor Jack could again play upon them with any degree of harmony.

Helen was with her husband for whatever portion of the day he needed her, whether it was to read aloud to him, or to converse, or to wander about the garden. She served each meal to him with her own hands, and watched the progress of his improvement so carefully that nothing remained undone. Yet, with deliberate intention, she was with him no more than this. Whenever she found him interested in something or with some one who engaged his attention for the time being, she slipped away so quietly that he scarcely noticed it and devoted herself to her own interests, which she was desperately trying to make fill the void in her life. Her music was her greatest solace, for in it she found a response to her every mood. In the dim-lit hall of the villa she sat for hours at the piano, her fingers running over the keys, her mind pondering upon her complex problem— each action apparently separated from the other, yet in exact accord. Sometimes it was a nocturne of Chopin's, sometimes an impromptu of Schubert's; but always she found in the unspoken, poetic expression of the composer's soul an answering sympathy which was lacking in other forms more tangible.

Inez interrupted one of these communions, when Helen supposed herself alone with Debussy. Lately she had found herself turning to the charm and mystery of his atmosphere, the strangeness of his idiom, the vagueness of his rhythms, and the fugitive grace and fancy of his harmonic expression with an understanding and a surrender which she had never before felt. The music reflected upon her its delicate perception of nature in all its moods—the splash of the waves upon the shore, the roaring of the surf, the gloom of the forests relieved by the moonlight on the trees.

"Don't, Helen—I beg of you!" Inez exclaimed, suddenly. "Say it to me, but don't torture me with those weird reproaches. Every note almost drives me wild!"

"Why, Inez, dear!" cried Helen, startled by the girl's words no less than by the suddenness of the interruption. "What in the world do you mean? You should have told me before if my playing affected you so."

"I love it, Helen," she replied; "but lately it has hurt me through and through. I can hear your voice echoing in every note you strike, and I feel its bitter reproach."

Helen tried to draw Inez beside her, but the girl sank upon the floor, resting her elbows on Helen's knees and looking up into her face with tense earnestness.

"You have been terribly unstrung these days, dear," Helen replied, "and you are unstrung now or you would not discover what does not exist. It is your instinctive sympathy for poor Mélisande that makes you feel so—you see her, as I do, floating resistlessly over the terraces and fountains, the plaything of Fate, a phantom of love and longing and uncertainty. That is what you feel, dear."

Helen took Inez' face between her hands and looked into her eyes for a moment. "People call it mystical and unreal," she continued, "but I believe that some of us have it in our own lives, don't you?"

Inez did not reply directly, and struggled to escape the searching gaze.

"Helen," she said, abruptly, "I simply cannot stay on here; I shall go mad if I do. Each time I suggest going you say that you need me, and it seems ungrateful, after all you have done for me, to speak as I do. But you cannot understand. I am not myself, and I am getting into a condition which will make me a burden to you instead of a help."

"I do need you, dear," Helen replied, quietly, "but certainly not at the expense either of your health or your happiness. The effects of the accident have lasted much longer than I thought they would. I wanted you to be quite recovered before you left us."

"If the accident were all!" moaned Inez, burying her face in Helen's lap.

Helen made no response, but laid her hand kindly upon Inez' head. After a few moments the girl straightened up. Her eyes burned with the intensity of her sudden resolve, and she spoke rapidly, as if fearful that her courage would prove insufficient for the task she had set for herself to do.

"Helen!" she cried, "I am going to tell you something which will make you hate me. You will want me to leave you, and our friendship will be forever ended."

"Wait, dear," urged Helen—"wait until you are calmer; then, if you choose, tell me all that you have in your heart."

"No; I must tell you now. I love Jack, Helen—do you understand? I love your husband, and, fight it as I do, I cannot help it. Think of having to make a confession like that!"

Helen's face lighted up with glad relief.

"I am so glad that you have told me this," she said, quietly.

Inez gazed at Helen in wonder, amazed by her calmness and her unexpected words.

"But I must tell you more," she continued, wildly; "I have loved him for weeks—almost since I first came here!"

"I know you have, Inez." Helen pressed a kiss upon the girl's forehead. "I have known it for a long time; but I have also seen your struggle against it, and your loyalty to me—and to him."

"You have known it?" Inez asked, faintly. Then her voice strengthened again. "But you have not known all! I did fight against it, as you say, and I was loyal until"—her voice broke for a moment—"until that day of the accident—in the cottage—I thought him dead—"

"Yes," encouraged Helen, eagerly.

"Until then I was loyal, but when I was alone with him, and thought him dead, I—oh, Helen, you will hate me as I hate myself—then I kissed him, and I told him of my love, and I—"

"Yes, I know, dear," Helen interrupted, her voice full of tenderness. "No one can blame you for what you did under such awful circumstances. I suspected what had happened when I found you where you had fainted across his body. But you can't imagine how glad I am that you have told me all this. I felt sure you would, some day."

"You will let me go now, won't you? You can see how impossible it is for me to stay."

"I need you now more than ever," replied Helen, firmly. "If you insist on leaving I shall not urge you to stay, but even you—knowing what you do—cannot know how much I need you."

"How did you know?" Inez asked, weakly.

"From what Ferdy said first, then from what I saw myself."

"Why did you not send me away, then?"

"I had no right to do so, Inez."

"Of course you were perfectly sure of Jack."

Helen winced. "Yes," she replied, quietly; "I was sure of Jack."

"But you understand now that I really cannot stay?"

"Jack needs you still."

"No; his manuscript is complete. He will not need me for the revision."

"You would stay if he did?"

"Why, yes."

"Then if you would stay if he needed you, surely you will do the same for me?"

"Oh, Helen!"

"Will you? When Jack is quite himself again I will urge no longer. Now that you have told me this, it will be easier for you. Will you not do this for me?"

"There is nothing I would not do for you, Helen!" cried Inez, throwing her arms impulsively around her friend's neck and kissing her passionately. "You are so strong you make me more ashamed than ever of my own weakness."

"Thank you, dear," Helen replied, simply, returning her embrace; "but don't make any mistake about my strength. It is because I lack it so sadly that I ask you to stay."

Dr. Montgomery found Armstrong's temperature considerably higher when he called later in the day, after the disquieting mental experience his patient had passed through. Armstrong also appeared to be preoccupied, and more interested in asking questions than in answering them. For the first time he seemed to be curious in regard to the nature of his illness.

"In a case like mine, is it possible for the mental convalescence to be retarded or to go backward?" he asked.

"Yes," Dr. Montgomery replied, "it is possible, but hardly probable, especially with a patient who has progressed so normally as you have."

"It is normal for the memory to have a complete lapse, as in my case?"

"Absolutely so."

"Is it possible for a knowledge of the events which occurred during such a lapse to be restored—say, weeks afterward?"

"Yes; under certain conditions."

"And those conditions are?" asked Armstrong, eagerly.

The doctor settled back in his chair.

"Let me see if I can make it clear to you: all memories are permanent—that is to say, every event makes a distinct, even though it may be an unconscious, impression upon the brain. Sometimes these memories remain dormant for months, or even years, before something occurs to bring them to mind; but even before this the memories are there, just the same."

"But you are speaking of every-day occurrences, are you not? My question is whether or not it might be possible for me, for example, to have a reviving knowledge of certain events which took place during a period of apparent unconsciousness."

"I understand. Yes, it would be quite possible for this to happen."

"What would be necessary to bring it about?"

Dr. Montgomery smiled at his patient's earnestness.

"Are you so eager to recall that period? But the question is a fair one. Some incident must take place similar to something which occurred during the unconscious period in order to revive the dormant memory. I doubt if you could do it deliberately."

"I have no intention of trying," Armstrong replied; "but I am interested in this particular phase of the case. Suppose, during the apparently unconscious period, some one had lifted my arm or placed a hand upon my forehead—would the same act be enough to restore the dormant memory, as you call it?"

"Quite enough—though it would not necessarily do so. I have known several cases where the repetition of such an act has produced just the result which you describe."

"And these revived impressions are apt to be trustworthy?"

"As a photographic plate," replied the doctor, emphatically.

Armstrong was silent for some moments.

"It is an interesting phase, as you say," he remarked, at length. "I think I may try the experiment, after all."

"The chances will be against you; but I imagine you have been pretty well informed of what has happened. Don't try to think too hard. It will be all the better for you to give your brain a little rest; it has had a hard shaking-up."

So this was the solution of the mystery for which he had sought so long! Armstrong found himself in a curious position after the doctor took his departure, leaving behind him a new knowledge of affairs which, six hours before, his patient would have considered absolutely preposterous. Helen was right, and had been right from the beginning. His one consolation was removed, and in its place was a complication which seemed past straightening out. To the blame which Armstrong had already taken to himself on Helen's account, he must now add the responsibility of having inspired this sentiment in Inez' heart, which meant unhappiness to all. Even though this had been done unconsciously, he told himself, it was no less culpable in that he had not himself discovered the situation and checked it before any serious harm had been done. Helen had seen it, the contessa had seen it, and he wondered how many others. He had been blind in this, criminally blind, and now he must pay the penalty.

But this penalty could not be borne by him alone—he could see that clearly. Helen and Inez were both hopelessly involved. And what a woman his wife had shown herself to be! Knowing of this affection on the part of Inez, she had suffered them to continue together in order that his work might not be disturbed. She had told him just how matters stood—not with recriminations, but with loving solicitude, offering to sacrifice herself, if necessary, to secure his happiness, drinking her cup of sorrow to the dregs, and alone! It was plain enough to him now. He thought of Helen as she was when they first came to Florence, and compared her with the Helen of to-day. He had brought about that change; he alone was responsible for it. She had craved the present, with its sunshine, its birds, its happiness, and instead of all this he had filled it for her with nothing but sorrow and suffering! He merited the scoring Emory gave him, even though the denunciation had gone too far.

As the bandage fell from his eyes, the character which he had assumed during these past months stood out clearly before him, shorn of its academic halo, and pitiful in its unfulfilled ideals. He had sought to join that company of humanists who had awakened the world to the joy and beauty of intellectual attainment. He had believed himself worthy of this honor, in that he believed he had understood and sympathized with their underlying motives. So he had in principle, but how wofully he had failed in his efforts to carry them out! Instead of assimilating the happy youthfulness of the Greek, together with the Grecian harmony of existence, he had developed his morbid self-centering and self-consciousness. His blind, unreasoning devotion to his single interest had resulted in folly and fanaticism. He had overlooked the cardinal element in the humanistic creed that knowledge without love meant death and isolation. Instead of singling out and joining together the beauties for which humanism stood, he had embraced and emphasized its limitations.

"I am an impostor!" Armstrong exclaimed, no longer able to endure his mental lashing in silence—"an arrant impostor! I have set myself up as a modern apostle, I have written platitudes upon intellectual supremacy and the religion of knowledge, when the one single personal attribute to which I can justly lay claim is insufferable academic arrogance. I have seized a half-truth and fortified it with fact; and in accomplishing this stupendous piece of fatuous nonsense I have stultified myself and destroyed the happiness of all!"

XXVII

Armstrong's first act, on the following day, was to send to the library for his manuscript. Helen looked upon this as an evidence that with his returning strength had also come a return of his all-controlling passion. This was a natural explanation of the peculiar change which she had noticed in him during the past few days, and his request fitted in so perfectly with a conversation between Uncle Peabody and herself the evening before that she almost unconsciously exchanged with him a glance of mutual understanding.

But the real motive was quite at variance with her interpretation. Armstrong had passed through his period of introspection without taking any one into his confidence. Fierce as the struggle had been, he felt instinctively that his only chance of restoring conditions to anything which even approached equilibrium was to make no new false step. He had come to certain definite conclusions, but was still undecided as to the proper methods to be adopted in his attempt to turn these conclusions into realities.

First of all, he had placed himself in an entirely false position with Helen. He had given her cause to believe him indifferent and neglectful. This, at least, he argued, could be remedied, even though it was now too late to spare her the suffering through which she had passed. But he could explain it all, and by his future devotion to her, and to those interests of which she was a part, he could make her forget the past.

With Miss Thayer the proposition was a different one. To her he had done an injury which could not be repaired. He had sought to take her with him into a world full of those possibilities which the intellectual alone can comprehend. Instead of leaving her there, inspired by the wisdom of such an intercourse, he had—unconsciously but still culpably—developed in her an interest in himself. The problem was to extricate her and himself from this compromising situation without destroying all future self-respect for them both; and the solution of it seemed far beyond his reach.

And besides all this, there was the manuscript. Despite his best endeavor, he could not recall even an outline of what he had written. After a full realization came to him of the extent to which he had misunderstood and misconstrued the basic principles of humanism itself, his interest in his work became one of curiosity to learn by actual examination how far he had accepted the half-truths, and how far he had wandered from the path which he had thought he knew so well. The whole volume must be filled with absurd theories, falsely conceived and as falsely expressed. He must go over it, page by page, and learn from it the bitter fact of his unworthiness to stand as the modern expounder of those great minds whose influence alone should have been enough to hold him to his appointed course.

When the manuscript arrived he devoted himself to it with an eagerness which added to the natural misunderstanding of his motive. With no word of comment, he took the package to his room, where, after bolting the door, he opened it and applied himself to his task. Hours passed by, but he refused to be interrupted. Helen tried to persuade him to come down-stairs for luncheon, but he begged to be excused. Uncle Peabody calmed her anxiety; so the day passed, leaving him alone with his burdens.

Armstrong approached his manuscript with bitterness of spirit. This was the tangible form of that inexplicable force which had drawn him away from those ties which stood to him for all future peace and serenity; this had been the medium which had fostered the new affection so fraught with sorrow and even danger; this was the proof of his absolute lack of harmony with those noble principles which he still felt, when rightly expressed, represented the highest possibilities of life itself. At first he hesitated to read it, dreading what it must disclose. Then he attacked it fiercely, passing from page to page with feverish intensity.

As he read, his bitterness and dread disappeared, and in their place came first surprise and then amazement. Was this his manuscript? Had he written these pages in which the real, wholesome, glorious spirit of past attainment and present possibilities fairly lived and breathed! His amazement turned into absolute mystification. He read of the important movement which liberated the rich humanities of Greece and Rome from the proscription of the Church; he saw literature itself expand in subject and in quantity; he himself felt the sundering of the bonds of ignorance, superstition, and tradition which had previously confined intellectual life on all sides.

Surely this was a simple yet sane presentation of the subject, Armstrong said to himself, as it had formulated itself in words after his long study. His error must lie in his application of it to the people. The manuscript unfolded rapidly under his eager inspection. It told him of the great step forward when writing changed to printing. He followed the convincing argument that this new art from its earliest beginnings was to be identical with that of culture, and a faithful index to the standards of the ages to come. It told him that the advent of the printing-press made men think, and gave them the opportunity of studying description and argument where previously they had merely gazed at pictorial design. He could see the development of the people under this new influence, growing strong in self-reliance, and confident in their increasing power.

He found himself unable to condemn his work thus far. In application, as in definition, what he had written seemed to ring true. Later on he must find expressions of those distorted ideals in the manuscript, just as he had found them in himself. With increasing interest he read of the benefits these people of the *quattrocento* reaped from the principles of Grecian civilization, now tempered by the inevitable filtering through the great minds of a century. With no uncertain note the manuscript portrayed the efforts made by this people to reach the unattainable, refusing to be bound down by limited ideals, and creating masterpieces in every art which expressed in the highest form the ethical spirit of the period.

The pages still turned rapidly. At times Armstrong became so absorbed that he forgot himself and the fact that he was analyzing the outpouring of his own soul. Then he recalled the present and the problem before him. He could not comprehend that this work was his own; he did not remember writing it; he was ignorant of the particular study or reasoning which had brought it forth. But there the words stood, in his own handwriting, a visible evidence of something which had actually taken place.

As the reading progressed, he became more and more bewildered. It was direct and convincing. The subject was handled with restraint, and yet he felt the force behind each sentence. Suddenly his eye fell upon this paragraph:

"After giving due credit to humanism for its vast contribution to the arts and to literature, there yet remains to acknowledge the greatest debt of all: it taught man to hold himself open to truth from every side, and so to assimilate it that it became a part of his very life itself. Thus making himself inclusive of all about him, his attitude toward his fellow-man could not be other than sympathetic and appreciative."

Armstrong read this over a second time, and, bending forward, he rested his head upon his hands in the midst of the sheets of manuscript and groaned aloud. This was his acknowledgment of the great lesson of humanism, and yet he had not applied it to his own every-day life! "It taught man to hold himself open to truth from every side," he repeated to himself. "Thus making himself inclusive of all about him, his attitude toward his fellow-man could not be other than sympathetic and appreciative."

At length he raised his head, and, rising wearily, he walked to the window, drawing in the refreshing air. The strain had been intense, and he found himself utterly exhausted.

"I see it all," he said, bitterly; "the fault is not with the book or with the principles themselves—it is with me! I have written better than I knew; I have preached where I have not practised. Oh, Helen—oh, Inez! Can I ever undo the wrong I have done you both!"

XXVIII

It was several days before Armstrong found himself ready to take up the unravelling of the thread. The shuttle had moved to and fro so silently, and its web was woven with so intricate a pattern, that he felt the hopelessness even of finding an end of the yarn, where he might begin his work. He watched the two girls in their every-day life as they moved about him; he studied them carefully, he compared their personal characteristics. Both were greatly changed. Miss Thayer continued ill at ease and unlike her former self in her relations to Helen and Uncle Peabody as well as toward himself. He felt that now he understood the reason; and beyond this it was natural that she should miss the absorbing interest which the work had given her, coming, as it did, to so abrupt an end and leaving nothing which could take its place.

But Helen had changed more. The girlish vivacity which had previously characterized her had disappeared, and in its place had come a quiet, reposeful dignity which, while it made her seem an older woman, would have appealed to him as wonderfully becoming save for the restraint which accompanied it. She held herself absolutely in hand. Her every action, while considerate in its relation to others, admitted of no denial. Armstrong felt instinctively rather than because of anything which had happened that were their wills to clash now hers would prove the stronger. There had been a development in her far beyond anything he had realized.

Comparing the two, as he had ample opportunity to do, he wondered if he had made a fair estimate of her strength in his previous considerations. Helen had considered herself unfitted to enter into his work with him. She had frankly stated her unwillingness to go back into the past, and to live among its memories, when the present offered an alternative which was to her so much more attractive. Inez seized with avidity the opportunity he offered, and had entered into his work with an enthusiasm second only to his own. Suppose Helen had done this, Armstrong asked himself. With her characteristics, as he was only now coming to understand them, she would not long have remained content to act as his agent—she would have become a definite part of the work herself, and would have helped to shape it, instead of yielding more and more to his own personality. Inez had helped him much, and his obligation to her was not overlooked; but he could see how this helpfulness had lessened, day by day, as her intellect had become subservient to his own. He had been glad of this at the time, but now he found himself asking whether Helen would not have shown greater strength under the same circumstances.

Since his accident the contrast had been greater. Helen had assumed definite control over everything. Inez, Uncle Peabody, Armstrong himself recognized in her, without expression, the acknowledged and undisputed head of affairs. It had all come about so naturally, and Helen herself seemed so unconscious of it, that he could not explain it. On the other hand, Inez had completely lost her nerve. The crisis through which the two girls had passed had produced upon them vastly differing effects, and Armstrong could not fail to be impressed by the result of his observations.

Finally he determined to talk the matter over with Helen, and here again he found himself counting upon her assistance in straightening things out with Inez. Had he realized it, this was the first time in his life that he had admitted even to himself that any one could aid him in any matter which he could not personally control. Dimly, it is true, but still definitely, he was conscious that he was making an unusual admission, yet he experienced a certain amount of gratification in doing so.

Helen had been reading aloud to him while he reclined upon his couch in a shady corner of the veranda. For some moments he had heard nothing of the spoken words, for his eyes, resting fixedly upon his wife's face, revealed to him a more impressive story than that contained within the printed volume. How beautiful she was! The clear-cut profile; the long lashes hiding from him the deep, responsive eyes, whose sympathy he well knew; the soft, sweet voice which fell upon his ear with soothing cadence; the whole harmonious bearing, indicative of a character well defined, yet unconscious of its strength—all combined to show him at a single glance how rare a woman she really was. As he watched her the definition which he himself had written came back to him with tremendous force. "It taught man to hold himself open to truth from every side. Thus making himself inclusive of all about him, his attitude toward his fellow-man could not be other than sympathetic and appreciative." What man or woman had he ever known who so truly lived up to this high standard as this girl who sat beside him, all unconscious of the tumult raging in his mind?

Then the storm passed from his brain to his heart. His affection, intensified by the struggles he had experienced, overpowered him, and he cried aloud in a voice which startled Helen by the suddenness of its appeal. Seizing her disengaged hand, he pressed it passionately to his lips.

"Don't read any more," he begged; "I must talk with you."

Startled almost to a degree of alarm, she laid down the book, regarding him intently.

"Can you ever forgive me for all I have made you suffer?" he continued, in the same tense voice; "can you ever believe that my forgetfulness of everything which was due you was not deliberate, but the result of some force beyond my control?"

Helen looked at him steadily for a moment before replying. "Yes," she said, at length, making a desperate effort to preserve her composure; "I forgive you gladly. Shall we go on with the story?"

"No!" he replied, almost fiercely, seizing the volume and placing it beyond her reach upon the couch. "I have been waiting for this moment too long, and now nothing shall take it from me."

Helen realized that it was also the moment for which she had been waiting, and which she had been dreading beyond expression. Now he would comprehend what she had meant, now he would struggle with her to prevent her from doing what she knew she must do.

"There is no need of explanation, Jack," she said, at length. "I understand everything, and have understood for a long time."

"Can you believe that I myself have only recently come to a realization?"

"Yes; it has come to you sooner than I had expected."

"Can you believe how sincerely pained I am that all this should have happened?"

"I have never for a moment thought that you would intentionally hurt me."

"Then you do understand, and will forget?"

Armstrong sat up on the edge of the couch and watched Helen's face intently.

"You don't know what you are asking," she replied, dropping her eyes.

"Yes, I do," he insisted. "I want to blot out the memory of every pang I have caused you by a devotion beyond anything you have ever dreamed."

"Don't, Jack," protested Helen.

"Why not? Don't you think I mean it? From now on I have no interest except you, dear; and I will make you forget everything which has happened."

Helen pressed his hand gratefully, and then withdrew her own.

"This is only going to open everything up again," she said, in a low, strained voice, "and that will be simply another great mistake."

"You don't believe me." Armstrong's voice was reproachful.

"I believe you feel all that you say now, Jack."

"But—"

"But you are not yourself now; that is all."

"I am quite myself; in fact, I am almost as good as new."

"I don't mean physically."

"And mentally as well. My mind is as clear as it ever was."

"I know, Jack; but you are far away from the influence which has so controlled you. That is what I mean."

"It is a mighty good thing that I am." Armstrong spoke with emphasis.

"For the time being, no doubt; but soon you will be able to return to it."

"I shall never return to it."

Helen looked up quickly. Armstrong's words were spoken so forcibly that they startled her.

"You must go back to it," she replied, with equal emphasis; "it is your life, and you must go back."

"I have passed through the experience once and for all time."

Helen found it difficult not to be affected by the convincing tone.

"I have made more mistakes than you know of."

"In your work, do you mean?"

"Yes."

"But this is only the first draft; you can easily correct them."

"They could be more easily corrected in the book than where they are."

"I don't understand."

"The mistakes are in me!" Armstrong cried. "I am no humanist; I am an impostor!"

"Jack! Jack!" Helen was really alarmed. "You are putting too much of a tax upon yourself. Remember, you are not well yet."

"I am worse than an impostor," Armstrong continued, excitedly, refusing to be checked: "I am a traitor to the very cause I set myself to further! I have been false in my duty to it, as I have been in my obligations to you."

"That is just the point," Helen interrupted. "I absolved you of your obligations to me weeks ago, so that part of it is all settled."

"But I did not absolve myself. I don't understand what I did or why I did it. Day by day I felt myself slipping further and further away from you. I was not strong enough to appreciate what was taking place, and was powerless to resist."

"But I understood it even then," Helen continued. "I recognized that our marriage was the first mistake, and decided that I would do my part toward remedying the error with as little pain as possible."

"Our marriage was no mistake, except my own unfitness to be your husband!" Armstrong cried, bitterly.

"Don't, Jack," Helen again pleaded. "You see, I have had a much longer time to think the matter out."

"I was all right until I came under the influence, which completely changed me, just as you told me it did, time and again. Then, instead of being developed by it as I should have been, I assimilated nothing but its limitations and began to go backward."

"You must have assimilated far more than that," Helen insisted, "for your personal development through it all has been tremendous. Otherwise this could not be."

"Listen, Helen." Armstrong was desperate. "Let me tell you how far down I have gone. You know how eager I was, when we first came, to accomplish some great achievement. You know how much I admired the works and personalities of those grand old characters of whom you have so often heard me speak. Well, I took up my work. I studied these characters, I wrote about them, I tried to assimilate their principles and to express them in words. At length the work was finished. Cerini praised it, and I felt that I had proved myself equal to the undertaking."

"And so you had," Helen interrupted. "Cerini told me so himself."

"Cerini knows nothing of how ignominiously I failed to apply these principles to myself. He has read the noble platitudes with which my book is filled; you have experienced the unworthy personal expressions as they have appeared in my every-day life."

"But you have said yourself that you could not help it."

"I should have been able to; that is where I showed my utter unfitness for the undertaking. Now do you understand?"

"Yes, Jack," Helen replied, slowly, after a moment's pause, "I think I do understand; but I also think that my understanding is clearer than yours."

"Does it not enable you to forgive me for it all?"

"Yes—I have already told you that. What you have said is exactly what I knew you must say when you had been long enough away from your work. I have never felt this influence of which you have so often spoken, but I have recognized its strength by what I have seen. I do not mean that you need necessarily continue in your present intensity, but I do mean that whether you recognize it or not this second nature is your real self."

"But I tell you that I have no further interest in my work."

"You think so, Jack, but you have been away from it for weeks. Perhaps by returning home you could smother your love of it for a long time, but it would be there just the same. And without it you could never express your own individuality."

"I would, at least, be the self you knew before we came here."

"Yes, but only that. With all the pain, Jack, I have not been blind to what it has done for you. With all the misapplication of the principles which you mention you have gained so much that you could never be the old self again. I could not respect you if you did. Surely it would not be following the teachings of these grand spirits were you to live a life below the standard which you have shown yourself capable of maintaining."

"Then let us live that life together, Helen," Armstrong begged; "let us begin all over again, taking my mistakes as guiding-posts to keep us from the dangers against which I have not been strong enough, alone, to guard myself."

"Oh, Jack!" Helen withdrew her hands and pressed them against her tired temples. "Don't you see that this is simply repeating the mistake which has caused all our trouble? Now, at this moment, we are to each other just what we were when we became engaged, forgetful of all that has occurred since. Why not recognize things as they really are, and spare ourselves the added sorrow which must surely come?"

"Can you not forgive what has happened since?"

"I have forgiven all that there is to forgive; but I can't forget the knowledge that has come to me."

"What knowledge is there which refuses to be forgotten?"

"A knowledge of your real self, Jack—and that self has never belonged to me. It is as distinct and separate as if it were that of another man. It has been developed apart from me; it is of such a nature that I cannot become a part of it."

"You are so great a part of it already, dear, that you could not sever yourself from it."

"No, Jack. It is your loyalty, your sense of duty, that is speaking now. Or perhaps you are far enough away from what has happened not to see it as clearly as I do. You have become a part of another life, and your future belongs to that life and to the woman who has also become a part of it."

"You can't mean this, Helen. Think what you are saying!"

"I do mean it, just as I meant it when I said so before, when you failed to comprehend. It is Inez who must be your companion in this new life."

Armstrong did not remonstrate, as he had done before. It was impossible to misunderstand the conviction in Helen's voice. He could no longer attribute it to jealousy or to caprice; he could no longer fail to understand the meaning of her words.

"I have fully deserved all this," he said, at length. "When you first told me of Miss Thayer's feeling toward me I did not—I could not—believe it. Never once, during all the hours we were together, was there anything to confirm what you said."

"You did not notice this any more than you noticed other things which happened, Jack; you were too completely absorbed. But that does not alter the fact, does it?"

"No; the fact remains the same. It has only been since the accident that I have realized it; and this is one of the two problems which I have to straighten out."

"Then you do know now that Inez loves you?"

Armstrong bowed his head.

"What is it that has at last convinced you?"

He hesitated for a moment. "It seems uncanny, Helen, but I have been 'seeing things.'"

She looked at him questioningly. "Seeing things?" she repeated.

"Yes; you will think I have lost my mind again, just as I did; but the doctor says it is not unusual. Inez was alone with me, after the accident, you know, in the cottage."

"Well?" encouraged Helen, breathlessly.

"She thought me dead, and—this is brutal to repeat to you, Helen."

"No, no—go on!"

"Why, she said she loved me—that is all."

"But you were unconscious, Jack—you did not know what was happening."

"Not then, but later. It came to me yesterday, while lying on the couch,—almost as in a vision. I spoke to the doctor about it, and he said that sometimes such things do happen. If you had not told me what you did I probably should have thought it nothing but an uncomfortable dream, but as it was, of course I understood."

"Are you sure now that it was no dream?"

"Yes; I questioned Miss Thayer about some of the details—not the most vital ones, of course—and she corroborated them. But telling you all this will only make matters worse."

"No, Jack; I know about it already. Inez has told me everything, and the poor girl is distracted. I am glad that at last you are convinced."

"You knew all this?" He looked at her in amazement. "You knew it, and have let her stay here?"

"It is right that she should remain," Helen answered, firmly.

Armstrong's voice broke for a moment. "And I said you were jealous!" he reproached himself. Then he continued his appeal. "But granting all this, it cannot settle the matter, deeply as I deplore it. My own blindness and stupidity are to blame for it, and I must accept the full responsibility; but my love for you has never and could never be transferred to her or to any one else. I have been criminally neglectful, I have been culpably dense, but through it all you, and you alone, have been in my heart. I have longed to say this to you even while the spell was on me. I have longed to fold you in my arms and ease the pain I have seen you suffer, but I found myself powerless in this as in all else. Can you not—will you not—believe what I say?"

Helen looked up into her husband's face before she replied.

"Sometimes I wish you were not so conscientious, Jack—but of course I don't mean that; only it would make it easier for me to adhere to my determination to do what I know is right. I was sure that this moment would arrive; I know your ideas of duty and loyalty, and I know that you would sacrifice yourself and your future rather than be false to either. I believe that you are sincere in thinking that your sentiments toward Inez are purely platonic—I am sure they would be so long as you were not free to have them otherwise."

"Then why do you insist that they are otherwise?"

"I don't insist—I am simply accepting things as they really are, even though I must suffer by doing so. You are the only one who does not realize it, unless it be Inez herself. Cerini told me, 'I have never seen two individualities cast in so identical a mould.' Professor Tesso, who saw you at work together at the library, said, 'There is a perfect union of well-mated souls'; you yourself, when we returned from that moonlight ride, said to her, 'You are the only one who understands me.' It has simply been your absorption in your work and your loyalty to me which has kept you from seeing it yourself."

"Cerini said that—Tesso saw us at the library?" Armstrong looked at Helen in bewilderment. "You thought my remark to Miss Thayer possessed anything more than momentary significance?" His face assumed an expression of still greater concern. "I have, indeed, been more culpable than I realized. Is it not enough if I tell you that you are all wrong—that I do not love any one except the one person I have a right to love?"

Helen smiled sadly. "No, Jack," she replied, kindly but firmly, "it is all too clear. When you return to your real life, as you must do, you will return to your real self as well. Then you will know that I have saved you from the greatest mistake of all. You and Inez are meant for each other, and always have been." She looked up with a brave but unsuccessful attempt to smile. "Perhaps our little experience together has been necessary in the development of us both, dear. If so, it will make it easier to believe that our mutual suffering will not have been in vain."

"I will never accept it, Helen!" cried Armstrong, desperately in earnest. "Your devotion to this false idea will do more than all I have done to wreck our lives. You must listen to reason."

"Don't make it any harder for me than it is," Helen begged, her voice choking. "I am trying to talk calmly, and to do what I know I must do; but I have been through so much already. Please don't make it any harder."

Armstrong longed to comfort her, but he knew that she would repulse him if he tried. He watched the conflict through which the girl was passing and was overwhelmed by the sense of his own responsibility. He realized how near the tension was to the breaking-point, and dared not pursue the subject further. Taking both her hands in his, he gazed long into her eyes now filled with tears.

"If to give you up is the necessary penalty for the sorrow I have brought to you," he said, quietly, his voice breaking as he spoke, "it shall be done—for your sake, no matter what it means to me; but my love for you is beyond anything I have ever known before."

XXIX

There had been many visitors at the villa during Armstrong's illness and convalescence. Cerini had called several times, being most solicitous for the speedy recovery of his *protégé;* and the Contessa Morelli, temporarily thwarted in the solution of her problem, took advantage of the proximity of her villa to be frequently on the spot, where she could observe the progress of affairs under the suddenly changed conditions.

Armstrong had long desired to question the contessa further in regard to the disquieting conversation he had held with her upon the occasion of their first meeting; but the rapidity with which his latent impressions had become definite realities made him unwilling to allow any new developments to add to the complexity of the situation as he had now come to know it. After his interview with Helen, however, he was convinced that matters had reached their climax, and he grasped any additional information as possible material to be used in the solving of his double dilemma. His opportunity came on the following day, when he found himself alone with the contessa upon the veranda, Helen having been called to another part of the villa by some household demand.

After Helen had made her excuses, Armstrong felt himself to be the subject of a careful scrutiny on the part of the contessa. He looked up quickly and met her glance squarely. Amélie had a way of making those she chose feel well acquainted with her, and Armstrong, during his convalescence, had proved interesting.

"Well," he asked, smiling, "what do you think of him?"

It was the contessa's turn to smile, and the question caught her so unexpectedly that the smile developed into a hearty laugh.

"I have been trying to make up my mind," she replied, frankly. "At first I thought him a human thinking-machine, all head and no heart, but I am beginning to believe that my early impressions were at fault."

"It gratifies me to hear you say that," Armstrong answered, calmly. "I presume those early impressions of yours were formed at the library, when Miss Thayer and I came under your observation."

"Yes," replied the contessa, unruffled by the quiet sarcasm which she could but feel. "You see, I have lived here in Italy for several years and have become accustomed to the sight of saint worship; but it is a novel experience to see the saint come down off his pedestal and prove himself to have perfectly good warm blood coursing through his veins."

"Don't you find it a bit difficult to picture me with all my worldly attributes even as a temporary saint?"

"Not at all," the contessa answered. "Most of the saints possessed worldly attributes before they attained the dignity of statues. But think of the confusion among their worshippers should they follow your example and again assume the flesh! I imagine their embarrassment would almost equal yours."

Amélie spoke indifferently, but Armstrong felt the thrust. It was evident that she had no idea of dropping the subject, and Jack saw nothing else but to accept it as cheerfully as possible.

"Why not say 'quite'?" he asked.

"Because the saints were wifeless. Perhaps that is what made it possible for them to be saints."

Armstrong laughed in spite of himself. "If modern women were to be canonized, you undoubtedly think they should be selected from the married class?"

"Canonizing hardly covers it," the contessa replied; "they belong among the martyrs."

"But you have not told me why you now feel that your early impressions were in error," Armstrong resumed, sensing danger along the path which they had almost taken, and really eager to learn how far his attitude had impressed others. The contessa regarded him critically.

"There are many kinds of men," she began, "and to a woman of the world it is a necessity to classify those whom she meets."

"Indeed?" queried Armstrong. "You are throwing some most interesting side-lights upon a subject which my education has entirely overlooked."

"Am I?" Amélie asked, innocently. "But your education has been so far developed in other directions that you can easily recognize the importance of what I say. A woman who meets the world face to face must be able to estimate the elements against which she has to contend."

"Into how many classes do you divide us?" Armstrong was interested in her naïve presentment.

"The three principal divisions are, of course, single men, married men, and widowers, but the subdivisions are really more important. For my own use

I find it more convenient to separate those I meet into four classes—the interesting, the uninteresting, the safe, and the dangerous."

"You have developed an absolute system," Armstrong asserted.

"Yes, indeed," Amélie responded, cheerfully; "without one you men would have too distinct an advantage over us."

"I wish you would enlarge on your classification a little more. It is gratifying to me to know that members of my sex receive such careful consideration."

"Well, suppose we eliminate the uninteresting—they really don't count except in considering matrimony; then we have to weigh the material advantages they offer against their lack of interest. This brings us down to the interesting and safe, and the interesting and dangerous."

"Have I the honor to be included in one of these two classes?"

"Yes," the contessa replied, frankly.

"May I ask which? You see, my curiosity is getting the upper hand."

Amélie threw back her head with a hearty laugh. "I was certainly wrong in my first diagnosis," she said. "A man who was merely a thinking-machine would possess no curiosity. Usually a learned man is entirely safe."

"Then you really consider me dangerous?" There was a tone in Armstrong's voice which caused the contessa to look up at him quickly.

"Most men would consider that a compliment, Mr. Armstrong."

Receiving no reply, Amélie continued:

"Your wife has such original ideas! I have found my acquaintance with her positively refreshing."

"How does this bear upon our present conversation?" Armstrong inquired, still weighed down by the contessa's estimate of him. Amélie's frankness showed that no doubt existed in her mind as to his attitude toward Miss Thayer, and he felt that denials would be worse than useless. If impressions such as these lay in the mind of a casual observer like the contessa it was but natural that they should assume greater proportions to Helen; and it was with a foreboding that he heard her name mentioned in the present conversation. Amélie, however, could not sense the effect of her words upon her companion.

"Because we once discussed the same subject," she replied to his question, "and her attitude was most unusual. She even said that were she convinced that her husband really loved some other woman she would step aside and give him a clear field."

"Did she say that?" Armstrong demanded.

"She did," asserted the contessa. "You are a very lucky man, Mr. Armstrong," she continued, looking into his face meaningly; "my husband is not so fortunate."

While Armstrong hesitated in order to make no mistake in his reply, Helen returned accompanied by Cerini, and the moment when he could have formulated an answer had passed. The old man held up a finger reproachfully as he saw the contessa.

"You have never made another appointment to study those manuscripts with me," he said, as he took her hand. "Tell me that your interest has not flagged."

The librarian spoke feelingly, although he tried to conceal his disappointment. It was such a triumph that his work should appeal to one so devoted to a life of social gayety. Amélie remembered her interview with him at the library and felt that she deserved the reproach.

"Surely not," she replied, with so much apparent sincerity in her voice that the old man believed her and was mollified. "I have even received a new impetus from listening to Mr. Armstrong's enthusiastic account of his work with you and his impatience to return to it."

Armstrong glanced quickly at Helen as the contessa attributed to him a desire so opposed to the definite statement he had made the day before, while Cerini smiled contentedly. Helen gave no sign of having particularly noticed the remark, but Jack felt keenly his inability at that moment to set himself right.

"I was just about to take my departure," Amélie continued, "and I am glad not to be obliged to leave the invalid alone. I know how delighted you will be to take my place," she said to Cerini.

The old man dropped into the chair the contessa left vacant, while Armstrong watched the two figures until they disappeared in the hallway. Then he turned to his friend—but it was to Cerini the priest, the father-confessor, rather than to Cerini the librarian. He felt the seriousness of the situation more acutely than at any time since a realization of its complexity came to him. Cerini watched him curiously.

"You are not so well to-day," he said, at length. "You must go slowly, my son, and give Nature ample time to make her repairs."

"I fear even Nature has no remedy sufficiently powerful to cure my malady," Armstrong replied, bitterly. "I would to God she had!"

Cerini was at a loss to understand his manner or his words.

"What has happened?" he asked, sympathetically. "Is there some complication of which I know not?"

Armstrong bowed his head, overcome for the moment by an overwhelming sense of his own impotency.

"What is it?" urged the old man, himself affected by his companion's attitude. "I have missed you sadly at the library these weeks, and I am impatient for your return."

"I shall never return!" cried Armstrong, fiercely. "I have proved myself utterly unworthy of the work I undertook with you."

"My son! my son!" Cerini was aghast at what he heard. Then his voice softened as he thought he divined the explanation.

"Slowly, slowly," he said, soothingly. "It is too soon to put so heavy a burden upon your brain after the shock it has sustained. There is no haste. Your friends at the library will be patient, as you must be."

Armstrong easily read what was passing through the librarian's mind, and it increased his bitterness against himself. Cerini's calmness, however, quieted him, and he was more contained as he replied.

"I wish that the facts were as you think," he said, decisively. "It would be a positive relief to me if I could believe that my mind was still unbalanced as a result of the accident, but it is so nearly recovered that I must consider myself practically well. But I am glad of this chance to tell you how we have both been deceived. It will be a comfort to have you act as my confessor, and if your affection still holds after my recital I know that you will advise me as to what future course I must pursue."

In tense, clear-cut sentences Armstrong poured out to Cerini the story of the past months as he looked back upon them. He was frank in speaking of what he believed to be his accomplishments, as he was pitiless in his arraignment of himself in his failures. He showed how he had assimilated the lessons of the past only in his capacity of scribe; he explained how self-centred, selfish, and neglectful of his duty toward others he had been in his personal life. He spoke freely of his companionship with Miss Thayer, of her unquestioned affection for him, and of the impressions which had been made upon Helen and the Contessa Morelli. He insisted simply yet forcefully upon his own loyalty to Helen, not from a sense of duty, as she firmly believed, but because his devotion had never wavered.

In speaking of his wife Armstrong went into minute detail, even going back to his early attempts to interest her in what had later become his grand passion. He described her personal attributes, her love of the present rather than the past, her protective attitude toward her friend even in the face of such distressing circumstances; her generosity toward him; and finally her unalterable conviction that their separation was imperative.

Cerini listened in breathless silence as Armstrong's story progressed. He himself had played a part in the drama of which his companion was ignorant, and a sense of his own responsibility came to the old man with subtle force. He recalled his first meeting with Helen at the library, he remembered their later conversations, and in his contemplations he almost forgot, for the moment, the man sitting in front of him in his consideration of the splendid development, which he had witnessed without fully realizing it, in this woman whom he had pronounced unfitted by nature to enter into this side of her husband's work, as she had longed to do. Now, as a result of his lack of foresight, she proposed to eliminate herself from what she considered to be her husband's problem. "It has been more far-reaching than even you realize," she had said to him at the reception at Villa Godilombra, and this was what she had meant.

It was several moments after Armstrong ceased speaking before Cerini raised his eyes, and to Jack's surprise he saw that they were filled with tears. He naturally attributed it to the librarian's affection for him and his sympathy for his sorrow.

"I should not have told you this, padre," he said, sadly, pressing the hand which the old man laid tenderly upon his. "The fault is mine, and I should not try to shirk the full responsibility by sharing it with you."

"It is mine to share with you, my son," Cerini replied, firmly. "You have erred, as you state. You have been to blame for not giving out again, as the example of the master-spirits of the past should have taught you, those glorious lessons which impart the joy of living to those who give as well as to those who receive. But my error is even heavier. I have lived all my life in this atmosphere, drinking in the knowledge and the spirit which have come to you only within the past few months; yet I failed to recognize in your wife the natural embodiment of all that the best in humanism teaches. What you and I have endeavored to assimilate she has felt and expressed as naturally as she has breathed. She has shown us humanism in its highest development, purified and strengthened by her own fine nature, even though we have given her no opportunity for expression. Thank God we have recognized it at last!"

"You really believe that?" cried Armstrong, recalling his own earlier and less-defined conviction.

"Beyond a doubt," Cerini answered. "Let us find her, that we may tell her what a victory she has won."

Armstrong placed a restraining hand upon the old man's arm. "Not yet," he said, gently but firmly. "There is much still to be done to prepare her for this knowledge. At present she would not accept it."

"We must convince her."

"First of all I must make my peace with Miss Thayer," Armstrong replied. "Until that complication is relieved there is no hope."

"Do you feel strong enough for that?" asked Cerini, anxiously.

"It requires more than strength, padre," Armstrong replied, seriously; "it requires faith in myself, which at present is sadly lacking."

The old man rose and stood for a moment beside Armstrong's half-reclining figure. Bending down, he took his face in his hands and looked full into his eyes.

"Let me give you that faith," he said, affectionately. "You have already learned by sad experience that you are not the master of Fate. Let me tell you that by the same token you are not the victim of Fate. Nature, unerring in her wisdom, is now giving you the privilege of being co-partner with her in the final solving of your great personal problem. Accept the offered opportunity, my son, and show yourself finally worthy of it."

XXX

Helen had not overlooked the contessa's remark to Cerini, even though she gave no evidence at the time of having heard it. Her conversation with Jack had given her thoughts much food to feed upon. His words were so welcome, after the long breach, his manner so sincere, that she had been nearer to the yielding-point than he imagined. She had wondered if, after all, her attitude was justified, in view of his expressed desire to return to the same relations which had previously given them both such happiness. Jack's statement that her insistence upon the present conditions would do more to wreck their happiness than anything which he had done, made its impression upon her. Nothing but the previous intensity of her conviction that she must yield her place to Inez had held her to the self-appointed duty which she found so difficult to perform.

When the contessa repeated to Cerini what appeared to be an expression of her husband's impatience to return to his work Helen felt all hesitation vanish. Jack sympathized with her suffering, and would do all which lay in his power to make amends. She knew that he would give up all idea of future work, no matter at what sacrifice to himself, rather than add another straw to the burden which he now saw was nearly bearing her down. Yet the affection which she felt for him refused to be strangled. His very insistence, even though she was convinced that it was prompted by his sense of duty, fanned the embers into flame at a time when she was certain that at last their fire had become extinct. It was further evidence of her weakness, she told herself, and she would make superhuman efforts to adhere to the duty which lay plainly enough before her.

As she was leaving, the contessa placed her arm about Helen's waist and whispered to her:

"Don't think me meddlesome, my dear, but you will make a great mistake not to stick close beside that big, splendid husband of yours. They all do it, and I imagine he has been almost circumspect compared with most of them. Send the girl away and see if you can't make him forget his affinity. He is worth the effort, my dear—believe me, he is worth the effort."

Helen was so taken by surprise by the contessa's words that she stood speechless, looking at her with dull, lifeless eyes as she stepped into the tonneau and waved a smiling farewell as the motor-car rolled out of the court-yard. So the contessa was aware of the situation, and was also convinced of Jack's attachment for Inez! This was too horrible—she could not endure it! Matters must be brought to a head soon or she would die of mortification! She could not return to the veranda where she had left Cerini and Jack together, but went up-stairs to her room, where she locked the door and threw herself upon the bed in a paroxysm of tears.

Armstrong, on the contrary, had gained strength from Cerini's sympathy. He would accept the offered opportunity and see if at last he could not prove himself worthy of such glorious co-partnership. Unlike his previous efforts, if he succeeded it would tend to restore Helen's happiness as well, and this gave him an added incentive.

It was the afternoon of the next day before he was able to make his opportunity. Inez had taken a book and secreted herself in Helen's "snuggery" in the garden, but Armstrong's watchful eyes followed her. Waiting until she had time to become well settled, he strolled around the garden, finally appearing at the entrance to prevent her escape. To his surprise she made no such effort, and appeared more at ease than at any time since the accident.

"Have you come to join me?" she asked, with much of her former bearing.

"If I may," he replied, advancing to the seat and taking the place she made for him beside her.

"How famously you are getting on!" she said, laying down the volume; "you are more like yourself than I have seen you since the awful accident."

"If I may say so," Armstrong replied, watching her closely, "I was just thinking the same of you."

Inez flushed. "You are right," she answered, frankly, after a moment's pause.

Armstrong was distinctly relieved by her unexpected attitude. As he looked back he realized that there had been a change in her bearing toward him, particularly during the past week; but until now he had not appreciated how rapidly her unnatural manner had been returning to what it was during the early days of their acquaintance. The apparent effort to avoid him had disappeared, although he knew of no more reason for this than he had originally seen cause for its existence. Whatever the reason, the change had undoubtedly taken place, and it made matters easier for him.

"We have passed through much together, Miss Thayer," he began. "I wonder if we realize how much."

"It has certainly been an unusual experience," she admitted. "I expressed this to you at the library—do you remember? As I said then, it could hardly occur again."

"I appreciate that now," Armstrong replied, in a low voice; "at that time I do not think I did."

"There was much which you could not appreciate then," continued Inez; "and as I look back upon it there is much which I cannot explain to myself. In fact, there is a great deal that I blame myself for."

"The blame belongs to me, Miss Thayer," Armstrong asserted, firmly.

"For being away from Helen so much?"

"Yes; and for many other acts of selfishness and neglect. I am to blame for all that you feel against yourself."

"Against myself?" Inez repeated.

Armstrong paused long before he continued. "You have passed through this spell with me," he said, at length. "You, better than any one else, know its power, and can understand the cause of my attitude toward you and Helen, which was as inexplicable as it was unpardonable. And because you understand this I believe that I shall find you the more ready to forgive."

"There is nothing for which you stand in need of my forgiveness," Inez said, in a low tone. "On the contrary, there is much for which I have to thank you. It was a new world to which you introduced me—one which I should not otherwise have known; and having known it, nothing can ever take it from me."

"If matters had only stopped there," Armstrong continued, "I should have accomplished just what I had hoped to do. The fascination of the work so held me, and my desire to further the principles which seemed to me to represent all which made life worth the living resulted in blinding me to the possibility that you, perhaps, were not affected to a similar degree. Your assistance was so valuable, your companionship so congenial that I never once realized that I was running any risk of not performing my full duty toward you as well as toward Helen."

Inez could not fail to comprehend the import of his words, and a feeling of thankfulness passed over her that this conversation had not come earlier. The days which had passed since she confided to Helen the secret which she had so long carried alone had, in their way, been as full of chaotic conditions as had Armstrong's; yet it was but recently that she had come to realize the full importance of what had really happened. The days at the library, as she looked back upon them, seemed as a dream. She could close her eyes and bring back the intoxication of those moments alone with Armstrong in which she had silently revelled, while he had applied himself to the task before him unconscious of what was taking place. She could not deny herself the guilty pleasure of recalling them, yet little by little these thoughts had become disassociated from the man with whom she now came in almost hourly contact. With this disassociation came a welcome relief. The dread which she had felt of seeing him and hearing his voice disappeared as suddenly as it had come. She wondered at it, but she accepted it eagerly without waiting for an explanation.

With her return to more normal conditions her solicitude for Helen increased. She was conscious of her friend's unhappiness, yet she, perhaps, of all the household, was least aware of the extent of the breach between her and Armstrong. Helen, naturally perhaps, had confined her conversation upon this subject to Uncle Peabody and her husband, so Inez had no thought other than that all would straighten itself out now that Jack had become himself again. She had believed that Helen alone shared her secret with her, so it was with surprise and mortification that she became aware that Armstrong himself knew of what had taken place. This was even more of an ordeal to face than when she made her confession to Helen, yet it was one which ought to be met with absolute frankness.

"I understand what you mean," she replied, the color still showing in her face, "and I am glad that this opportunity has come for me to speak freely, even at the risk of losing your esteem. It is quite true that I, too, found myself beneath a spell—but besides this one which influenced you there was also another and a different one. I see no reason why I should be ashamed to say that this other spell was unconsciously exerted by a great scholar, a noble friend, a loyal husband. The effect of it was for a time overpowering, but now I can acknowledge it without injuring any one and express my gratitude for an influence which must always act for my best good."

"Miss Thayer!" Armstrong cried, overwhelmed by the revulsion which the girl's words brought to him. "I beg of you not to make virtues out of my errors; I cannot accept a tribute such as that, knowing myself to be unworthy of it. Can you not see that I should have guarded you from that spell, both for your sake and for Helen's?"

Inez smiled in real happiness that the break had at last been made. "You have given me far more than you have taken away, dear friend," she replied, gratefully; "now that the experience is past I appreciate it more than ever. But promise me that you will not give up this work because of what we all have been through."

Armstrong shook his head. "I shall not take such chances again," he said.

"It could never repeat itself," Inez urged. "Because one has been wounded by the thorn he failed to see is no reason why he should never pluck another rose."

"But suppose that in plucking the rose something fell out from next the heart which was inexpressibly dear to him and was lost forever?"

Inez looked up quickly. "What do you mean?" she asked.

"Do you not know that Helen insists upon a separation?"

"A separation!" Inez repeated, rising to her feet; "why, she worships you! Surely there is some mistake."

"No; she is convinced that our marriage was all wrong, and that she stands between me and the continuance of this work, which she argues is essential for my development and happiness. It is ridiculous, of course, but I cannot move her."

"She is right about the work," the girl said, decidedly; "but there is no one in the world better fitted to enter into it with you than she, if she but knew it. As I said, you will never take it up in the same way again, but having learned what it means you can never eliminate it from your life; and this should draw you and Helen even closer together."

"My one remaining labor is to convince her of this," Armstrong replied, feelingly.

"And I will help you do it."

Armstrong looked at her steadily for a moment. "There is another point upon which she insists, of which I have not told you," he said.

Inez waited for him to continue.

"She believes that you and I are foreordained for each other," Armstrong said, bluntly, "and she proposes to step aside to make the realization of this possible."

The girl gazed at her companion in silent amazement. So this was the cause of Helen's suffering—this was the price she was willing to pay as a tribute to her friendship for her and her love for her husband!

"The brave, brave girl!" Inez cried, almost overcome by her emotion. "I must make her understand that the Jack Armstrong I loved was killed at the foot of the hill of Settignano. Dear, dear Helen! it is now my privilege to give her back her happiness as she gave me back mine!"

XXXI

It had been to Uncle Peabody that Helen had turned during all this period, but it was for comfort and strength rather than for advice. The problem was hers, and she alone must finally solve it. She had thought it settled until her conversation with Jack, which caused a momentary wavering. She repeated Armstrong's words to Uncle Peabody, and his absolute conviction that her husband's present attitude was a normal and final expression encouraged her to question whether there might not be some other solution than the one upon which she had determined. Still, it was only a questioning; as yet she was unprepared to share Uncle Peabody's conviction.

"Don't lean too far backward," he had said to her, "in your efforts to stand by your principles. I have seen things which were called principles at first become tyrants and do damage out of all proportion to the good they would have done had the conditions not changed."

"It is the conditions I am watching, uncle," Helen had replied. "I have no 'principles,' as you call them, which will not joyfully yield themselves. I must not—I will not—stand in the way either of Jack's happiness or of his development. If I can make myself see any way by which we can stay together without accomplishing one or the other of these mistakes, God knows how eagerly I will again pick up the thread of life."

Uncle Peabody had folded her in his great arms again, as he had done so many times lately.

"People have sometimes told me that I am a philosopher," he said, huskily. "They have seen me meet death in a dear friend, or even one closer to me, with calmness, sending the departed spirit a wireless 'bon-voyage' message and considering the incident as fortunate, as if he had received a promotion. But when I see one as dear to me as you are, gasping for breath in what has seemed to be a hopeless and prolonged struggle for that life which love alone can give you, I must confess that my stock of philosophy, such as it is, seems sadly inadequate."

Now had come the necessity of repeating to him what the contessa had said, which gave Helen double pain, knowing, as she did, how much relief her last conversation had given him.

"I can't believe it, Helen," Uncle Peabody said, decisively. "Whatever else one may say of Jack Armstrong, he is honest, and I can't believe him insincere in what he said to you."

"It is not insincerity, dear," she replied, wearily. "He is trying to deceive himself.—What is it, Annetta?" she asked, almost petulantly, of the maid as she approached.

"Monsignor Cerini—" began the maid.

"Mr. Armstrong is on the veranda," Helen interrupted.

"But he asks for the madama."

"For me?" Helen was incredulous. "Show him out here, Annetta."

The librarian's face beamed genially as he greeted her and Uncle Peabody.

"Has the maid not made a mistake?" Helen asked. "Is it not our invalid whom you wish to see?"

"No, my daughter, it is you whom I seek. I have come to make a full though long-delayed acknowledgment."

Helen glanced over to Uncle Peabody, thoroughly mystified.

"Your husband and I were talking of you yesterday," he continued, "and we both are deeply concerned to find how erroneous have been our estimates and how slow we have been to recognize the truth."

So Jack had sent him to plead his cause, Helen told herself, and in her heart she resented the interference. It was unlike him to intrust so important a matter as this to another, yet perhaps it was a further evidence of the new conditions.

SO JACK HAD SENT HIM TO PLEAD HIS CAUSE, HELEN TOLD HERSELF; AND IN HER HEART SHE RESENTED THE INTERFERENCE

"Shall I not leave you to yourselves?" queried Uncle Peabody.

"By no means!" Cerini cried, hastily. "It is most fitting that you should hear what I am about to say. Do you remember the first day I met you at the library?" he continued, addressing his question to Helen.

She closed her eyes for a moment, and an involuntary shadow of pain passed over her face as she replied, quietly:

"Do you think I could ever forget it?"

Cerini saw it all, and it touched him deeply. "I was unkind to you that day, my daughter—even cruel. I thought I understood, but later events have shown me that my judgment led me far astray."

The old man had come to a realization at last! This, at all events, was a comfort to her.

"Only in part," she replied, trying to speak cheerfully. "The character-building was going on just as you said."

"It was," Cerini said, forcefully—"to a greater extent, I believe, than any one of us knew. My only excuse is that I was possessed with a preconceived idea—the very thing which I so much object to in others."

"I don't think I quite understand," Helen replied. "Do you mean that, after all his efforts, my husband is right in his conviction that his work has been a failure?"

"It is not of your husband that I am thinking now," the librarian answered; "it is of myself—and you."

"Of me?" Helen was genuinely surprised. "But I have never entered into the consideration at all, where the work at the library was concerned."

"You should have done so; that is just the point."

"I wanted to," Helen cried; "but you told me that I was quite incapable of doing so."

"I know I did," replied the librarian, bowing his head; "and that is where I made my great mistake."

"It would have stopped their work where it was—you said so yourself."

Cerini again bowed his head. "All part of the same mistake," he admitted. "Had I encouraged you at that time you would not only have added much to the work itself, but you would have saved your husband from his own great error. I have been much to blame, my daughter, and you must not hold him responsible for a fault which is really mine."

Helen tried to fathom what was in the old man's mind. She could not question his sincerity, yet his words seemed a mockery. Jack had evidently taken him freely into his confidence, so there was no reason why she should not speak freely.

"Mr. Armstrong has apparently told you how unfortunately his experience has ended in its effect upon our personal relations. Knowing this, I am sure you would not intentionally wound me further by seeking to restore matters to a false basis; yet I can understand your words in no other way. As you said of my husband, that day in the library, this time it is your heart and not your head which finds expression."

The librarian gasped with apprehension. "Daughter! daughter!" he cried, "have I not made myself clear! Then let me do so now before any possible misunderstanding can enter in. I am a humanist by profession—until now I believed myself a modern humanist. When I first knew your husband, he was a youth full of intelligent appreciation of those ancient marvels which I delighted to show him. Imagine my joy, twelve years later, to welcome him again, grown to man's estate, and to find that the early seeds which I had planted within him had sent out roots and tendrils so strong as to hold him firmly in their grasp. Then he brought Miss Thayer to me—at first I took her for you, as she was the kind of woman I had expected him to marry.

She entered into his work with him with the same spirit as his own, and my foolish old heart rejoiced that such splendid material had been placed in my hands for the moulding."

"Why repeat all this?" Helen interrupted; "I know it all and accept it all, but what agony to pass through it still another time!"

"Forgive me, my daughter," Cerini replied, quickly; "we are past the period of your sacrifice now, and have reached the point of your triumph."

"My triumph!" cried Helen, bitterly. "Why do you hurt me so?"

"Patience, dear," Uncle Peabody urged, quietly. "Monsignor Cerini has some purpose in mind which makes this necessary, I am sure."

"I am unfortunate in my presentation," the librarian apologized. "The point I wish to make is that up to the time I met Mrs. Armstrong I had known but one kind of humanism. I myself had studied the master-spirits of the past, and had assimilated the principles which they taught. Mr. Armstrong and Miss Thayer assimilated their lessons in the same way as I had done; but we all failed to recognize in this dear lady the natural expression—the personification—of all that we ourselves had labored so assiduously to acquire."

Both Helen and Uncle Peabody were listening to the old man's words with breathless attention.

"You mean that Mrs. Armstrong is a natural humanist?" Uncle Peabody queried.

"The most perfect expression of all that humanism contains which I can ever hope to see," Cerini replied, with feeling. "I, more than any one, have prevented the expression of these attributes which are your natural heritage; now let me help to merge them with your husband's undoubted talents."

"You cannot mean it," Helen said, weakly, sobering down after the first exhilaration of the old man's words. "I am no humanist, either natural or otherwise. Monsignor Cerini evidently means to give me a new confidence, but it is a mistaken kindness."

"You must listen to what he says, Helen," Uncle Peabody insisted. "I have known Cerini for many years, and he would make no such statement unless he felt it to be true."

"It is all as unknown to me as some foreign language I have never heard before," she protested. "I know, for I have tried to understand."

"Does a bird have to know the technique of music before it can sing?" asked Cerini, quietly.

"Oh, this is agony for me!" cried Helen, in despair. "I can only see in it another opening of the wound, another barb later to be torn from my heart."

"Be reasonable, child," urged Uncle Peabody, soothingly. "It seems to me that instead of all this Cerini has brought to you—to all of us—the solution of our problem. Let me ask him a few questions, while you control yourself and try to understand."

Helen acquiesced silently. Cerini's words had seemed to give her hope, yet she dared not allow herself to hope again. Limp from exhaustion, worn out by her ceaseless mental struggle, she had no strength even to oppose.

"Mrs. Armstrong has taken her present position," began Uncle Peabody, "because she feels absolutely that her husband's real expression of himself is that which he has shown her while under the influence of this spell which his love of the old-time learning has woven about him."

"She is right," replied the librarian, "except that by an unusual combination of circumstances this influence overpowered him by its strength, and he should not be held wholly responsible for his abnormal acts. This is not the first time I have seen this happen. There is a peculiar languor in the atmosphere, here in Florence, impregnated as it is with the romance of centuries, which is absolutely intoxicating to the mind, but it is rarely that it succeeds in making itself so felt upon an Anglo-Saxon temperament. Mr. Armstrong ought never, for the sake of his own individuality, to give up his fondness for the *literæ humaniores*, but it is entirely out of the question for him ever again to become so subject to their control."

"She senses this quite as strongly as you do; but beyond this she feels that he can never retain the development which has come to him here except in an atmosphere filled with a comprehension of all which he holds so dear."

"Mrs. Armstrong is still in the right," assented Cerini, gravely; "but there is one point which she still fails to understand. Her husband's work has been humanistic, but he himself is but just ready to begin to be a humanist. She is the one best fitted in every way to join him at this point, and their two personalities, thus united, can but produce splendid results."

"I cannot believe it," Helen interrupted, speaking with decision. "It has been from Inez and not from me that he has received his inspiration. Things are no different now from what they have been: Inez is still the one to inspire him to attain his best."

"You are wrong, dear," spoke a low voice behind them, as Inez threw her arms about Helen and embraced her warmly. "I surmised what you were discussing, and took this first opportunity to do my part toward straightening things out."

Helen sat upright and looked steadily into Inez' smiling face, completely freed for the first time in many weeks from its care-worn expression.

"You—you could not look like that if you understood," she stammered, still startled by her friend's sudden appearance.

"Mr. Armstrong and I have talked it all over, and at last I understand what should have been clear to me long ago. You are a dear, brave girl, Helen, and deserve all the happiness which is in store for you."

"Happiness—to me! Oh, Inez," Helen cried, "why do you all mock me with that word? There can be no happiness for me, and, unless I do what I propose, it means misery for every one instead of for me alone."

"No, dear," Inez replied, softly, gently smoothing Helen's hair as she rested her tired head upon her shoulder. "No—there can be nothing but happiness, now that all is understood."

"But you—you love Jack, Inez."

The girl colored as Helen spoke thus freely in the presence of others, but her voice was firm as she replied.

"Helen, dear," she said, "here in the presence of Mr. Cartwright and Monsignor Cerini I ask your permission to keep in my heart the image of the man I learned to love while we both were beneath the spell. That man no longer exists in the flesh, but I still worship his memory. He can never exist again except as a part of an experience which could never be repeated. Is this asking too much, dear?"

"What does it all mean?" cried Helen, gazing at her helplessly—"what does it all mean?"

"It means that there have been two Jacks, Helen—one of whom became transformed for a time into a veritable master-spirit of the past. To this man, I admit, I gave a devotion which I shall never—could never—give to any other; but he died, Helen, when the spell broke against that wall at the foot of the hill of Settignano. This man, even during his existence, gave me no devotion in return, and knew not the passion which he inspired in me. He had no heart, but it was not his heart I worshipped. To me his mind—broad, comprehensive, and understanding—stood for all that life could give. The other Jack—the man you married—has never wavered in the love he gave you from the first. He has suffered from the influence of the second personality in that he was forced into the background by the greater strength of this sub-conscious self; but he has also gained from its influence in the development which we all have seen. My Jack is dead, but yours still lives. He needs you, and he longs for the return to him of the wife he has always loved."

Inez paused after her long appeal, eager to read a favorable response in the pale face still gazing at her, but no change came over the set features. Once or twice Helen started to speak, but no words came. Uncle Peabody and Cerini had followed Inez intently, realizing that she was pleading the cause far better than they could. Affected by the scene before them, they found themselves unable to break the silence. At last Helen's voice came back to her.

"He longs for the return to him of the wife he has always loved?"

She repeated Inez' words slowly, in the form of a question.

"Yes, dear," her friend replied; "he is waiting for you now."

"Oh no, no, no!" Helen cried, brokenly, covering her face with her hands; "it is all a mistake. You are all doing this for my sake, and it is not the truth—it is not the truth!"

"You are ill, Helen!" cried Inez, alarmed by her appearance as well as by the wildness of her words; "come, let me take you to your room."

Unresistingly Helen suffered herself to be led into the house, leaving Uncle Peabody and Cerini looking apprehensively at each other.

"He longs—for the return to him—of the wife—he has always loved," Helen murmured over and over again, as Inez and Annetta undressed her and gently put her into bed. She seemed indifferent to what Inez said to her, and conscious only of the words which she kept repeating. Thoroughly frightened, Inez left her in Annetta's care while she rushed down-stairs to summon the doctor.

XXXII

For a few days Helen's condition was grave enough to warrant the anxiety which pervaded the entire household. Dr. Montgomery was again pressed into service, and found his skill taxed to the utmost to meet the condition in which he found his new patient.

"This is a great surprise to me," he remarked to Uncle Peabody, shaking his head ominously. "I have made it a point to watch Mrs. Armstrong throughout the shock and the strain of her husband's accident, anticipating that this nervous reaction might occur; but the time when it would naturally have happened is now long since passed."

Mr. Cartwright reluctantly explained to the doctor enough of the facts to assist him to a proper understanding of the case, and with sympathies fully enlisted his efforts were redoubled. The patient herself proved to be his greatest obstacle. Try as he would, he could not arouse in her any interest in her recovery. She accepted his services and those of the nurse without question, but in an apathetic manner. Armstrong, Inez, and Uncle Peabody hovered about the sick-chamber, eagerly grasping such information as the nurse and the doctor were able to give them, the anxious lines in their faces becoming deeper as the hours passed by.

But it was naturally upon Armstrong that the burden rested most heavily. He had been given the fullest details of the conference in the garden which immediately preceded Helen's collapse, and her replies to Cerini's appeal showed him, better even than his last conversation with her, how seriously she had been affected. For this he alone was responsible, and he was equally responsible for the illness which came as a final result of it all. He had hoped that when Cerini awakened her to a knowledge of her own splendid development she would accept his plea that they take up their new life together, but this expectation had been in vain.

"It has come too late," he said, bitterly, to Uncle Peabody. "We can only imagine the tortures through which the poor girl has passed by the severity of this reaction. She has been forcing herself to make this supreme sacrifice, which she believes is necessary, and has succeeded at last in destroying that love which I know she felt for me even through the worst of the crisis."

"She loves you still, Jack," replied Uncle Peabody, whose complete sympathy had been won by Armstrong's attitude during the trying days they were passing through together. "It is this which has made it so hard for her."

"It is only your ever-present optimism," the younger man replied, sadly. "Now that I see myself as I have really been during these past weeks, I cannot share it with you, much as I wish I could. If I, having actually experienced this spell and knowing its force, find it so impossible to explain to myself this long series of inexplicable events, how can I expect anything other than this generous but unfortunate conviction that her self-sacrifice is necessary?"

His face contracted as he spoke, and the veins upon his forehead stood out boldly against the fair skin, still colorless from his prolonged illness.

"And the worst of it all is that I can make no sacrifice which can possibly accomplish anything," he continued. "She—she must suffer on indefinitely for my selfishness, for my neglect."

"Let me speak to her just once more," Inez pleaded, in real pity for the man beside her. "When she is strong enough, perhaps I can make her understand."

"No," he replied, firmly, yet showing his appreciation of her thought for him, "she has endured enough already. The very mention of her husband can only revive unhappy memories. She shall at least be spared any further pleading on my behalf."

At last the doctor pronounced the danger-point passed, and the relief which the announcement brought gave Armstrong the necessary strength to enable him to take upon himself the details of packing and closing up the house, and getting everything in readiness to leave for home as soon as Helen should be strong enough to travel.

"The place has been hateful to her all these weeks," he explained, "and she must be freed from every scene which suggests what has passed."

As he went from one part of the villa to another, he was constantly reminded with painful forcefulness of the days which they had first enjoyed there together. The flowers in the garden, the singing of the birds in the trees, the distant view of the city—each possessed a personal significance. "I love the present," she had said to him—"I love the sky, the air, the sunshine, and the flowers."

Happy, buoyant nature—the natural humanist! She assimilated all that was best in life, and had he given her the opportunity would have breathed it out again to those around her richer and more inspiring because of its contact with her own rare self! Fool that he had been! With the riches of the past lying at his hand to be drawn upon for material, he had selfishly insisted that his own methods of using them were the only ones, recognizing too late the inspiration and the real assistance which she was amply able to give him in transforming these riches into even purer gold by the magic touch of the present. Armstrong groaned as the irony of it came to him.

Helen recovered slowly, and with a sweetness which touched the hearts of all about her. Inez and Uncle Peabody were with her much of the time, but Armstrong, true to his conviction that he had become distasteful to her, waited to be asked for; and Helen did not ask. The only event which happened to interrupt the even tenor of the days was a call from the Contessa Morelli, who was solicitous for her condition.

"Make some excuse," Helen said, quietly, to Inez, who announced the visitor. "Don't say anything to hurt her feelings, but I really can't see her. She does not understand the life I know and love, and I don't want to understand hers."

So it was Jack whom the contessa met as she took her departure.

"I am so relieved to know that your wife is in no danger," she said, sympathetically.

"So are we all," Armstrong replied, in a perfunctory way, still feeling ill at ease in the contessa's presence. "This villa will soon be considered as a hospital if any more of us become invalids."

"Miss Thayer is not ill?" inquired the contessa, smiling archly.

"She is quite well, I believe," he replied, coldly, but with an effort to be civil.

"How fortunate!" Amélie continued. "With Mrs. Armstrong in no danger and Miss Thayer in good health, you will soon, no doubt, resume your charming *tête-à-têtes* at the library?"

The contessa was endeavoring to be mischievous, but Armstrong was in no mood for her pleasantries. He resented the words no less than the expression upon her face. Yet he himself was partially responsible, and this thought kept back the words upon his lips which if spoken would have been regretted. He looked intently into her face before he answered, and the contessa's smile faded.

"Instead of replying to your question," Armstrong said, quietly, with his eyes still fixed upon her, "may I not ask you a favor?"

"Surely you may ask it," she replied; "but that does not mean that I must grant it, does it?"

"You need not grant it unless you choose," pursued Armstrong; "but at least I shall have the satisfaction of asking it: will you not add one more class into which you separate the men you meet?"

The contessa laughed merrily. "What a curious request to be made so seriously!" she exclaimed. "Of whom shall the new class be composed?"

"Of those men who are husbands and who love their wives," Armstrong replied, feelingly; "who despise intrigue and disloyalty and hypocrisy in either sex; who consider honor and life as synonyms; and who, even for the sake of civility, cannot allow misinterpretations to cast a shadow upon the sanctity of marriage."

"*Mon Dieu!*" cried the contessa, making a pretty *moue* as she rose and moved toward the veranda; "and I thought he had no temperament! Shall I put you in this exotic class? Oh no; you would be so lonesome!"

"I could not expect you to understand," Armstrong replied, in a low tone, biting his lip with vexation.

Amélie watched his expression intently, a complete change coming over her manner. The flippant bearing was gone; the smile, aggravating as it was attractive, vanished. She took a step toward him as she spoke.

"But I do understand," she said, slowly, in a low, tense voice. "Perhaps I ought to feel shamed by your contempt and indignant at your criticism. On the contrary, I am glad that I incurred both, for by it I have learned that a man can be honest, and that appearances are not always the safest guides. What you have said is what a woman understands by instinct; anything different is what she learns—from men. Will you forgive me? I shall not offend again."

His surprise at this new and unexpected view of the contessa's character was so great that it was only instinctively that he pressed the dainty hand which was held out to him. For a moment their eyes met.

"I wish that you and your wife might both have come into my life earlier," she said, simply, and then turned quickly to the door and was in the tonneau of her motor-car before Armstrong could offer to assist her. So, as the machine moved away, he stood on the veranda, bowing his acknowledgment of her radiant smile into which a new element had entered.

Then Armstrong turned back into the hallway, where he met the doctor and Uncle Peabody coming down the stairs.

"Has she asked for me yet?" he inquired, eagerly.

"Not yet," Dr. Montgomery answered, with that understanding which is a part of the physician's profession. Armstrong turned away to conceal his face, which he felt must show all that was passing through his heart.

"I wish you would go to her, anyway," the doctor continued.

"You don't know what you are suggesting, doctor—I want to do it so much—but I must not."

"It will be necessary to talk with her soon about our future plans, Jack," Uncle Peabody said, seeing a way to accomplish their purpose. "Dr. Montgomery says that Helen is strong enough now to discuss the matter."

Armstrong looked from one to the other with uncertainty. "You are right," he said, at length. "She must be consulted about that, and I am the one to do it."

He chose the morning for his visit to her—a morning filled with the sunshine she loved so well. He plucked a handful of the fragrant blossoms from the garden, hoping that the odor might recall to her some of the happy moments they had experienced together. The very perfume rising from the redolent petals seemed to accuse him as he stood before her door awaiting the nurse's response to his knock.

"May I come in?" he asked, looking across the room to the bed where Helen lay propped up with pillows, so that she could look out of the window into the garden, even though the tops of the trees alone rewarded her gaze.

"Of course," Helen weakly replied, yet with a smile, and the nurse discreetly left them to themselves.

Armstrong seated himself on a chair near the bed and gazed in silence at the thin, pale features of the woman before him. This was the wreck of the beautiful girl he had married and brought here to Florence for her honeymoon. What a honeymoon!

"I am glad you came to me at last," Helen said, quietly, interrupting his convicting thoughts.

"At last!" The words brought him to himself. Mastering his emotion as best he could, he took her thin hand in his, and the fact that she did not withdraw it gave him courage.

"I have longed to come to you each day, but you asked me not to make it harder for you."

"I am glad you came to me at last," she repeated.

How should he begin? The sentences he had thought out carefully, which might convey his necessary message and yet spare her, seemed too cold, too meaningless. He glanced up at her helplessly, and the expression on her face helped him to his purpose. Impulsively drawing his chair still nearer to the bed, he poured out to her the self-incriminations which had haunted him for days. In a torrent of pitiless words he pictured himself without mercy. There was no plea for reconsideration, no thought of future readjustment. The one idea was to let her know how fully he realized all that had happened, how powerless he felt himself to make restitution, and his determination to do what now remained to make her future as little overcast as possible by the events which had already taken place.

"I would not have come now except that it is necessary," he said, brokenly. "I know that to see me must recall unhappy recollections, but there are some matters which we must talk over together. I have not come to plead for any reconsideration—you were right in what you said the last time we talked about it, as you have been in all else. Our marriage was a mistake, and it is I who have made it so. I no longer ask that we try to restore matters to their former position. The only sacrifice within my power is to give you a chance to recover as much as you can of what I have made you lose. The penalty is hard, but well deserved."

He did not look into her face as he spoke, lest he lose his courage before all was said. "Cerini has told you what you have taught us both, which is another debt I owe you. It should be some little consolation, dear, to know that your expression and your understanding have been so much clearer than those of this librarian, whom I have considered infallible; than those of your husband, whom in the past I know you have respected and loved. Thank God for that love!" he repeated, abruptly.

"Then it is really true that my 'dear present' is worth something, after all?"

"Your 'dear present' is the saving clause. Without it we limit ourselves beyond the hope of recovery, just as I have done. The glories of the past are as splendid and as important as I ever painted them, but they must be awakened with the breath of present necessities. You have always felt this and expressed it; I have known it only since you taught it to me."

"I am glad," she answered, simply.

"But I am forgetting my errand," Armstrong continued, bracing himself for a final effort. "As soon as you are able to travel you will, of course, wish to return home. It may be that, for the sake of appearances, you will wish me to go with you, in which case I shall make it as easy as possible for you. Or you can return with Uncle Peabody, as he tells me you once spoke to him of doing. He is eager to do anything you wish, but he has plans which need to be arranged after you have once decided."

Helen's gaze rested firmly upon her husband's half-averted face, watching the changing expressions, reading the unspoken words. "He longs for the return to him of the wife he has always loved" rang in her ears, and now for the first time it seemed to ring true. Her mind was moving fast as Armstrong ceased speaking, and even when she replied, a moment later, it was not an answer.

"What is Inez going to do?" she inquired.

"As soon as we close the villa she will go to the *pension* where the Sinclair girls were."

"She will stay in Florence?" Helen asked, surprised.

"Yes; she has arranged with Cerini to work with him upon his *Humanistic Studies*."

Helen withdrew her hand from his as she leaned back upon the pillow and closed her eyes. Armstrong regarded her anxiously, fearful lest their interview had been too great a strain upon her returning strength; but as he looked her eyes opened again.

"You must know at once whether I prefer to return home with you or with Uncle Peabody?" she asked, faintly.

"Not at once," he replied, leaning nearer to catch the low-spoken words— "not until you are strong enough to decide."

Suddenly he felt both her arms about his neck, and in his ear she whispered, "Let me go with you, Jack; but not to Boston—take me to Fiesole!"

THE END